The Fourth Wife

The Fourth Wife

LINDA HAMILTON

KENSINGTON PUBLISHING CORP.
kensingtonbooks.com

KENSINGTON BOOKS are published by

Kensington Publishing Corp.
900 Third Avenue
New York, NY 10022

ISBN: 978-1-4967-5690-9 (ebook)
ISBN: 978-1-4967-5689-3

First Kensington Trade Paperback Printing: April 2026

10 9 8 7 6 5 4 3 2 1

Printed in the United States of America

The authorized representative in the EU for product safety and compliance
is eucomply OU, Parnu mnt 139b-14, Apt 123
Tallinn, Berlin 11317, hello@eucompliancepartner.com

To every woman who ever sat in a hard pew and wondered if God heard her silent cries

CHAPTER 1

Salt Lake City, Utah Territory
1882

A loud crash followed by a screech cut through the walls of the house, startling me on the piano bench. My fingers hit a sour note and I scowled at the sheet music in front of me. Even at this early-morning hour there was rarely a moment of quiet in the home of a large plural family. Echoes of the baby's screams reverberated through the papered walls from a room above as I straightened my shoulders to continue my practice over the noise.

With my fingers stretched out across the keys, my body melted into the instrument until we were conjoined as one. My hands moved and the music swelled around the parlor. My heart lightened as the notes rose from my fingertips. I disappeared into the music I alone controlled. Perhaps the only thing in my life I controlled—the only place I felt safe to be myself.

Behind me, Aunt Emma clicked her tongue. "Hazel," she demanded. My music slowed but didn't stop. "Must you make such a racket right after breakfast? You've disturbed your sister."

I couldn't help the leap of guilt in my chest. It was always there, like another force pumping through my veins. My hands stilled on the keyboard. But a piece of my defiance struggled through.

"It's music," I responded in a quiet voice. "I wouldn't call it a racket."

"It's selfish to play at all hours of the day."

Selfish. Once again, I was told I was sinful. Part of me wanted to roll my eyes, but another part was racked with shame. I swiveled around on the bench, my dark blue skirt swishing against the piano legs. No amount of proper petticoats ever made me feel that I was much older than a child, even after my twenty years of life. A pulse of frustration hit me again and I bit my lip to stay quiet. Good Mormon women were never cross or disrespectful. Silence beat between us as I stared up at Aunt Emma's serious face, her baby balanced on her hip.

"But how am I to improve if I don't practice?" The words leaked out though I knew arguing would only lead to trouble.

Aunt Emma's cheeks lit up at my impertinence. "You play well enough already, Hazel. You can play all the hymns and entertain just fine. What more could you possibly be practicing for?"

Her words stung like a physical blow.

"Yes, Aunt Emma," I replied quietly. She was right. I already knew almost every hymn by heart, and I could play easily when called upon for gatherings. Nothing more would come of my music, no matter how much I loved it. Mothers and wives in Zion had other duties far more important.

A part of me held, unrelenting, to my silent desires. My head swam night after night with colorful dreams of my hands on the magnificent Tabernacle organ, my music bringing audiences to tears. And Elijah in the front row watching me with adoration. I wanted more from life than I was allotted—but this was a sin. So I shamefully pushed the dreams back again and again.

My sister squawked again from Aunt Emma's hip.

Aunt Emma let out a sigh. "Don't you have somewhere else to be?"

"Yes." I stood, towering over her even in my shortest heeled boots but feeling small as a mouse. "Father needs me at the printing office."

She clicked her tongue again in obvious disapproval. "Then hurry off. There's no place for idleness." With that, she spun on her heel and marched away, her hips swinging back and forth, uneven with the weight of her daughter.

"Good day, Aunt Emma," I called after her. She made no move to acknowledge me as she disappeared around the corner to the kitchen. "And don't stop there," I murmured under my breath. "Walk right on out the door and down the street and never return."

A mixture of shame and terrifying pleasure at the thought warmed through me. The last year had become almost unbearable with that woman and her growing brood of children under Mother's roof. If only Father wasn't so distracted with his newspaper these days, then maybe he could finally find them a new home after circumstances forced them out of theirs, and Mother and I could go back to pretending he didn't spend half his nights with another family.

Our family. My siblings.

I shook away the thought. I'd barely had breakfast and already too many emotions swarmed through me. I balanced on a tightrope knowing one jolt would send me plummeting over the side. The emotion I feared most buzzed in my chest—panic. I drew in a long breath, staring around the parlor, trying to calm myself.

Like any sensible Mormon woman, Mother kept her house in perfect order. It was a sign of our industry and refinement despite the harsh conditions of the valley. Matching maroon chairs and sofa surrounded the hearth in a warming circle. Embroidered stools welcomed the younger children beside the wooden table where Mother placed the family Bible and an intricate box that she kept stocked with tiny molasses sweets. The walnut grand piano tucked against the far wall beneath a family portrait and my framed sampler from childhood bearing the words *Home Sweet Home.*

And one day, Mother hoped, my own home would look much the same. My life was already laid out—become a plural wife and mother with little else to occupy my energies than the cause of the church and family.

Across the room on the mantel sat Mother's favorite blue dish. My heartbeat pounded quicker. Attempting to stamp out the growing panic—a panic I couldn't justify—I crossed the room on silent feet, my full skirts bobbing around me. Gingerly, I reached out and touched the beloved blue plate. Father had given Mother this set for their wedding many years ago and though the other pieces had been lost or broken, this one plate remained—the last physical evidence that once my father had loved his first wife before all others. Now it sat proudly displayed on the mantel as if she needed the daily reminder.

Someone cleared their throat, interrupting my thoughts, and I pulled my hands back as if the plate had scalded me. Another sin, distraction, to add to my list for the day. Slowly, I turned to find Mother standing in front of me, her fingers clutching a white envelope. She didn't smile.

"I have news." Mother's unusually stern voice matched her perfectly set hair, drawn back on her head in a tight bun, not a single strand out of place. "From Elder Crowther."

"Elder Crowther?" My heartbeat ratcheted. One of the apostles, the most powerful men in the church and entire Territory.

"He wishes to speak with you this morning."

At once, the air seemed to disappear from the room.

"Now?" My voice cracked. Elder Crowther was Elijah's father. Elijah, the boy I'd spent my childhood with, the boy who grew into the man I loved.

But Elijah was gone. *My* Elijah. For years he'd been away serving the church as a missionary in England, reduced to nothing but letters and memories. Did Elder Crowther have news of him? Of our future plan for our happiness together? The thought of Elijah with me once again was exhilarating, almost to the point of physical pain.

"You must hurry to the Council House to meet with him." Mother didn't move from her spot, but the envelope wrinkled as her grip on it tightened.

I tensed with the movement. Mother never acted this stiff and severe.

"What's wrong?" I asked.

"There's no indication that anything is wrong." She didn't meet my eyes. "Only a call to come at once."

I nodded, but I wasn't persuaded. Worry gripped my stomach. "There's something wrong, isn't there? What happened? Did he get hurt on his mission?" The invisible tightrope beneath my feet drew tighter, my pulse rushing faster. My mind took off, too many thoughts zipping through it to settle on any one.

Elijah's handsome face. His last letter tucked away in my trunk upstairs. His fingers intertwined with mine. His body broken and bleeding on the cobbled streets of London. Oh no, had he died? The image sparked a tiny yelp that I tried my best to swallow. He was dead, surely, killed by dark-cloaked street thieves or . . .

"Hazel." Mother snapped her fingers.

I had always been like this—unable to suppress my thoughts and stay focused, no matter how hard I prayed for relief from this burden. Everything distracted me, and often I found myself elsewhere entirely without ever having moved my feet, frequently assaulted with images and worries that weren't true but somehow felt so keenly real.

Panic swelled in my chest, outpacing my lungs. I opened my mouth gasping for air as dread overtook me. Was I dying? Squeezing my hands together as tight as I could, I pushed back the rush of tears.

"Hazel, what's happening?" Mother studied me with concern.

"N-nothing," I protested, the words barely coming out.

"The Devil is trying to overtake you again. You must fight him."

I nodded, my heart beating like it attempted to leave my chest. "I am, I promise."

I could feel his wicked claws around me trying to tear me

apart. Why was I so weak? Why did I have to always fight this battle? I lived with my head drowning in a sea of worries I couldn't drag myself from, and then all at once, this raging panic would overcome me—Satan and his legion ripping through me. I was nothing but an abominable young woman and these attacks only proved it.

"I need to go," I said, and stumbled toward the doorway. My world was suddenly a pinprick of vision, but if I kept moving and fought through this, the assault would end. And then I could pray for forgiveness for my weakness, my ineptitude, my failings.

"Hazel, are you sure?" At last, her voice had softened to her typical kindness.

I forced air into my lungs, dampening my unreleased sobs. "Yes, I'm fine. I'm not giving in to this weakness of the flesh." I slid back through the doorway to the entry, where our neat row of hats hung along the narrow wall. "I'll find my hat and be off."

As I moved, I sensed the Devil hanging on my chest like a millstone. Each breath in felt unworthy, but I forced myself through it. I had to prove I was capable of the perfection God demanded of me. At last, my heart slowed some.

Aunt Emma strode back into the entry, her eyebrow raised at the remnants of my display.

"Elder Crowther's office?"

Of course, she would be listening in. I busied my fingers with retrieving my hat and tried to focus on more air, the only solution to lessening the weight pressing down on me.

"That's over ten blocks. She shouldn't go alone in this pathetic disposition. I'll fetch Ammon."

"I don't need him to accompany me. I'm strong enough."

"Are you truly, Hazel?" Her eyes shot accusations at me, ones I knew were all too true. I was pitiful. "You need your brother to escort you for your own good." She looked over at Mother, who reluctantly met her gaze. "Don't you agree it's proper, Sister Mary?"

Mother's eye twitched but she otherwise maintained her calm demeanor, unable to defend even her own daughter if it meant causing disagreement. "Thank you, Sister Emma. How generous of you to loan us your son."

Aunt Emma smiled in triumph. "Ammon! Ammon, come down here now to escort your sister." She climbed up the stairs two at a time to fetch him.

I gave my mother an expectant look, ignoring the dizzying in my head that often accompanied one of my panics. "This isn't necessary. He's only sixteen, not exactly a chaperone. And I need to hurry."

"He's your oldest brother," she said.

"Living brother," I whispered to myself.

I often imagined my brother Heber and I would've been great friends if he had lived past our childhood. If he and the other lost babies had lived, then perhaps Father would never have needed to marry Aunt Emma and produce more children for Zion. I shifted my weight between my feet, forcing a damper on thoughts of things I couldn't change, and continued. "Please, I can't delay and I'm not required to have a chaperone. She's only trying to rub it in—"

"It's best not to argue with Sister Emma," Mother cut me off but gently touched my shoulder. "Contention is a tool of the Adversary. A proper Mormon woman doesn't cause arguments or disputes. If you learn nothing else from me, Hazel, remember that it is your calling as a future wife and mother to be a helpmeet and a source of peace. Don't waste your time trying to be right. It's better to simply be quiet. . . ." She trailed off, biting her lip as she looked away.

As always, Mother was right. I needed to improve, even with my wicked panics. Better yet, I needed to be smaller, less of a person to worry about. And yet, I couldn't resist the undercurrent within me, to be more and find a life unfettered. But such desires were only my sinful nature—something to be squashed and scorched away.

Ammon slouched down the stairs, dutifully shoving his arms into his worn brown coat. Spring in Salt Lake was a constant see-saw between threats of snow and blazing heat, and today the sun was hidden behind a thick layer of gray clouds. With a forced smile, I fixed my hat over my pulled-back curls and threw open the door.

Our house was a fine two-storied brick home, much like the others stretching down the street. Father's occupation at the newspaper made us stable enough to never want, though we were far from the wealthiest of the Saints in Salt Lake. Ammon clamored behind me down the wooden porch steps and onto the sidewalk lining the dirt street.

I pivoted sharply without saying a word to him, headed toward the center of our bustling Deseret—the true Mormon name of our territory. Despite the itch of guilt at my pride, I didn't bother to wait for Ammon, but his lanky legs caught up with me in a flash.

"You don't have to walk me," I said, allowing my fizzling worries to morph into frustration. "You can run off to see your girl and I won't tell your mother." Out of the corner of my eye, I saw a bright flush of pink overtake his face at my teasing.

"No, I'll mind my task."

I bumped him with my elbow as he passed, the tension between us simmering. He was already taller than me and would probably grow even more by the end of summer. His golden-brown hair matched mine, as well as his chestnut eyes. We'd both inherited our father's nose, and he, Aunt Emma's stiff chin, while I favored our father's soft features around the mouth. In any other city in America, a gentile passerby would've easily taken us for full siblings and left it at that, but here everyone knew we were truly two out of thousands of children in families throughout the Territory, all mixed up and gathered in the crucible of plural marriage.

Ammon slowed his steps again as we crossed the block. "You worried about Elder Crowther's summon? Bet you an extra dessert helping you're in trouble."

"Betting, little brother? Then perhaps we should skip this excursion altogether and go to a gambling den. I'm sure the bishop would love to hear about that adventure."

His mischievous smile dimmed. "I'm sure he'd also love to hear about the book I found under your pillow."

My boot slipped on an uneven edge of the sidewalk, and I caught myself by grabbing the edge of his sleeve.

No one was supposed to know about the hidden dime novel I kept with its story of daring romance. "Promise me you'll never tell anyone about it, especially not the bishop. I swear, I'll throw it away. I meant to, that is. I didn't mean to—I wasn't planning to—"

"Golly, Hazel, you're always so dramatic. I was only joking."

Certainly, to him it was only a lark. Though only sixteen, Ammon was still a man and as such, entitled to the priesthood—God's power given to men on earth to pronounce blessings and to govern over the church. All men deemed worthy were given the priesthood through religious rite, regardless of their occupation. That priesthood allowed them to rule not only over the church in all positions of authority but also over their families, wives, children, and eventually, eternal kingdoms in the life after death where they would become gods.

Ammon would never understand what position he held over me and my whole sex simply by virtue of being born male. A man reported with a scandalous book was worth a stern talking-to at most. A woman was branded a whore.

I immediately buried the weight of that reality. My church and my God demanded that I be more than I was, and I hated myself for my failures. A good Mormon woman was submissive, faithful, and always joyful. She never complained or caused contention, and she certainly never questioned the authority of those over her. She read books of the highest virtue and spoke in the sweetest tones. She obeyed her husband's command and reared children to do the same. And only then was she acceptable.

It had to be this way. God willed it so, and I had to obey or risk losing my eternal soul. I shoved down the possibility that there was another way, another life. My hand fiddled in my pocket searching for something it'd never find as we walked on in silence. Mormonism was all I knew. I had to be this remarkable woman. I had no other choice, surely.

A trolley bell dinged as it ambled down the center of the road on its metal rails, toward the heart of Salt Lake. The noises of the city center were picking up now: horses braying, carts rolling against the dust of the street, the distant din of hammers and chisels from the Temple builders. I relished in the familiarity. This was home.

Everything in Salt Lake spread out from the center square of the rising granite Temple like appendages, every block neat and organized into exact squares across the city. Carts and horses drove past tall, redbrick buildings and shops lining the road. Between all the bustle, women walked in their long, simple dresses with baskets for errands, and men in their starch suits or dirt-covered clothes for a day of labor.

The prophet Brigham Young's particular vision for his beehive oasis in the desert lived on past him. His imposing fingerprints were all over every nook and cranny of the great Utah Territory, from its cooperative enterprises to far-flung towns to hardly secular governments. This spider's web was his creation—a home for Mormons in the toiling hard soils of the west, far from the persecutions and influences of the hostile gentiles.

I'd heard many visitors who came to Salt Lake were surprised to find a hustling, modern city, despite its curious residents and our peculiar polygamist way of life. But to myself, Ammon, and many other Mormons milling in and out of the houses and stores surrounding us, it was the only way of life—the uncompromising bastion of our religion worth bleeding for when we were told. No threats of Eastern sensitives or federal government interference would wrangle this beast from our hands. Plural marriage was God's principle and command, and our people would rather lie down in death than surrender to man's laws.

Ammon took the last block almost at a jog. The Council House appeared ahead of us as we passed the Lion and Beehive Houses, where Brother Brigham used to live. As a child, I would try and peek in the windows of these magnificent homes hoping to catch a glimpse of the prophet's many elegant wives. But the family had moved out since his death, leaving only the ghosts of their past refinement behind.

I looked up at the house and a shiver rolled down my spine. The curtains covering the upper far-left window rustled and parted open. I paused, uncertain for a moment about what I saw.

A woman's face, her expression long and mournful.

I blinked and the figure was gone, the window as empty as it was before, the drapes shut up tight.

I shook the image from my head. My mind was too much in a whirl this morning for sense, a remnant of my earlier panic. But Elder Crowther was waiting for me and I couldn't delay any longer to ponder on it.

We arrived at Council House and I motioned for Ammon to wait as I pushed open the white picket gate of the church's headquarters. The two-story brick building was nothing particularly grand, but its position directly across from the growing Temple marked its importance.

Ammon collapsed onto the bench near the road. "I'll be waiting here." Like his ancient scriptural namesake, he was ever dutiful. With one last glance over at the Temple, the pumping center of my world, I walked silently toward the door.

Chapter 2

Elder Crowther opened his door halfway through my knock, as if he'd been standing right there waiting for me. The apostle's smile was even, if a little severe, when he motioned me inside and clicked the lock shut behind me. His eyes looked painfully like Elijah's.

"Sister Russon, please have a seat." He took his place across from me at the expansive oak-painted desk.

"Thank you." I sat back into the surprisingly stiff seat. Its plush padding had long since lost its comfort—or perhaps the lack of reassurance was by design.

The office was both orderly and devoid of personal touches, save for the photograph of his sizable family hung on the wall behind him. Even the air tasted stale. Books of Mormon and other sacred volumes lined the brown shelves, but everything in the office pointed your attention back toward the man occupying the desk.

Elder Crowther propped his fingers beneath his long, peppered beard and stared as if drinking me in. His penetrating gaze never wavered.

I hated this part of interviews. Church leaders gave me the distinct impression they could see into the very essence of my soul. It was as if I'd been stripped naked while he probed the depths of my mind and spirit. A bead of sweat dripped down the small of my back.

"Do you wish to speak about Elijah?" I blurted out. "I mean, is my friend all right? Or is he hurt, or—or—" The image of Elijah's broken body crumpled and blood-soaked in a dingy London alley conjured again in my mind.

"No, nothing is amiss." Elder Crowther finally blinked. "Elijah is still faithfully serving the Lord."

A wave of relief pulsed inside me. Elijah was safe. "Yes, of course. How silly of me."

Silence beat for more excruciating moments. I wished he would cast his eyes somewhere, anywhere else.

"May I ask why you called me here?" I asked.

"To deliver a message."

"From Elijah?"

"And the Lord."

God had a message for *me*? Only apostles and prophets could speak for Him, and I never imagined a high priesthood leader would ever deliver such an important call to unimportant me.

Elder Crowther went on in his solemn tone. "It's come to my attention that you and my son had a private attachment to each other."

Heat burned in my chest. "We've always been the closest of friends, as you know."

"Yes, but it appears you two weren't simply friends before he left."

I saw myself leaning against the old apple tree behind my house, Elijah's arms around my waist. His lips whispered his confession—he loved me, he'd always loved me—and I answered him with a kiss. I wanted to be his wife—his only wife. Our secret desire would be a sin before his father and perhaps God

Himself, but we held fast to it in our letters back and forth across the ocean. We didn't want a life in polygamy. We only wanted each other.

"Sister Russon."

I snapped back to the apostle, the joyful memory interrupted.

"The first message I must deliver is that my son no longer wishes to pursue such an arrangement."

The floor dropped from beneath me. "He . . . he . . . what?"

"He's informed me of your prior promises by letter and no longer wishes to continue them. He desires to follow God's commands to live the Principle and so will find companionship elsewhere, as you're not amenable. He asked me to speak to you of this so he would not have to send such a distressing letter to your family, exposing your rebellion."

His words cut straight through me and I wrapped my arms around my waist to stop myself from splitting open. I dropped my eyes to the floor, blinking back tears I knew I shouldn't cry. Emotional women were unseemly, according to the Brethren.

"I'm sure this is difficult to hear, but all is not lost."

How could it not be? I'd loved Elijah since we were children. He made up such a large piece of my existence. And now he asked his father to tell me that he wished to end our attachment? That he wanted a life in polygamy with someone else? Nothing added up. My mind beat with too many thoughts out of rhythm, each filled with self-loathing.

"But why did he change his mind?" I tried fervently to keep my sobs from escaping.

Elder Crowther's penetrating stare returned. "Because he's been converted with full purpose of heart."

"What if I change? What if I pray more? Perhaps I could be converted as well."

"I believe you could."

A miserable, desperate kind of hope clutched at my chest.

"But not with Elijah," he continued.

I shrank back.

He seemed to lean closer over the desk. "I've been praying about this and I have another message to deliver. The Lord needs me to give you a commandment."

"A commandment? For me?"

"Have you ever thought of the things the Lord may be calling you to do?"

"My calling is to be a wife and mother in Zion," I responded on cue, as if called on in a Sunday school class. My legs refused to stop shaking beneath my petticoat.

"This is good, Sister, and pleasing to the Lord. I will speak freely then. There is a man in the Twenty-First Ward by the name of Brother Manwaring. Jacob Manwaring. He's a good man with a generous income who honors his priesthood. I've spoken to him about you, and I wish to counsel you to accept him."

"Accept him for what?"

"As a husband."

The walls seemed to collapse in on me. I couldn't breathe. Elijah didn't love me anymore and my consolation was to be called to marry a stranger?

"I've never met Brother Manwaring. Why would he want me?"

"The only thing that matters is that the Lord told him to marry you. Such arrangements are not unusual. I've counseled many couples to be sealed together."

Sealing. The highest form of marriage that brought a couple together not only for this life but after death into the eternal life beyond. The most important religious rite that was required for our eternal salvation.

But I was supposed to be sealed to Elijah.

Anger gushed through me, hot and piercing. How could he be telling me this? What had I done to earn Elijah's scorn so suddenly? The fervent ire hollowed me out; I felt like nothing but an empty shell.

"Are you certain?"

The apostle sat up straighter, giving him the appearance of growing larger in his chair. "As certain as the Lord lives. Brother

Manwaring is a loyal man of God and he deserves such a reward. He'll be called to much higher positions very soon. Together, your blessings will increase a hundred-fold."

I tried not to wince, knowing well enough the meaning behind his words. A *reward* was a plural wife.

"How many wives does Brother Manwaring have already?"

"Three," he said with an air of indifference. But that number made all the difference to me.

A sob escaped my lips. I'd been called by an apostle to become the fourth wife of a man I'd never met. Me. Useless, worrying, sinful Hazel Russon with impossible music and ambitions hiding in her sinews. Me, who was deeply in love with Elder Crowther's son. A son who'd written beautiful letters of promise and longing for years, only to smash it all to pieces suddenly.

A hundred questions ran through my head, along with a rather violent urge to be sick. Once more I sensed the weight of the Devil pressing on my chest, the panic rising.

"Come now, it's not so hard. Pray for faith, Sister Russon. You'll understand God's will and see that this is what will refine you. Remember, to obey is better than sacrifice." Elder Crowther's words sounded as if they were miles away.

Tears escaped down my cheeks.

But Elijah, my heart beat back. He'd been my support and confidant for as long as I could remember. He never berated me for my errant wishes or moments of defiance. He was the only one who saw me for not only who I was but all I could be. He even supported me through my panics without judgment. But now, I didn't have Elijah and never would again. He didn't want me. I was alone.

And what good was a woman alone in a world that required a man for safety and eternal blessings? Without a sealing to a righteous priesthood man, I couldn't be saved in God's Celestial Kingdom and receive the highest degree of eternal glory.

"Sister Russon. Think carefully about your future. You can't marry Elijah. But you can marry a good man. Brother Manwaring will take care of you. He told me he has an elegant, large home prepared only for you. Couldn't you imagine yourself presiding with your husband over such an estate? I know you're fond of the piano. I'm sure he would be happy to let you play for him and his guests."

A performance. My throat tightened. And yet, I hated how easily I conjured up the image of myself seated at a grand piano, wearing elegant skirts while a small audience clapped at my music. A husband who actually wanted me at his side, in a magnificent home. A home only for me. My head dizzied. It was all too real. All I had to do was say yes and become a plural wife.

I tried to swallow my tears. "This is the Lord's will for me?"

"Yes. Forget Elijah and be faithful."

As if I could forget the man I'd carved into my own flesh. But he had forgotten me and left his father to break my heart without explanation. Fury pulsed in my blood now. If he didn't want me, then I would purge him from me. If Elijah didn't want my heart, then what did it matter if I became a fourth wife or a hundredth wife? If I did this, perhaps everyone would finally accept me. Maybe the torturing worries and guilt would finally subside. Perhaps the panics would disappear at last.

The apostle looked at me expectantly. I could demand more time to seek my own revelation from God on the matter, but I sensed that asking for His sign would only lead to more heartbreak. I knew I had to give Elder Crowther the right answer, to obey immediately as I was taught.

"Yes, I will accept him." My words lanced through my heart. Perhaps it would never truly beat again.

Chapter 3

Two weeks later

The wagon creaked out of the city, moving toward the mouth of the canyon in the distance. I glanced once more over my shoulder at the receding view of Salt Lake and its sprawl of businesses and homes. Farms and fields of green and grain stretched around us now, and with every passing mile the homes grew fewer. Soon we'd be on the farthest edges of the valley, huddled against the towering mountains.

Jacob Manwaring shifted closer on the bench and the space between us lit up. I could sense every inch of him, heating me through. This morning, we'd knelt across the altar from each other while Elder Crowther performed our marriage and sealing. We murmured covenants before God and angels binding us together for time and all eternity. Not even death could separate us now.

Even though I was now his wife for this lifetime and the next, he was a mystery to me. My husband wasn't the bearded, aging man I'd first conjured in my mind. He wore fine suits tailored perfectly to his trim physique, and his boots were polished as a regal army general. His hair, though graying at his temples, was full and dark blond with a matching thick mustache. His deep blue eyes stood out in stark contrast to his hair.

Everything about him radiated respectability. His entire person was somehow unearthly. Elijah had been heat, with rocky and jagged edges, solid and real. But my husband was cool, removed, silken like a character from a forgotten storybook. I found him painfully intriguing.

I couldn't help the twitch of hope stirring inside me. I married a stranger, but at least he was kind. Love grew from marriages. All the women who spoke in Relief Society of their husbands did so with conviction and strong testimony of plural marriage. To speak ill of the Principle was akin to blasphemy itself. Surely, that meant they loved it and their husbands. They wouldn't lie about their happiness.

I thought about the first time I met Jacob, less than two weeks ago. Pink rose in my cheeks. We'd gone for a walk together, the late-spring breeze picking up stray white blossoms from the nearby apricot trees, which oddly reminded me of floating popcorn. I recalled how he kept his pace slow and steady, always walking between myself and the street. He offered his arm over puddles and did his best to keep the conversation lively even as I stayed as neutral and pleasant as possible. Mother's teachings hounded me; men didn't want women who were too forceful or inquisitive. That could be seen as divisive and disobedient, so I held in all my probing questions to do my duty to please him.

Besides, the men in my life had already offered what I needed to know. Elder Crowther spoke of his lovely home reserved for me and his piano I could entertain with. Father had inquired through his connections and told me of his wealth and rising status in the community, rumored to be called soon to higher priesthood offices. Anything more of importance to share Jacob would surely tell me. I wasn't raised to doubt or question those who held the sacred priesthood.

I learned that he liked licorice candies and reading thick volumes on scripture. His favorite color was inexplicably black, or perhaps he was only teasing me when I asked such a silly question. His voice was a rich baritone, and he hummed snippets of hymns under his breath whenever the conversation lulled. "Come, Come, Ye Saints" was his favorite, just like mine.

After some coaxing, I shared my love of music and piano, my dislike of baking, and my secret annoyance at being patient. To my surprise, he didn't scold me for such thoughts, only laughed playfully.

"I find you quite fascinating," Jacob said. He replaced an errant lock of hair behind my ear. "And absolutely beautiful."

My heart skipped a beat. "You don't need to flatter me." I tried to force from my mind the way Elijah had looked at me when he called me beautiful, and the anger and longing the image stirred up.

"I assure you, I'm not an idle flatterer. You'll always get the truth that you need to know from me, Sister Hazel. Life's too short to be mucked up in weariness and dramatics, don't you think?" He reached his hand out tentatively toward my arm. "May I?"

My lungs felt squeezed too tight. "Of course."

I gripped his offered elbow and allowed myself to be pulled against his side. His body was warm. Solid. It hummed against mine. For once, a surge of confidence struck me. Here I was, peculiar and often wicked Hazel, on the arm of a respectable, worthy man.

Jacob grinned as we neared my house again. "There's a lovely smile now. I hope to see it often. Heaven knows a husband needs the cheerfulness of his wife."

"Are your other wives not happy?" The words came out faster than I could recall them.

His gait slackened for a moment and embarrassment rattled through me. The biggest rule of polygamy, as my mother taught me, was to mind your own business, and I'd broken it already. But almost as soon as he'd slowed, Jacob picked up his pace again, squeezing my fingers in the crook of his arm.

"My greatest occupation is to bring you happiness, my dear Hazel. Anything you ask of me that I can give is yours. I'd give all my worldly riches away to bring out that alluring smile of yours."

We reached my porch and he stopped. Carefully, he took my hand from his arm and shifted to face me, drawing my hand against his chest. My heart beat faster as I felt his own pulse beneath my palm. Elijah's heart had beat like this once in time with mine.

He leaned down until his lips brushed against my ear. "You've positively bewitched me already."

I froze. Jacob's honeyed words weren't like Elijah's fumbling ones, but what did that matter anymore? Perhaps that's why they were so intoxicating to hear and filled my chest with a sticky hope that maybe soon the Elijah-shaped gash in my soul would heal.

With a brush of his lips against my knuckles, he bid me good night. But as I went to open the front door, my hand rested on the doorknob unmoving. My chest lurched. *No, please, not now. Why did it have to be now?* My head swam with images—Elijah. Jacob. A faceless row of wives. My heart burst out of my chest.

As hard as I tried to muster the strength to push open the door and disappear, I couldn't find it. Air sucked from my lungs as the panic rose. Devils clawed at me. Sinful, stupid me. I sank to my knees on the doorstep.

"Hazel?" Jacob said.

No, he couldn't see this. He couldn't see the manifestation of my unworthiness. I didn't turn around, wishing I could sink lower into the porch and disappear altogether.

"Are you all right?"

His hands took my shoulders, and he pulled my back against his chest. The contact was a rush. He wrapped his arms around me, holding me tight. Tears leaked down my cheeks as I tried desperately to force air into my lungs, to breathe evenly before I drowned.

"I'm here, it's all right," Jacob repeated over and over. Each time his words solidified in me. He was a pillar, a rock, allowing me to cling to him even as a storm tried to destroy me. Slowly, my breaths steadied, my heartbeat slowed, my sobs softened.

After what felt an eternity, he let me go. I turned, unable to meet his eyes. "I'm so sorry," I said. "I shouldn't have—I didn't mean to—"

"It's fine, Hazel." Jacob's tone was certain. I dared to look at his face. He didn't frown or scowl like I expected. Instead, his forehead was creased with worry. Care. I swallowed the last of my frantic tears. "Does this happen often?"

I nodded. "I understand if this changes your intentions."

"Change them? Certainly not. It only endears you to me more."

I searched his eyes for a sign of deceit, but he only watched me with sincerity. That sticky heat returned to my chest. "It does?"

He stood and offered his hand to help me up. "It means you need me to protect and help you. I will do that, I promise. If this is your storm, then I'll be your anchor."

My heart jumped again, but this time not from panic. It was . . . hope.

That same hope moved through me now as the wagon carrying us jostled across a hole on the dirt road. I studied Jacob as he clicked his tongue at the horses, a sense of anticipation shuddering through me. My husband. My anchor.

"It sure is lovely out here. You can get away from the bustle of the city and be your own person." Jacob's face met mine and I blushed. "I'm sure you're eager to see your new home and begin our life together. I know I am. It'll be wonderful to finally have you all to myself." He gave a low chuckle, sending warm shivers down my neck.

"I could tell you were eager," I said.

He tilted his head, questioning.

Embarrassment gripped me. "I mean—I only meant, we left so quickly after the wedding luncheon instead of staying in town.

I didn't . . . I didn't expect that." I gripped the board beside my knees and prepared for my reprimand.

Again, to my surprise, he only smiled. His mustache twitched like he was holding back another laugh.

"Can you blame me for being in a hurry with your beauty?" His palm rested on my knee and a flush moved through me. "The luncheon wasn't particularly extravagant or crowded, in any case."

Plural marriage was God's law, but not man's. Though the government tried to fight it, make it illegal, even threaten arrest and prosecution, the Principle continued on, if only clouded in more silence.

"Well, plural wives don't typically receive much fanfare. Especially now with persecutions rising. I know my place."

The wheels of the cart crunched over a fallen branch.

"Your obedience to the Principle is commendable, dear. It's what brought our souls together, I'm certain of it." Jacob's fingers wove circles in my skirt. "We'll be happy out here, alone in the beauty of the valley."

The wind tossed back the word again and again as if trapped in an echo—alone, alone, alone. My cheeks bloomed with heat. I'd finally reached the pinnacle of my creation's purpose with Jacob. At last, now I'd be loved and accepted. I would walk this life with him by my side, alone.

Until I met his wives.

I tried to banish the three women I'd yet to meet from my mind, but they held on to the corners of my consciousness, lingering just at the edge of my imagination.

"When will I see your, I mean, at what point will I encounter—when will I meet your other wives?" I managed to ask at last.

Jacob removed his hand from my skirts and turned his attention to steering the wagon onto a less worn path. Large stalks of desert weeds whipped past us, close enough to hit the sides of the cart.

I wondered if he was ignoring my question.

"Meet them? Well, I imagine they'll grant us privacy tonight, but I'm sure they'll want help with breakfast in the morning." He clicked his tongue to hurry the horse's pace again.

"You mean, they will be at the house to greet us?"

"Well, they live there, so yes, I suppose so."

I swayed with the cart and had to grab the bench to keep from pitching over the side.

"They all live . . . you mean, you keep one house?"

Most men kept their wives separately in houses throughout the valley and even into the territory beyond. Few plural wives were able to tolerate one another, let alone live together, and most families found it simpler to keep the peace by dividing their assets and time. After all, marriage was a matter between a husband and wife only—even when that man was married to another. But Elder Crowther had said he had a house prepared *only* for me. Had I misunderstood? Would I have chosen differently if I realized?

"It's far simpler that way. I'm building an eternal kingdom and we will all be together in worlds without end, so why start off apart now?" He raised an eyebrow at me.

Together. I would live with all his wives. Why had I never asked him to confirm the apostle's words?

"I didn't realize," I said, my mouth full of gravel.

"Your father keeps one household."

"Temporarily," I responded quickly, my face growing flush. "Aunt Emma used to run her own home, but she had to come live with us when the landlord needed the house. She'll be gone again soon. Father's especially concerned about the new act from Congress."

"I don't worry about the acts of man, only God. I didn't realize this would upset you, Hazel." His voice edged with disapproval.

I struggled to reel myself back in as I'd been taught. No disagreements. Be smaller, quieter.

"Forgive me." I pressed a smile onto my face and leaned in

closer to him. "It was only a momentary surprise. A happy one, certainly. I look forward to meeting them." The lies slid out so smoothly that perhaps even I could be convinced of their truth. It'd been ridiculous of me to assume I would run my own home. My husband had every right to preside over his family as he saw fit.

"I promise you will get your fair share of my time, Hazel," said Jacob.

My stomach unclenched, though my stubborn heart continued to race. Plural marriage was God's command to His people and I needed to be more faithful. And at least, I would be Jacob's plural wife—Jacob, my anchor. My chest swooned recalling his grounding touch. If Jacob promised me a good life, then surely his wives were content.

The dirt road snaked along the river, cutting toward the mountain pass beyond. Above the towering wall of the mountain range, dark clouds gathered, ready to roll into the valley with menacing force. I swallowed the last of my doubts and finally glanced up at Jacob's stubbled face. Faint lines pulled up in the corners of his eyes as he smiled ahead. A heat surged between us, charged as the lightning waiting in the inky clouds above.

Warmth moved through my limbs as I recalled the image I'd had in the apostle's office of a happy life. I'd clung to those brief words, perhaps too scared or too heartbroken to pry deeper. Even though he'd been mistaken about the house, surely he was correct about the rest.

"Elder Crowther said you have a piano?"

Jacob paused. A cloud shifted across the sun, casting half his face into shadow. "I'm afraid I do not. You'll have to forgive me. I know how much you love to play."

"Oh," I said in a tiny voice. Elder Crowther had been wrong again.

The cloud continued on and his face was bathed once more in sunlight.

"But I could get you one, Hazel," Jacob said.

I glanced up again, biting my lower lip with tentative hope.

"I'd love to spoil you, my dear. A wife who fills a home with virtuous music is a great blessing."

A smile stretched across my face. "Thank you, Jacob. That means, well, quite a lot to me."

"I know. That's why I'll do it, my dearest." He leaned over and pressed a kiss to my temple.

Dearest. I was someone's dearest. I settled into his side, allowing myself to experience the thrill of warmth where we touched. *His* dearest.

Chapter 4

Silence hung between us as the road split again and Jacob guided the cart off to the left. A patch of cottonwood trees lined the slight bend of the road, marking the edge of a property. The dirt road became bumpier, though I could see Jacob was doing his best to steer the horse and cart around the largest potholes. A sense of finality sunk into my stomach. We had arrived.

Around the last tree, a house came into view. My mouth dropped open at its magnitude. This house rivaled Brigham's houses in size. A pointed tower sprouted up toward the heavens with a twisted weathervane perched at the top. Alongside it, impressive gables protruded up and out, revealing a line of large windows. The house was a mix of dark red brick and white painted boards. A porch with ornate lacing around the top and short wooden steps leading up to the front door completed its charm.

This house, in the far-flung reaches of the Salt Lake Valley, was something out of a dream. It was no wonder he kept three—now four—wives in this home. It could have fit an entire congregation. Elder Crowther's promises seemed to be true.

Another pothole jostled me. I dropped my eyes from the lofty heights of the house to the land around it. Neglect hung on the trees surrounding the drive, their branches either buckling from overgrowth or shivering, brittle and naked from the lack of new sprouts. Those closest to the house seemed to defy the laws of gravity, appearing as though only one strong gust of wind would send them crashing to the ground.

As we drew up to a stop at the front of the house, uncertainty coiled through me. Though the May afternoon was plenty warm, a shiver ran down my spine as I took it all in. Jacob jumped down from the cart, but I made no move to remove myself.

Thick bushes that looked as if they'd once been planted and tended with care grew feral and tangled around the front porch. Wild tawny vines crawled up the sides of the house, choking the lower windows and their weatherworn shutters, as if the terrain were trying to reclaim the home as its own. Cracks zigzagged up the red brick and fissured out from the window corners like derelict latticework.

The half-dozen windows on the second floor seemed to loom inward as if to get a better look at me. The house watching me with blighted eyes.

I shook my head to displace the image. Houses didn't move or watch, and they certainly didn't have eyes.

Jacob appeared at my side, his arms held up to lift me down from the cart. For a moment, I held my breath, allowing my jumbled and thorny worries to root inside me.

It wasn't that the house being in disrepair offended my sensibilities. It was a whisper of concern that something about it—its strange, forsaken structure—didn't measure up. Both Elder Crowther and Father had assured me that Jacob was wealthy, and he himself had promised that he could take care of me. Too many women across the Territory suffered in silent poverty brought on by polygamy, but I had been promised that wasn't my fate.

"This is your house?" I asked.

Jacob's hands wrapped around my waist. Their warmth as he lifted me from the wagon fought the foreboding feeling throbbing against my rib cage.

"Indeed, it is. *Our* house, Hazel." His fingers held me firm as he lowered me to the ground. He gripped me tight an extra moment before releasing me and stepping back with an outstretched hand. "Welcome to Manwaring Manor."

A manor. Such places existed only in fairy tales, though this one appeared trapped in a dark story, long forgotten and eaten back up by the forest. The house creaked and I had the distinct impression that it listened for my response. I swallowed the strange thought.

"It's a fine house, isn't it? I bought it from a man who built it and then abandoned it. Some railroad speculation gone wrong. And don't worry about how it appears now. I've got so many plans for it, just you wait. I think you'll find it's plenty comfortable."

"It's lovely," I said, recalling my earlier convictions. "Some paint will brighten it right up. Perhaps some new shutters?"

A curtain fluttered in the top window of the spire, drawing my attention. Somebody stared back at me through the narrow gap, lit by a soft glow. Then, just as quickly as they had appeared, the curtains closed and they were gone.

"Come, let's get inside before the sun sets and we catch a chill."

Jacob held out his hand. I ignored the pang of discomfort at being watched and gladly took his steady arm.

The wooden steps creaked as we walked up to the door. A thin layer of moss grew across the edges of the porch, and the boards sagged beneath our weight. I drew in a soft breath.

And as I exhaled, so did someone else. I heard it distinctly, sharp in my ears. It felt cold, almost impossibly so, on the back of my neck.

I spun around, but there was no one there.

It was only a breeze.

The broad doorframe was trimmed in a fading spring green with a muted pattern of pink flowers painted across the top, suggesting that once someone had loved this place enough to paint it with strokes of care and hope. But now the decoration moldered away to almost nothing, forlorn from neglect.

I gasped as Jacob swept me up into his arms. My body seized up tight at the shock of being quite literally in his embrace, our bodies pressed against each other as they never had been before. All thoughts of the house flew from mind as I remembered that this was also my wedding night.

I dizzied at his scent—the residue of lavender soap and musk of sweat from the day. Everything about him was so much more real and solid as I breathed him in. The warmth I'd felt earlier in the wagon ride once again swept through me. I dared to wrap my arms around his neck and leaned in closer, trampling the image of Elijah's face that motion conjured.

His chest rumbled against my ear as he carried me across the threshold. His heartbeat seemed to mimic mine in a tight but wild rhythm. With me cradled in his arms, we studied each other. His eyes traced mine, etching back and forth until they dropped down to my lips.

The thought of savoring his lips against mine was maddening, enticing even. I blinked. Elijah's lips had tasted of the crisp apple we'd pulled from the tree to share minutes before our first embrace. I tried to flick the memory from my mind, to burn it to ashes.

"Jacob?"

A soft voice cut through our trance. His breath hitched. Our eyes lifted from our tangled stare toward the call. In the entry room, across from the grand staircase leading upstairs, a figure stood in a doorway. She was illuminated by a beam of golden sunlight falling through a nearby window. My cheeks flushed from our almost-kiss.

The voice belonged to a woman—a quite pregnant woman. My stomach twisted. I was bearing witness to the consequences of my own plural marriage for the first time. Watching the Principle growing up didn't prepare me for this visceral pain.

Jacob released my knees and placed me back on the floor. I smoothed my skirt with shaking hands, praying she wouldn't notice my tremor. She was short and slender except for her swollen belly protruding underneath the cream apron tied beneath her bust. Her sunflower-blond hair tousled in waves over her shoulders giving her an otherworldly glow in the early evening light. She was beautiful—far more beautiful than me.

"Prudence, so nice to see you." Jacob's tone stayed firm but jovial, as if he were greeting a casual friend in passing, and not the woman so clearly carrying his child while he brought his new bride through the doorway. "How are you feeling?"

"Fine," she said in a gentle voice. Her eyes brushed me up and down, and heat crawled up my back. She might hate me, the horrid voices whispered in my head. I'd just burst through the door of her home in the arms of her husband. My husband. Our husband.

My chest tightened.

Another face popped around the corner, severe and angular enough to cut you with only a glance.

"Prudence, why do you insist on standing there? Can't you see my hands are full of laundry?" A willowy woman stepped up behind the other with a large basket in her arms. Her graying hair pulled up in a tight bun, exaggerating her sharp features. With glasses balanced on her nose and the scowl on her lips, she reminded me of a strict schoolteacher. She bristled when she noticed me, straightening her shoulders as she raked me up and down. I fought the urge to cower behind Jacob.

"Who is this?" she asked in a tone that suggested swallowed surprise. Why would she pretend not to know?

"Flora, hello. How are you?" Jacob's pleasant tone didn't change as he shuffled a step closer to me. His hand rested on the small of my back, the intense warmth beneath his fingertips like fire.

"I'm well," she said, not taking her eyes off me. Her gaze dropped to my waistline and she clicked her tongue as if sizing me up. His grip tightened on my bodice like he sensed it too.

Tension clouded the room, so thick I was certain we would

soon see it as a fog. It brought with it a rush and electric silence, like the minutes before a mountain thunderstorm. No one spoke. I choked at the invisible weight lodging in my chest. I tried to take in more air as discreetly as I could. Why did the Devil have to take me now with his panics?

Shrill laughter cut through the room. A new voice. The others turned their attention to the grand staircase across the entry as if they knew exactly from where she would come.

Another woman descended the stairs and sat on the bottom step, her arms resting atop her knees. She appeared casual and calm, watching the show unravel before her. Her face was unreadable, a queer smile dancing on her lips.

Three voices, three wives.

Though this woman was probably more than a decade my senior like Jacob, she was breathtakingly beautiful. Fiery red curls framed her face, bringing out the punch of her gemstone-green eyes. A constellation of freckles dotted her porcelain cheeks and the bridge of her nose. Even without having said a word, her presence was commanding. She filled all the space around her; she knew she was mesmerizing.

The wife on the stairs laughed again.

"So, you brought home another wife. How charming." Her tone was peculiar. I couldn't tell if she meant to be scathing or condoning.

Jacob didn't relinquish his grip on me. "Yes, I have. This is Hazel."

"Pleased to meet you," I said between shallow breaths.

The panic couldn't happen, not now, not here. I needed to make a good impression on my new family.

"Ah, so that's where you've been spending your evenings then." The woman on the stairs didn't take her eyes off our husband. She dropped her hands to her sides and leaned back, fully revealing her large bosom and trim waist.

I tried my best not to stare, instead turning toward the other pair of wives, who were averting their gaze.

"You didn't know?" I asked, then turned back to Jacob. "You hadn't told them you were getting married?" I thought for a moment that the floorboards quaked beneath my feet.

"We trust that Jacob knows best as the head of this family," the tall wife—Flora, was it?—cut in.

The other beside her nodded in agreement.

Jacob beamed. "My family knows that their patriarch holds wisdom beyond their own. What a great blessing you all are to me."

"As you are to us," Flora said, shooting a look at the unnamed wife on the stairs.

"Yes, and isn't it exciting how the Lord chooses to bless us next?" The wife on the stairs pushed herself to standing, towering over us on her perch. "Why, you're even younger than the last. We're going to have to build another nursery."

I wasn't certain if that was an insult to my age or a suggestion about my womb. Her kind smile didn't ease the weight on my chest as I tried harder to breathe.

The room took on a purple hue in the growing dusk. The unnamed wife walked down the stairs, stopping directly in front of Jacob and me. No one had offered her name yet and I was too afraid to ask. A ripple of fresh panic crested through me. I was trapped between my husband and his wife. I wasn't prepared for any of this.

She tilted her head. "Oh dear, is she all right? I'm not sure she's even breathing."

Jacob's arm slid around my shoulders.

"Hazel is fine." He glanced down at me. "I'm here, dear. You can calm down."

"I'm just—it's only—"

The wife grabbed my hand and tugged it toward her.

"Long day, my dear?" she said.

She sounded sincere. I simply nodded as she worked to unclench my fisted fingers.

"I understand it's overwhelming on one's *special* day. But it'll be fine. You're here with us now and we'll all make the best of it. Welcome, little Hazel, to Manwaring Manor."

"Yes, welcome," the short wife—Prudence?—said in agreement. The tall wife nodded solemnly as if accepting her fate.

Welcome. They said I was welcome. I'd come unannounced and unexpected, and they welcomed me. Surely that meant this was a good place, that I'd made the right choice of husband.

"Thank you," I said, leaning into Jacob's side. My anchor in this new storm.

The wife Flora tutted loudly as if signaling an end to the party.

Prudence smiled softly. "Sister Hazel, it's late and I'm sure you're tired, so we can save all the introductions for tomorrow."

"Yes, you better go on up to your room for this important night," the still unnamed wife from the stairs added, giving my fingers one final sharp squeeze. "Sleep well, Sister Manwaring. You're in good company."

With a flick of her wrist, she removed her hand and brushed past us, disappearing through the open doorway. After a quick shuffle of bodies and last glances over at me, the others followed close behind her.

Sister Manwaring. One of four. This was my life now.

Chapter 5

The bed tucked in the corner of the room seemed enormous with its thick wooden headboard and four tall posts. Its blue and yellow patchwork quilt shone like a beacon, reminding me that in marriages, beds were not only for sleeping. I tore my eyes away to assess the rest of my room.

The neatly made bed appeared to be the only piece of furniture that had seen any cleaning in quite some time. A delicate vanity table encrusted with dust sat along the wall beside the window. Its ornately carved mirror was covered in a film of dirty smudges. On the opposite wall, an armoire covered in faded green paint sat empty, its door ajar. I turned toward the hearth, at least expecting a bit of life there, but the mantel displayed only more dust, the fireplace a pile of forgotten ash. The brass clock in the center would certainly be no help with its hands stuck at midnight.

The room was large and empty enough that the sound of my boots echoed as I walked. Cobwebs stuck in the corners of the ceiling. A chilled draft blew through me and I shuddered. I fought an overwhelming urge to cry. None of this was how I'd imagined my wedding night.

I crossed the room and pushed the curtains aside, desperately needing a view of something else. The darkness of night stared back at me, but I could tell my room faced out toward the valley and I imagined my entire universe—every corner I'd ever known—stretching out before me. An ache clenched in my chest. In my mind I saw the corner store, the bricked walls of the newspaper office, the silvered dome of the Tabernacle. And my family. Somewhere out in that great distance my family gathered for dinner with one less chair at their table. The realization hit me that it'd be many months before I'd pass another meal with them. Desire for their familiar presence suddenly clawed at me.

Be good, my girl. My mother's final words as she embraced me one last time came back to my mind. *Be an obliging wife as I taught you and all will be well. Even if it's hard, you must do what God commands.*

I would write her right away, assure her that I was doing my best. Perhaps she'd be proud of me in her response. The thought of her intimate handwriting and kind words was suddenly of desperate importance. How could I survive this strange place without something well-known to buoy me?

The floor creaked behind me, sparing me the ruin of thinking further on such saddening things, and I spun around. Jacob stood in the doorway, his arms full of my case and hatboxes. He flashed me a smile like a well-trained porter and shut the door with the heel of his foot. My stomach lurched in anticipation. Without taking his eyes off me, Jacob crossed the room and placed my things by the vanity. He ran his finger across the surface and examined the dirt that came off with a click of his tongue.

"I apologize for the state of the room. I didn't realize it'd gotten so bad." He brushed the offending dust off on his trousers.

"Oh no. It's fine. It's a lovely room." I turned back toward the window, my hands pinching tight together. Though my earlier panic had subsided, I still sensed it simmering inside, my body a string pulled too tight. "Besides, now I'll have the chance to make it up as I see fit."

Jacob smiled as I studied his reflection in the window glass.

"This is what I love about you, my Hazel. Always so obedient and cheerful. You look on the pleasant side of life."

I smiled back. If only he knew the secret horrors always crawling through and staining my mind.

He drew a step closer, growing larger, distorted, in the glass. Behind us, a sole candle flickered by the bedside, though I couldn't remember lighting it.

"But I also have my struggles." I tried to keep my voice steady as he stopped close enough for his shallow breaths to raise the hair on the back of my neck. Warmth gathered in my center.

"You saw them yourself," I said, silently praying he'd repeat his words from before. I would need his promised shelter in this storm.

His gaze raked down my neck, his mouth slightly agape, his breathing growing heavier. "We all have our troubles, my dear. And the Lord will try us until they are refined. But don't worry yourself more on it. Everything will work out in the Lord's time."

Behind us, the candle flared.

Jacob cleared his throat as if to end the subject, but his righteous counsel didn't bring relief as it should. I watched his eyes trace me up and down in the window's reflection, unable to linger in any one spot for too long. Heat bloomed in my cheeks. I needed to ignore my discomfort and focus on better things, like the warmth of his body hovering against my back, scant inches between us now.

"Is there anything I can do to make you feel more at ease?" His breath brushed my ear as he rested his chin on my shoulder. "Name it, and it's yours."

"I would like something." Could I truly make demands of my husband on our first day of marriage?

"And what is that?"

Jacob didn't sound upset, so I continued. "I want to make sure my letters to my family reach them quickly. We're so far away out here. Will you deliver them the next time you ride into town?" I imagined Mother's letter, brought back in only a few days to encourage me.

"I think that could be arranged. . . ." His words drifted off as his hands wrapped around my waist, locking me firmly against him. My heart pounded out of time, unsure of which rhythm to follow. I could feel his own heart hammering faster against my back.

We were as close now as we'd ever been. The embrace was inviting, warm, everything I imagined a husband's touch would be. I forcefully shoved the hope for familiar reassurance from my head. I needed to be here now—to be a true wife to my husband. Though the thought intimidated me, I sunk back into him and felt our bodies connect against each other. A new momentum built inside me. Part of me wanted to softly moan like I had when Elijah kissed me that first time, but it seemed a strange inclination so I bit my tongue.

"Hazel, are you all right, darling?" Jacob brushed kisses against my shoulders. Each touch of his lips sent fire down to my toes.

"Yes, perfectly fine," I said.

My hands trembled as his roved lower down my sides. Only Elijah had touched me this intimately before. I sensed we stood on the edge of a forest, ready to set it ablaze. Fingers twitched below my waistline.

"Don't be frightened, my dearest. Trust me."

Jacob's words dripped in my ear like soft rain.

I nodded in silent agreement as he spun me to face him. Wrapping my arms around his neck, I tugged us close. But in the back of my mind, Elijah embraced me. Heat zinged and splattered in the tiny spaces between our pressed bodies. Jacob's mouth searched for mine, eager and trembling. My lips found his, sparking against the darkening room. In my memories, Elijah's tongue bid my lips open. I sagged against Jacob's chest.

Deep in my center, primal need awoke and swelled and consumed. I was here in my husband's arms, but I couldn't contain the unbidden thoughts that moved through me. In my head, Elijah's body held me close, his honeyed words trickled in my ears, his lips worshipped my skin.

Lord, forgive me my sins.

Jacob snored. His shoulders rose and shook with every noisy breath as he lay beside me on the bed. I held back a snicker. Shifting away from my husband, I stared into the darkness. Unlike my bedmate, I couldn't sleep. My body ached with exhaustion, but my mind refused to silence itself. The day relived itself over and over through my head—the binding promises, the dilapidated house, the unknowing wives, the blistering passion.

Cold air seeped through the crack of the windowsill and, even beneath the covers with my husband's warm body so close, I shuddered. Only the occasional groans of the old house interrupted the midnight stillness. But instead of feeling tranquil, the quiet closed around me in an oppressive vise grip.

My body seized, every weight of the long day constricting around me. I'd fought it since I dressed that morning for my wedding, but now the panic finally overtook me.

My head felt heavy against the pillow. A force unseen was pressing down on me. It sat on my chest, threatening to cut off my air. I would die in this bed by invisible hands if I couldn't find my breath.

I opened my mouth wide, gulping at the cool air. The Devil couldn't defeat me, not now. Not when I was at last married and my life had truly begun. I sparred with the unseen monster on my chest; my frantic heart struggled to slow.

A loud creak echoed across the room. My eyes flew open. A distinct groan forced life into my limbs and I shot up. Now my heart beat out of time for another reason.

I peered around the room. In the darkness, lit only by the faint moonlight from the window, everything was the same as it had been when I'd first entered the room. A shiver climbed my back. My eyes traced the dark walls and blackened shadows to the door.

A muted brightness pierced through the gloom—a thin line of light illuminating from beneath the door. I clutched the blankets in my fists, dragging them tighter against me. Someone lurked in the hallway. They'd come to spy on me. Perhaps even to see if they could hear any sounds coming from our marriage bed. My stomach twisted into a knot.

I listened for footsteps, a knock, a murmured voice, but there was nothing. The silence stretched on. Eventually, the light flickered, then faded gradually from sight. I heard no footsteps, not even a rustling. The midnight visitor as good as a ghost.

Chapter 6

Morning light filtered through the fraying curtains, casting strange shadows across the room. I sat up, momentarily uncertain of where I was. As my memories returned to me, I settled back into our bed. Jacob was gone, but in his place a long-stemmed wildflower sat on the pillow. I picked it up with careful fingers, a giddiness spreading through me.

Clutching Jacob's gift, I took in the room in the light of day. The view from the bed was so different from that of my childhood bedroom. The peeling cream wallpaper was a far cry from the neat blue walls I'd grown up with, and the room felt devoid of life.

In fact, the entire house did. Except for the occasional close of a door or the patter of distant footsteps, the house seemed uncomfortably silent. I swung my legs over the edge of the bed. Part of me wondered if I stayed here, hidden away, this house would all turn out to be a strange dream.

The hinges of the armoire squeaked as the door swung slowly open and I startled.

"It's only old furniture, Hazel," I scolded myself, and placed my feet firmly on the floorboards.

"I suppose you're trying to tell me to get up?" I said to the armoire with a laugh. Of course, it made no response.

"Only one day here and already I'm speaking to furniture," I grumbled as I stood.

A whisper of movement brushed against my ankle. I shuddered.

"Rats," I murmured, scanning the floorboards around the bed. "Of course, there's rats."

I placed Jacob's flower on the dusty vanity, a bright reminder of budding hope against a marred world.

My clothes were still packed away in my case, so I knelt and pulled out the dress on top—a checkered black and white print on a simple skirt that I hoped would show I was humble, practical. I needed to show my husband—and his wives—that I was trying. That I would be the perfect plural wife.

I cocked my ear toward the door as I did up the buttons on my bodice. There were no sounds, no children squealing or running, no mothers scolding or teaching. Surely, there were many people in this house? But Jacob had never spoken of his children, or even formally told me the names of his wives. And I'd been too afraid to ask, even now.

But one of them stalked my door last night.

The door of the armoire moaned again. I jumped.

This was my new reality. Staring at myself in the dusty, cracked mirror, I raised my chin.

"I can do this," I recited to myself.

Based on the light pouring through the window, it was late in the morning. I rushed toward the door. The other wives would certainly dislike my delay. Or perhaps they never spoke to one another and wouldn't notice me at all? Even though they were forced into the same house for the last year, Mother ignored Aunt Emma as much as possible, leaving her to tend her own children and household as if they didn't share the same four walls.

Sucking in a breath to fortify myself, I stepped out into the hallway. There was only one way to prove myself in this strange house.

"Jacob?" I called out softly and waited. No one responded. "Jacob, are you there?"

Only the floor creaking beneath me returned my call.

A line of doors mirrored one another down the hall until it veered off into another wing. Sunlight streamed through the twin set of windows at the end of this wing of hallway, providing some light in the absence of gas lamps. A yellowing carpet covered parts of the floorboards, though it appeared pieces of it had moldered or been ripped away. I shifted back toward my own room, which was closest to the stairs.

A door shut loudly somewhere down the hallway and I whipped my head around.

"Who are you?" a tiny voice said.

I looked down at a small boy, no more than four, in front of me. His hair was matted on one side as if he'd only recently woken from sleep, his clothes disheveled like he'd fought as he dressed. He stared up at me with wide blue eyes—Jacob's eyes.

"Oh, hello." I tried to make my voice sweet and calm as I'd heard my mother do. "My name is Hazel. I suspect I'm your new aunt."

I bent down to his eye level with an even smile.

"Hmm," he responded, rubbing his hand in his eye as he studied me. "Like the other."

"Yes, like your other aunts."

There was something odd in the way he stared at me, like he couldn't believe I was there. His unblinking eyes and solemn expression were unsettling in a child so young.

"What's your name?" I asked. By virtue of being the eldest daughter in a plural family, I'd spent most of my years caring for younger children. I enjoyed their little minds and quirks, though this child struck me as rather particular.

"Edward."

"Edward, nice to meet you." I stood slowly, extending my hand toward him.

Squinting, he poked at my palm with a single finger.

Yes, a very particular child. I smiled again, though strangeness wrapped around me.

"Edward, do you think you could show me to where the others are?" I asked.

He nodded and started down the stairs.

The steps squeaked and sagged beneath my feet as I followed him. Below, the entry appeared the same as the evening before, only empty and teaming with sunlight from the high stained-glass windows. Mosaiced diamonds filtered the light in a variety of colors but did little to bring life to the stale room. What should have been a place of welcome and respite was oddly bare and uninviting. Mother would've hated it. I bit my tongue to keep from laughing, or perhaps crying, at the thought of her circling the room with a severe frown.

I looked up at the chandelier above, more rusted than sparkling, a hundred unseen eyes scrutinizing me in its tarnished jewels. Edward grabbed my hand, tugging my gaze away from the foreboding entry.

"You're slow, Aunt," he stated.

I resisted the urge to stick out my tongue like I would with my little brothers. "Maybe you're simply too fast, little sprite."

That seemed to please him and he grinned, dragging me across the entry to the doorway the other wives had disappeared through after our strange introduction the night before. We walked down a hallway lined with fading floral wallpaper until it opened into an expansive room.

"Is anyone here?" My voice echoed off the high walls. The only response was another tug of my hand. This time I followed even more slowly, allowing myself a moment to take in the room.

Despite the expectation of grandeur, this main parlor lacked what I envisioned for a fine home. Fraying and mismatched furniture cast the room into chaos, as if the family had gathered every scrap they could find without thinking of how it would look assembled together. There were two high-backed red chairs with fabric so bare it almost looked white, a large rocking chair beside a small one, a once-elegant checkered pink sofa with a wood-tipped back, and an assortment of embroidered stools all bearing different stages of age. Three side tables of various sizes and wood colors sat here and there among the seats. All of it begged the question—exactly how many people lived here? And when was the last time they all gathered in this unkept room?

I couldn't help thinking of Ammon as I brushed over the many footstools to the fireplace. He always loved a place to stretch out his lanky legs. Perhaps one day he could come and visit to try them out. The thought didn't balloon into hope, though, only a vague dread.

The hearth was massive, an impressive arrangement of brick and stone beneath an ornate beam. A row of books lined the mantel, though it looked as if they hadn't been picked up in some time. It seemed almost blasphemous to see such lovely books settled within a layer of dust.

A few framed pictures hung on the cream-splashed walls of hand-drawn nature scenes, but most hung askew, and none were family portraits. No heirlooms or bobbles or treasures adorned the empty spaces. There was nothing at all really to distinguish Manwaring Manor as belonging to its own.

"Do you usually spend time here as a family, Edward?" I asked, not taking my eye off the gaping hearth. If I wasn't thinking sensibly, I would think the fireplace yawned like it could swallow me into its depths. Still, hair rose on my arms.

The boy shrugged, prodding me toward the next doorway.

"No, it likes it quiet."

I swallowed. How strange his words struck me. What should've been the heart of the home was unnerving. Unnatural.

At last, I followed Edward through the next doorway. A large dining table took up most of the space. Long rows of mismatched chairs ran along the table, each more out of place than the next.

Some were cushioned and well-used, others wood with fading stain, and one appeared to be a repurposed armchair.

"Ah, the dining room," I said as my mind flooded with memories of the dining room back home. My *mother's* home, I corrected.

"We spend a lot of time here eating," Edward said. "It doesn't mind that. Usually."

It?

"I'm glad to hear you eat then. I was worried." I laughed nervously, but he didn't join me. "Where is everyone this morning?"

"Here." He pointed to one of two further doors. "You'll find the other."

I nodded.

"Good morning, is anyone there?" I asked as I approached, my voice hoarser than I anticipated.

The door thumped. Someone was inside, but there were no voices.

"Edward, are you sure?" I turned back, but the young boy was gone, a giggle reverberating as he disappeared back into the depths of the house.

"What a strange child," I whispered, pushing the door open with a creak.

A ferocious bath of sunlight stunned me, stopping me in the doorway. When I regained my sight, no one greeted me. The room was empty. I released a slow exhale. The boy had played a trick on me. Heat twinged in my ears. It was silly of me to follow him in the first place. Perhaps the whole family was in on the joke.

Fighting the sudden urge to cry, I looked around the room. It was small with two windows stretching nearly to the ceiling. Judging from the shape of the room, this must've been the base of the turret I'd seen outside yesterday.

A loudly ticking, standing clock counted out the moments as I studied the room. Shelves took up most of the walls, each covered with haphazardly placed tomes and curious items. Leftover cups and dark transparent bottles of liquids that by strict definition shouldn't have been drunk in a Mormon home lay between stacks of books and rolled-up parchments. But not all adhered to the Word of Wisdom health code exactly—even prophets and apostles—so I couldn't judge their use. Riding gloves sat with empty glass jars, and what appeared to be a discarded long knife.

More thin dust layered over it all. The only part of the room that appeared cared for was the line of black and brown books of scripture on the highest shelf.

A heavy desk consumed the center of the room. Two well-worn brass oil lamps suggested a lot of late-night readings. A map of what appeared to be a mine took up a majority of the desk's surface and was surrounded by three high stacks of paper. A quill and ink lay askew as if dropped in a hurry. All of it left an unsettling knot in my stomach.

This had to be Jacob's personal study.

I ran my fingers across the dated globe beside me. It grunted and protested, unable to spin. Retracting my hand, I turned to the only frame hung in the room. The probing eyes of the prophet Brigham Young glared back. Even in portrait, he saw straight through me. It was strange Jacob didn't have a single picture of his family in his study, only this man.

This disordered space contrasted peculiarly with the gentlemanly manner I'd seen from my new husband, and none of it was welcoming. In fact, it felt forbidden. What if he discovered me snooping around his private things? Surely, this place was off-limits.

The floor was solid beneath me and yet somehow unstable. It felt like I stood on a piece of earth that shouldn't have existed. Even the air tasted off, sharp with a tang. This room was . . . wrong. The urge to leave and never return pumped through my veins.

I took a step back toward the door, but a dance of light flickered across the highest shelf. Without thinking, I reached up and ran my fingers along the line of holy books. I lingered on the last black spine. A shock sizzled in my fingertips and I yelped, drawing my hand back to my side, both amazed and confused at what had just happened.

All at once, cold slipped down my body like I'd jumped into an icy river. I gasped and stumbled back until I flattened against the door. Frigidity settled in my bones and I shivered uncontrollably. I fumbled for the doorknob.

"This isn't real."

I nearly fell as I thrust open the door and spilled back into the adjoining room. Warmth spread through my iced veins. I blinked around the dining room, needing to recall where I was. Slowly, my breathing calmed and my memory of the unexpected freeze dissipated into a moment of silliness. But my heart didn't settle.

This massive house was—peculiar. Frightening. Intoxicatingly strange.

Or perhaps I was the strange one. This was my husband's house and all I found were faults.

I moved toward the last doorway in the dining room. For the first time all morning, I heard familiar voices. My chest tightened. At last. I needed to stop wandering and see to my duty. The other wives were on the other side of this door.

CHAPTER 7

The door croaked as it opened onto the spacious kitchen. A long brown table took up the center of the room, surrounded by shelves of dry goods and a large iron stove. At the far end of the room was a dark-bricked hearth hung with drying herbs.

Someone cleared their throat. The pregnant wife—Prudence, I recalled—sat at the end of the table closest to me, her face fixed in a tiny smile. The tall wife—Flora—loomed right behind her, staring down her nose as I stood in the doorway.

Words dried on my tongue. My hands twitched in my skirts as silence stretched between us. They'd been here all morning, but never heard me calling through the house. Or they'd been ignoring me. Where was Jacob to anchor me through this new storm?

"Good morning." Prudence's soft voice at last broke through the quiet.

"Yes, good morning, Sister," Flora grumbled. She didn't bother to hide her disdain, tutting her tongue audibly.

"Good morning," I said.

Prudence waved me in. "What is your name again, Sister?" There was a warmth lining her tone and her faint British accent was charming.

"Hazel," I said, praying my voice gave off some kind of confidence.

"Nice to meet you formally, Sister Hazel." She coaxed me another pace into the kitchen, but I stood unsure if I was welcome at the table or if I should remain standing until told otherwise.

"I'm Prudence, and this is Flora."

Flora promptly turned on her heel to the sink.

"I'm pleased to meet you formally." My eyes dipped to Prudence's protruding stomach. She must've been close to bearing her child, and the thought cracked at a place unexpected within and let out a hum of jealousy. I did my best to ignore it and the uncomfortable thoughts that came along with it.

"I was looking for Jacob, but I see he's not here," I continued, feeling sillier by the moment.

"Yes, Jacob usually leaves early to get about his work on the property or at the mine. It's not unusual for him to be gone for days at a time," Prudence said.

Days? Had he left me already to fend for myself with his wives?

"But today, I imagine he'll be back around dinner."

I exhaled. Being useful would distract me until then—from unwanted feelings, from being sinfully idle, from the ridiculous thoughts that the house watched my every move.

"May I help with something?" At least this room didn't appear to be in complete disarray, though it was sparse for serving a large family.

Flora scoffed from the sink. "You could've helped if you'd been up as expected."

"Forgive me for oversleeping," I said. "This certainly isn't how I intended to start things off."

"I should hope not."

Prudence jumped in. "Sister Flora, she must be tired after all the . . . excitement. She only arrived last night." Her words came out sweet as honey. My hope rose. Maybe she meant to be kind to me. "Don't worry another moment about it, Sister Hazel. We're glad you're well rested after your busy day yesterday. Wedding days are quite the production, are they not?"

"Oh yes, it was very . . . interesting."

No one acknowledged the unspoken truth about the previous night—my wedding night. Fractured pictures conjured in my mind, a paralyzing jumble of skin, mouths, and bright-hot sensations.

"For a fourth wife? I doubt it." Flora's cold tone cut like a knife.

Prudence grimaced. "Flora, please—"

"Please what? You should care the most, Sister Prudence. You're no longer his newest wife."

"Unlike you, I care nothing for position over others, Sister Flora, so you can stop your tirade." She appeared surprisingly unphased by the tension brewing around us, and by Flora's menacing stare, but it tore at me.

Every household had a hierarchy of wives. It was an inevitable but unspoken reality of polygamy, with the older wives typically ruling over the newest, though sometimes the wife with the most children took that place. Either way, there was always a superior or a favorite. Mother had been Father's favorite, much to Aunt Emma's chagrin. I couldn't yet sense what stakes were at play in my new home, but the strain between the two women struck me with uncertainty. How could these women allow such discord to take root in their hearts?

"It's not my intention to cause any extra strife," I said. The impulse to immediately begin bailing water out of a sinking boat was innate.

Prudence shifted again in her seat. "No, and we would never think it of you."

"But you didn't know I was coming and—"

"And why should we?" Flora said. "Marriage is between a man and his wife, not his *wives*."

My shoulders drooped. This woman's manner was practical, but laced with unrestrained anger. She wasn't one I wanted to fight with ever. She also appeared to be working the hardest.

Behind us, the door closed with a thud, but before I could swivel toward the sound, an arm draped across my shoulders.

"Well, she's here now, isn't she? No reason to spend another moment fretting over it." The unnamed wife from the night before leaned against me.

Her strawberry hair was braided neatly down her back, and her dress was a vibrant pink floral. Her unconventional attire stood in stark contrast to the dark hues and tight hairstyles of the rest of us. From so close, I could see thin lines of worry etched across her face, but they did nothing to detract from her beauty. Her grip was tight, her fingers digging into my skin. It was both soothing and frightening at once, and I again didn't know what to think of her. Of any of them.

"I realize that scoundrel of a husband didn't properly introduce us last night. He's so silly, teasing me like that."

Had Jacob not named her on purpose? But that wouldn't make any sense.

"My name is Abigail. Though you may call me Abby as he prefers. The others do." Another knot loosened in my chest. "Instead of chiding her, Sister Flora, give her some bread. I'm sure she's starving."

As if on cue, my stomach gurgled in agreement. I hadn't eaten since the luncheon yesterday and even then, I managed to only nibble on the spread.

"If she'd been on time—"

"She'd have gotten a full meal, yes. So, she'll just have to manage with some bread until dinner." No smile traced Abigail's lips, but she spoke confidently, unquestioningly. She pushed me to the table.

Flora seemed to consider her words with annoyance, then bent over and retrieved a scrap of bread from a bowl. Glaring at

Abigail, she plopped the morsel onto the table and then went back to her original task. Abigail was clearly the leading and first wife, but it didn't appear Flora entirely agreed with her position beneath her. Whether that meant that Abigail was unfairly domineering or Flora was jealously ambitious, I wasn't certain, but the last thing I needed was to make an enemy of either.

I rubbed my palms down my skirt. "I don't need this much fuss. I'm fine, truly."

"Nonsense. Eat."

I didn't dare look up as I took the piece of bread and popped pieces into my mouth as if I were being force-fed. Anything to end this tension that clawed at me.

"Good. Now, I've just got the children started on their morning reading. Prudence, why don't you have Hazel help you with hanging the washing after she's finished eating. I'm sure you young women have much in common."

Abigail's eyes flicked down to Prudence's stomach.

Her instructions were met with only silence and her face drooped into a scowl.

"You all act as if you've just been invited to a funeral. Cheer up."

She teased out a loose curl from her hair and her lips ticked up into a queer smile. It was beautiful, but cold. "Just because your husband found someone new to fondle doesn't mean we have to be so rude. Grow up, children."

I kept my eyes set on the grain of the wood in the table as the door crashed behind us, signaling Abigail's departure. No one spoke, or dared to breathe loudly, for some time. I wished I could disappear into the floorboards altogether. We all knew the realities of marriage, but I'd never heard anyone speak of it so plainly.

Still, if Abigail was the first wife, I wanted to make a good impression and follow her word. A good plural wife was helpful and cheerful—not quarrelsome.

"Don't start by making a habit of siding with Abby, Sister Hazel. She's ridiculous, as you can see," Flora said as if she could sense my thoughts.

"At least she is kind to me," I said, louder than I intended. I quickly picked at my bread to hide my red-hot cheeks.

Flora laughed. "You'll find that kindness has little to do with usefulness."

The bench scraped across the floor, striking through the conversation and moving me with it. "Let's get started on the washing, Sister Hazel." Prudence avoided my eyes as she spoke.

I followed her out the door, eager to leave behind the suffocating presence of Sister Flora.

Chapter 8

I hefted the large wicker basket of laundry on my hip, trailing a waddling Prudence from the back porch to the crisscross of hanging lines tied between trees and the house. The garden was even more overgrown back here, like the mountain forest beyond was coming to slowly retake the land. Only a space directly behind the house was cleared for laundry, the kitchen garden, and chopping wood. On the outskirts of the yard, one path edged in uninviting brush lead into the wilderness. I immediately prayed I would never have to take it.

The tension from the kitchen clung to me. Each step away from the house seemed harder, as if we plunged through ever-thickening mud. As I walked away from it, I sensed the home rising up behind us. I shook my head against the ridiculous thought.

Prudence signaled where to drop the basket.

"It'll be much easier to do this with your help. Bending over isn't my greatest strength these days." A whistle of a laugh escaped between her teeth as she handed me a handful of clothespins.

"Certainly, I intend to be useful here." Once I proved myself in this family, then I could ask those harder questions probing at me. Trust was earned in worthiness and obedience in Mormonism. "Simply instruct me what to do," I said with perhaps too much forced eagerness.

Again, she laughed softly.

"I would tell you first to relax. We can be friends. Flora often acts as if our situation is a competition, but I think that's silly."

"I appreciate your friendship, though you'll discover that relaxing isn't one of my great strengths."

She gestured for me to retrieve a dress from the basket for her. "Then I'll try my best to teach you how."

"I'll happily let you try," I said.

Perhaps between Jacob's love—sparked in his passion the night before and solidified in a placed flower this morning—and Prudence's friendship I could gain some surer footing.

"It's only nerves from the newness. I'm lucky to have married Jacob after—"

I cut myself off. Elijah wasn't a topic I could broach ever again. Instead, I bent to retrieve the dress and changed the subject, as if I'd said nothing.

"May I ask when you are expecting?"

"Should be about two more months." Her face brightened as she stroked her belly.

"Your first?"

"It'll be my second," she answered. "My eldest, Edward, is almost four."

I recalled my strange tour this morning. "Edward? I met him this morning."

"Oh good, he's a darling."

I returned her smile, though I was uncertain of what to say. He was darling—and very odd.

"I've found that children are a great comfort in plural marriage, so don't lose hope if it seems overwhelming right now," she assured me.

A jolt rushed through me at the thought of bearing Jacob's child. But why was the only image I saw of Elijah bouncing a tiny bundle in his arms? I bent over and retrieved a small pinafore from the basket, determined to throw out the thought. Becoming a mother in Zion was my calling, what every good Mormon woman was raised to do, so of course it would happen with Jacob. Only Jacob, my husband.

"The house is so quiet. Are there many children?" I dared to asked at last.

"Oh yes. They're all either at work around the property or in Sister Abby's school right now."

Abigail or Abby? It'd sounded as if she preferred Abigail, but all else called her Abby. Perhaps I'd been mistaken.

"I haven't heard so much as a giggle from them. My own siblings are always making noise whether working or sewing, or simply sitting."

"Oh, the house is so large I swear it swallows all sound. You won't hear much of anything, I'm afraid." Her explanation made some sense, though it didn't bring me much relief. How could a house muffle all sounds?

I glanced up at the imposing manor as I hung another pinafore. The twisted vines climbing its sides covered almost every inch of the back wall of the house.

"How many children?" I asked, without taking my eyes off the vines for fear they'd wrap themselves tighter around the structure.

Prudence held out her hand for another item.

"Well, I have Edward, and Sister Abby has the eldest, Nephi and Esther. Flora has three, Aaron, Joseph, and Vilate, though I know she wants more."

Prudence's words soured some on mentioning Flora, but she quickly brushed past it.

I bent down to retrieve another shirt, Jacob's guessing by the size of it.

"You're the youngest wife?" A worm of guilt wriggled in my head at peppering her with questions. "I hope you don't mind me asking," I added.

She pulled a clothespin from her mouth.

"Oh, don't worry. I know the older ladies always tell us to mind our own business, but really, how will we form a true sisterhood that way?"

I recalled Mother reciting that exact reprimand. For the first time in a long time, I wondered if perhaps she wasn't entirely right about everything.

"To answer your question, though, Jacob and I have been married for nearly five years. Sister Abby is the first wife, as you can probably guess, and Sister Flora the second."

Prudence must've sensed the tension held tight in my shoulders as she looked me over hanging the next garment, and her voice softened into almost a coo.

"I know we're a bit unconventional, all living far out here together. And with the threats from Congress—but it's truly rather blissful most of the time. Jacob prefers living the Principle this way, and honestly, so do I."

"You do?"

To my mind, the burden of plural marriage stained every interaction, every conversation in this house, as evidenced by the simple act of breakfast this morning. It couldn't be easy to live with.

"Oh yes. It's easier to work together, rather than apart," she said. "Sister Hazel, have you ever considered the benefits of plural marriage?"

My hands hung lamely in the air over the line.

"Benefits." I bit my cheek to keep from releasing a nervous laugh. "Well, I mean, our faithfulness to the kingdom of God is inspiring. And raising up righteous seed to the Lord." I snapped my fingers back to work. "It's simply a commandment and our way of life."

"Well, yes, but truly, plural marriage can be a heaven of its own," she insisted. "Women all have different talents and interests, do we not? When many women work together for the good of the family, then each woman can individually find freedom in what she likes. Sister Emmeline Wells taught me that." There was an uptick of pride swelling in her voice.

"I'm afraid I don't quite follow." The name sounded familiar, but I couldn't quite place it.

"Sister Flora is an excellent cook, and Sister Abby is a wonderful teacher. I can leave those tasks to them and focus on my own strengths, the things I wish to do. It's like a kind of harmony. Every woman is free to follow her own pursuits because her sister wives will pick up any leftover pieces."

Prudence rattled it off as if it were the most obvious thing in the world. Gears spun in my head. Mother and Aunt Emma lived apart for most of their marriages, so I hadn't seen much harmony, but in a permanent single household, it sounded plausible. Perhaps this explained the state of disarray in the manor; all the wives were too busy pursuing their own goals to scrub it.

My heart skipped over. What if that was why Jacob had married me? To be the permanent housekeeper? It'd been rumored Brother Brigham had done the same to find his family a devoted cook. I shoved the disheartening thought away.

"And what is it you wish to pursue?" I asked.

Her face shined with a smile of excitement. "I want to be a midwife."

"You're not worried about taking yourself away from your home and children?" Natural fear crept up my back. Her words teetered into a territory I'd never dared to venture.

"Though it requires training, it's a very acceptable role for a woman. Someone must deliver all those precious babies from God."

I matched her smile, her enthusiasm contagious. "I've only known you a few hours, but that just seems to suit you. I'm sure you'll be a wonderful midwife."

"Isn't there something you wished to do?" She cocked her head at me as she accepted another item to hang.

I swallowed. I'd never met a woman who openly spoke of her own desires without a flush of shame.

"Well, I do enjoy music," I said.

"I will have to bring you to our next meeting so you can meet Sister Emmeline then. I'm certain there will be a place for you."

"Meeting? You mean Relief Society?" I hadn't imagined the wives traveled into the city much.

"Oh no, our local suffrage meeting. That's what I'm most passionate about. Utah women may have secured the vote for now, but we must retain it. We need to show the world that we aren't oppressed or ignorant just because we live plural marriage."

Now the name from earlier clicked in my mind: Emmeline Wells, one of the wives of the mayor of Salt Lake and notorious for her support of the rights of women. Even in my most whimsical thoughts, I'd never given much credence to worry about voting rights. The possibility seemed far away, like a mythical problem for adults—of which I firmly was now one. I forced back the sudden wave of insecurities.

"I look forward to going with you and meeting her," I said quickly.

I would gladly attend any meeting—anything at all to get out of this strange house for a few moments. And certainly, I wanted to be closer friends with Prudence.

A light breeze rippled through the line of the freshly cleaned clothes around us, bringing with it a scent of strong pine and harsh dirt. We worked on in steady silence. As I turned Prudence's words over in my mind, the wind whipped the sheet I was holding into my face. I brushed it back with my hand and was straightening it on the line when movement in the top window of the house caught my eye.

A figure hung in the window, the cream curtains tucked around them like a shroud. An odd light clung to their person as if they lifted a lamp in the broad daylight. They looked down on me, strangely motionless, but for a moment, I swore their eyes met mine, sending a shock like lightning coursing through me. Before I could see who it was, the curtains billowed up around them and then they were gone, leaving only the empty window frame.

My spy was back. Perhaps it was Flora waiting to see if she could understand my character or my flaws to bring up in complaint to Jacob. Something hard lodged in my throat.

"What are you watching?" Prudence's question made me jump.

I tore my gaze from the upper window.

"Oh, nothing. Someone was watching us from above and it surprised me, that's all." I tried to sound as nonchalant as possible.

"Oh?" Her eyebrows knit together in confusion as she examined the house.

After a moment's pause, she set back to work, urging me to join her with a gesturing clothespin. I nodded, unwilling to break the tentative silence. The easy conversation now felt awkward, something unseen dampening the air between us. Without either of us saying a word, we worked quicker.

And still I couldn't shake the distinct sensation of being watched.

Chapter 9

In the early evening, I watched from my bedroom window as the light slipped across the valley. The day had been overwhelming, to say the least, and Jacob hadn't yet returned. My body seemed adrift without him in this strange house.

Too eager to receive a reply, I'd written a quick letter to Mother, letting her know I'd arrived and all was well, and tucked it into my pocket like a charm. I didn't dare write the truth of it—that the manor puzzled and drained me, that I knew I was already failing before I even learned all the rules.

I stretched my fingers out over the windowsill. What I truly longed to do now was play the piano. Twilight was the hour of imagination, my favorite time to play.

My fingers tapped the wooden sill as if it were the piano keys, one invisible note after another. I let my mind wander and saw Jacob standing beside me at a grand piano, his beaming smile warming through me. He loved me and he'd bought me a piano as kindly as he'd brought the flower. It felt like an oasis in this strange desert.

I struck a pretend chord. With my eyes closed tight, I could almost hear the notes rising around me. I played another, its sound echoing distantly. My hands moved of their own accord, plucking out the notes of Jacob's favorite hymn. As I played without sound, it felt so real, so certain. A song coursing through me, livening me.

My eyes fluttered open and my fingers stalled out over the wood of the sill.

I *could* hear the notes. The chords floated unquestionably around me, the same as if sitting in church. Somewhere in the house, a piano sounded out a hymn:

Come, come, ye Saints . . .

Jacob had brought home a piano—my piano. A smile cracked across my face. He'd been true to his word, and so quickly too. I dropped my hands from my intangible instrument and made for the door, my heartbeat clicking in rhythm with my footsteps.

The music was distinctly louder in the hallway. I listened to ascertain its origin.

No toil nor labor fear . . .

I dashed down the stairs, expecting to find Jacob and the magnificent instrument sitting in the entry awaiting my arrival. I skidded to a stop on the bottom step, confusion clouding my enthusiasm. The entry was just as empty and sad as it had been earlier in the day.

But with joy wend your way . . .

My neck snapped back to trace the ceiling above me. No, the sound was certainly coming from above. Maybe the piano had been brought upstairs while I completed chores with Prudence all afternoon. I hadn't yet explored any of the other rooms, and many larger homes had additional sitting rooms or music rooms. My heartbeat thrummed in time with the music echoing from above.

Though hard to you this journey may appear . . .

I climbed back up the stairs. Down the darkening hallway every door was closed, each room's occupants talking low or silent as the grave. Perhaps my new family was gathered altogether now awaiting my arrival. I turned into the next wing of the hallway. There were two more closed doors, and then, nothing.

Grace shall be as your day . . .

No one waited to greet me. With a throb of disappointment, I pressed my ear to each door but heard no music emanating out. I tilted my head, listening intently. The music came from higher still. I shifted between my feet. Perhaps I was being fooled by a trick of the mind.

Tis better far for us to strive, our useless cares from us to drive . . .

Yet the hymn played on. I fought the panic rising up, the worry that the Devil played with my mind, and I leaned back against the wall at the end of the hallway. It was odd that it ended where it did, with no bright window. As I pressed against the wood, something hard lodged in my lower back. I inhaled sharply.

Behind me was a small handle painted nearly the same color as the wall. I stepped back, eyes widening. My fingers traced along an almost-imperceptible groove in the wallpaper. This was a *door.*

Leaning in again, I listened.

Do this, and joy your hearts will swell . . .

The piano was behind this door. With heat trickling down my back, I grasped the nearly invisible handle.

A hand closed around my elbow and I startled, stifling a scream. Jacob held on to my arm. His eyes traced me up and down, then flickered to my hand on the wall. The music had ceased, as if the piano's fallboard had suddenly snapped shut.

"What are you doing, darling?" Jacob's voice was sharp but soft.

I let my eyes rove once more over the wall, but what moments ago had been so plainly a door now appeared merely a dirt-streaked wall. Had I imagined the music altogether? There was no sound but the pulse of blood in my ears.

"I heard music. You didn't tell me you already brought the piano." I gently tugged my elbow from his grip. Jacob's expression didn't change. I dropped my fingers to thread through the folds of my skirt.

Jacob let out a booming laugh.

"Heavenly Father must've spent too much time on making you pretty to give you sensible ears."

"I—" The sudden urge to cry caught in my throat.

"It was only a joke, dear. No need to be so sensitive about a jest." His mustache shifted up with his smile. "Did you get the flower I left you this morning?"

I blinked back unexpected tears. This was the man who gave me flowers, who called me pretty, even when I was being overly sensitive.

"It was lovely. Thank you. But the music—"

"You are mistaken, Hazel. I told you before, I don't own a piano."

His eyes blazed.

"Hazel, darling, you're tired. The journey, our new home. I know you love music, but we don't have a piano yet. I'm working on it, though."

My hands froze in my skirts. I strained my ears again for the hymn but heard nothing. The house was as still as an empty church once more. If my husband said there was no piano, then I had to believe him. He knew his house far better than I.

I was so caught up in my daydream of playing that I imagined the entire thing. Mortification shook me. I was a fool, as usual. Lost in the world within my head and the Devil had made it his playground.

I forced a smile to my face, praying the guilt of my growing panic wasn't etched too obviously on my face. "Yes, that must be it. I'm so sorry, I'm probably much more tired than I realize."

Jacob studied me one final time, then smiled. "Come, let's go to bed, darling. You'll feel better in the morning."

His hand pressed on the small of my back as he led me back down the hallway. Unexpected warmth spread from his touch and the memories of our night before pulsed through me. A part of me wickedly hungered for the chance again to pretend, to close my eyes and kiss my husband while I imagined Elijah.

"Oh, and Hazel," he said as we walked slowly. "Don't try that again. There's nothing for you behind locked doors."

I nodded, torn between the desire flaring awake and the meaning of his words. There *was* a door then . . . And there was no music, he'd said, but I could've sworn I heard the final chords:

All is well! All is well!

Chapter 10

The enormity of the front of the house rose up in front of me, taller and stranger than I remembered. My feet shifted, sinking into the spongey soil beneath me. Above the peak of the weathervane, the sun hid behind a tumultuous sea of black clouds. I looked around. Pockets and grooves marred the dirt drive around me, but the twisted roots of the overgrown plants were gone, and the trailing vines that had tried to reclaim the house were missing. The property appeared more like the magnificent house it should've been.

I took in a deep breath that burned my throat. An odd tang hung in the air. This vision wasn't right.

A gust of wind whipped my unpinned hair around my face. I wore my nightgown, though it was clearly day. Uncertainty took root, but I continued to stand there watching the house like I was waiting. It inspected me back. Out of the corner of my eye I noticed someone appear beside me.

Abigail.

I opened my mouth to apologize for my state of dress and confusion, but no words came out. She paid me no attention, staring at the house with shining eyes. Her copper curls fluttered behind her like butterfly wings, loose and carefree. Her face was smooth and tan with a youthful flush underlying her freckles. I held my breath, temporarily stunned by her beauty.

I tried to speak again, but there was no sound. A terror crept up and settled in my chest.

Abigail brushed back her locks, then took off toward the house, an easy skip in her gait. My chest lurched as if dragged by an invisible chain. I fought to keep my feet planted, but the weight tugged against me until I gave up and followed the command. In a blink, I was behind Abigail at the door.

The porch was no longer dilapidated. Fresh green paint lined the door as bright as the first blooms of spring. She paused to run her fingers over the rose-colored flowers decorating the lintel.

Abigail pushed the front door open and continued inside. I moved after her, drawn by the unseen thread between us. As I crossed the threshold, the door shut with an echoing thud, locking us inside. The air shifted around me, hanging heavier with a pregnant uncertainty. It pressed against my shoulders and I rocked back on my heels to steady myself.

She didn't seem to notice the change, however. She stared around as if looking for someone. That's when I noticed the bundle in her arms—a black leather book she pressed tight against her bosom. With a snap of her head, Abigail ended her brief survey and bounded up the stairs. Taking them two at a time, I stumbled after her, my feet barely touching the floor.

At the top of the stairs, she stopped in front of my door. She still hadn't noticed I was right beside her, that she wouldn't find me in my room. Without hesitating, she stepped inside. Horror spread through me as I lunged behind her, bidden by invisible hands. She was prying into my affairs and was about to come face-to-face with her husband in my bed. As I followed her into the room, I tried begging her to stop, but my tongue remained tied.

But my room was empty. There was no sign of Abigail or that

she'd ever come in. A stiff silence ate up the stale air. Everything was as I remembered it, my still-packed cases in front of the armoire, the layer of dust I hadn't yet had time to clean. But my chest refused to settle as I looked around. This wasn't right. All at once, I was hit with a smell of rust, of wrongness.

"Hazel?"

That voice. My body froze. It couldn't be.

Perched on the edge of the bed was Elijah. His worn brown suit hung loose on his shoulders like he'd recently lost weight. His face was stubbled, and his mop of brown curls desperately needed a trim. But his honey eyes were bright as they traced me up and down. The ache I hated to give admittance to pooled hot and rapid in my stomach.

And there was no sign of Jacob anywhere.

"Elijah?" At last, I found my voice. I couldn't say if I was angrier at him or at myself for being pleased to see him. "What are you doing here?"

He smiled, revealing his dimples. "I'm here for you, Hazel. Why else?" The ache moved lower into my center. Elijah had come back for me, but the elation I expected from the thought didn't take flight inside me.

"You didn't want me." The words came out jagged and low.

He winced.

"That's not true. Of course, I want you."

My feet shuffled closer of their own accord, betraying my own want.

He eyed me with a hopeful smile. "Always."

"Elijah, no—" My throat choked my words. He couldn't be here, shouldn't be here. "I . . . I love Jacob now."

"I don't believe you." His voice rumbled through me, and I didn't stop him when he reached out to grab my waist. "See? You love me. You want me."

The words were possessive, almost feral.

"I can't." With trembling hands, I reached out and brushed

my fingers against his cheeks. My usual inhibitions rolled off me like water. "I can't, but I do. Elijah, I need you."

My hands dropped to his shoulders. I ran them up the length of his neck and through his tousled hair. He moaned as he drew me closer. Hunger growled within me in response. I climbed onto his lap, locking my legs around his and pulling us together, one chest beating firm against the other.

Our lips met, a river of heat fueling me. His fingers traced up the sides of my thinly covered ribs, cutting grooves with feverish heat into my skin. He trailed his fingers across my chest and palmed my breast. I gasped into his mouth, unable to control my breathing. Unlike the kiss we'd shared before he left, full of only promises and innocent longings, this was raw and potent—the color of rubies cut sharp and alluring. I wanted more of him, all of him. I wanted in ways I'd never allowed myself to want.

Elijah locked his arms around my back and rolled me over until his weight pressed me against the bed. I should've trembled, but I craved and moaned. His lips traveled down my throat and across the top of my collarbone. The pulsing need deep within me sped up. My hands cut grooves into his back.

A droplet hit my hand with force enough to interrupt my rapture. Then another plopped onto my forehead. It must've started raining, but I ignored it, desperate to return my focus to Elijah's lips now whispering into the crook of my neck. Another drop landed on my arm and slid down my elbow. A tangy smell overcame my senses. And then I realized—we were inside.

I forced my eyes open. The roof was there above as it should be, but more drops fell onto my face. I lifted my hand from Elijah's back as he kissed lower, his fingers gripping the white fabric of my nightgown like he might rip it open with impatience. I blinked, all thoughts of pleasure fleeing my mind. My wrist dripped with scarlet. I brought my hand closer to my face to inspect.

Blood.

My scream reverberated through the room, but Elijah didn't

stop. Drops of blood now covered his back, his hair, my arms. I felt them oozing down the sides of my face and sticking warm between our bodies. The taste of dark rust cut my tongue.

"No, no, you must stop," I pleaded, trying to force him off me by the shoulders. He needed to see the sky was leaking blood as if in a biblical plague. But he didn't stir, his tongue now exploring the tops of my breasts. I gasped again, stuck between this grip of pleasure and terror.

"Please, Elijah, the blood—"

He lifted his head and my words dried in my throat. Elijah was gone. Staring back at me, with his piercing, iced eyes was Jacob. He gripped my waist too tight, his fingers digging into my barely clothed skin.

"Mine," he murmured, his tone biting through me like windchill. With a single motion, he tore away the fabric of my nightgown. I opened my mouth to cry out, but my tongue drowned in blood. His fingers slid over the peaks of my breasts. My back arched into him, restirring the desire in me.

I wanted him too.

My eyes closed in reverie as he continued his exploration, our panting breaths filling the room. But I could hear the constant drip of the bright crimson cascading from the ceiling. I forced my eyes open again. Blood seeped down the walls, a sickening coat of paint. But neither of us stopped our passion play. Instead, my vision blackened as we were covered in a torrential downpour.

The red mess soaked through the sheets, tangled in our hair, stuck thick to our skin. Soon it filled my mouth, my throat, my lungs. I tried to scream, but I could only gurgle as I choked on blood.

"Hazel!"

Two hands held my shoulders firm. My eyes flew open and I shot up. I was in my bed. Jacob leaned over me, his eyes tracking back and forth rapidly in the darkness. I forced in a deep breath. Nothing blocked my airway.

"Are you all right, darling? You started screaming." Jacob spoke softly, his slightly shaking hands gripping my upper arms.

I looked around the dark room, blinking in the low light. No blood painted the walls. I shook off his arms and brought my hands to my face. No crimson stained my skin. I patted the sheets around me. They were clean and white. I swallowed. No taste of rust.

It was only a dream.

First, stalking Abigail through an imagined world.

And then those carnal wants. Elijah's words hit me again: *Always*.

I took in another breath and exhaled slowly like I could force every horrible anxiety trembling through me to leave my body. My heart began to slow and a wave of foolishness hit me. It was a dream, nothing more, and I'd screamed as though a child.

I couldn't meet Jacob's gaze.

"I'm sorry. It must've been a nightmare. Forgive me for waking you."

I dropped back onto the pillow, hoping that would end the conversation. I didn't dare confess the hunger that had nearly devoured me.

Jacob laid back down beside me. "You should dream of nothing but joy, my dear."

His arm wrapped around me, cocooning me against him. Warmth whispered through me. My husband had me secure in his embrace. Entwining my fingers with his, I sunk back against his body.

"I'll do better tomorrow," I murmured. "I promise."

Soon his snores again filled the room. I tried to hold on to the sense of comfort his closeness brought, but sleep fled from me. One day in this home and already I was floundering. But I would prove my worth as a wife.

Chapter 11

I snuck from the bed without waking Jacob just as the first streaks of light filtered through the fraying curtains. Dressing quickly, I slipped out of the room. There was work to be done.

The cool morning air sank into my skin as I searched through the kitchen for a broom and cleaning rags. Without the other wives nearby, the silence surrounding me was almost palpable, like I could reach out and hold it in my hands. I pushed away the thought that the quiet stillness breathed in and out with me in a mimicking rhythm.

In the parlor, I dropped my supplies to the floor as I surveyed the damage. First, I would need to rearrange the chaotic furniture, then I would scrub until it shined. Surely, this would show my sister wives that I was useful.

I hummed beneath my breath as I worked pushing armchairs and tables. The pink-checkered sofa here and the tattered red armchairs there. I looked around to examine my handiwork and frowned. I hadn't moved the furniture much at all. If I didn't know better, I would've thought the pieces had all shifted back to their original positions.

"Perhaps I'll start cleaning first," I said to myself. Resuming my hymn, I bent and began to scrub.

The floorboards creaked behind me. "Up early, little Sister?"

I startled.

"Sister Abigail," I squeaked more than spoke. She peered over me with her hands on her hips. "Yes, I wanted to clean the parlor for you."

"For me?"

"Oh, well, I mean, for the family, of course." I squeezed the rag in my hand.

She stared with pursed lips as if contemplating telling me a secret, then giggled high and birdlike.

"Very well then. Thank you, Hazel." Crossing the room, she flopped onto the sofa, sending dust into the air. "I shall keep you company then."

"Thank you," I replied with uncertainty.

She sank into the cushions and stretched her legs over the sofa arm, her dress riding up to expose the white fabric of her sacred temple garments from her ankles to her knees. I turned away from her improper position and vigorously scrubbed my rag down a chair leg.

Another skirt stepped into my view.

"What's going on here?" Prudence smiled down at me. "Sister Hazel, are you cleaning before breakfast?"

"She wanted to clean the parlor for me," Abigail said.

My ears heated. "Well, for the family."

"That's very kind of you, but you shouldn't have to—"

"Oh hush, Prudence," Abigail scolded, a glint in her eye. "Let Hazel enjoy being Jacob's new Cinderella."

I glanced between the pair of wives, not wanting to acknowledge what her words meant.

"Abby, you're incorrigible." Sister Flora swept into the room as a storm cloud. She scowled at Abigail's position and knocked her feet off the sofa arm as she passed. Abigail only replaced her legs, her garments that should have stayed hidden still hanging out for all to see.

Flora frowned. "Really, Abby. Have you no decency?"

"Poor little Hazel is scrubbing our floors and you're being positively ungrateful, Flora."

"Why should I be grateful she can't even arrange the room properly?" Flora said.

Embarrassment crept up my neck. I knew there was something wrong with the furniture.

"Is there a different way you'd like me to clean, Sister Flora?" I said.

Prudence shook her head. "No, dear. You're doing fine. There's more than one way to skin a cat."

"There's only one way that's proper," Flora muttered.

I sat back on my heels, wringing the rag. Could I do nothing right?

Abigail threw up her hands. "Proper this and proper that. Heaven forbid we upset our slaver!"

"Really, Sister Abby?" Prudence questioned.

Cinderella, Cinderella, that wicked voice taunted in my mind. *You're only the next piece in a household collection.*

"It's only harmless teasing," Abigail said.

"What's harmless teasing?" Jacob's voice cut through the room.

Everyone froze, except Abigail lounging blithely on the sofa, who stared right through him.

"We're simply initiating your newest acquisition, dearest." Nothing in her tone suggested she held her husband particularly dear, though.

"By showing off your sacred garments?" Jacob reached down and tugged her skirt.

Abigail sat up swiftly. "I'm instructing her on cleaning."

"How kind of you," he said flatly.

Jacob's face found mine as I sat paralyzed, uncertain how to defend her—or perhaps it was best to say nothing at all. After a moment, he shifted to Flora. "I believe it's time to start breakfast. The children are already stirring upstairs."

"Of course, forgive the delay." Turning on her heel, Flora disappeared into the kitchen.

"Prudence, darling, could you see to the children?"

She smiled back at Jacob, her hand gliding down her belly. "Certainly." As she waddled away, her fingers squeezed my shoulder, her touch comforting.

I rose slowly. "I wanted to clean the parlor this morning for you and the family."

"I see." He cast Abigail another look of frustration. "Though you're the most beautiful woman I've ever seen cleaning, I wouldn't disrupt the order of things, my Hazel. Breakfast and the children first."

I'd broken another unspoken rule. But Jacob also called me beautiful in front of another wife. Perhaps I was Cinderella, but I was *his*. A greedy stitch of satisfaction surprised me at Abigail's sour face, but I buried the sin away.

"Why don't you go and help Flora in the kitchen?" he said.

"Yes, of course. I'll just return the rag and bucket."

He didn't take his eyes from his first wife. "Abby can do that for you."

Panic clawed at my chest. "I can do it."

"Oh no," Abigail said. "Let me do it. I live to serve the harem, after all."

I flinched, but Jacob didn't. We watched as Abigail rose from the sofa and bent slowly to retrieve the bucket.

The wind rustled through the chimney.

"The children will need you, Abby," Jacob warned.

She lifted the bucket with a pasted-on smile. "Then I'd better hurry to my tasks."

I wiped my hands on my apron as she left. "Are you sure you don't want me to help Sister Abigail?"

"Abby," he corrected.

"Abby," I repeated on impulse. It tasted awkward in my mouth. I had been mistaken from her introduction.

I shook the thoughts away. "I'll go and help Sister Flora."

Jacob nodded. "Thank you for your generosity, my dear. I don't deserve a wife as wonderful as you." He pressed a kiss to my lips and my heart fluttered.

A thud broke us apart.

A fallen book.

"I've been needing to fix that shelf," Jacob said.

I swallowed. "Yes, of course. I'll see to breakfast now."

Our hands brushed as we walked away. I tried to ignore that the shelf wasn't broken at all as I passed.

Afternoon light poured through my bedroom window as I scrubbed and scrubbed. Morning chores were now properly finished and I wanted to impress Jacob tonight with a shining and orderly room. But the layers of grime were stubborn. My fingers pinkened raw, but I tried to stamp out my frustrations with the unyielding house as I shoved the vanity table screeching across the floorboards to clean beneath it.

"You must work harder," I murmured to myself, as I'd been reminded an untold number of times in my life. Nothing was wrong with this house, only with me.

I dragged the chair over to the wall and grabbed my broom. Perched up on my toes, I swatted at the cobwebs in the upper corner. Dust scattered in the stream of light from the window as I swiped furiously. By the time I'd finished all four corners, a bundle of glistening strings hung off the end of the broom. I stepped down, but my ankle collided with something hard. Losing balance, I slipped off the chair and caught myself awkwardly before I fell to the floor.

I looked at the chair and gasped.

The vanity table was directly behind it, not where I'd pushed it across the room. I gripped my broom tighter and inched away. My mind roared into a frenzy as I sank back onto the bed.

My own imagination was an untrustworthy place, I knew that. But that table had moved! Hadn't it? Who had done it?

"Who's there?" I asked the room, unable to believe my own words.

"It's only me."

I yelped.

Flora leaned in the doorway, her arms crossed.

"I didn't see you there." I forced myself to take a breath. How long had she been watching me?

"I told you there was a proper way to these things, which I suppose I'll have to teach you. You've been in this room for far too long. It shows your vanity for your own earthly things rather than the rest of the family."

Vanity. My heart thudded out of time. The vanity table *moved*. Across the room. Had Flora moved it? But why? How hadn't I heard her?

She tsked her tongue at my silence. "Come, it's time to prepare dinner."

I nodded, nearly tripped over my own feet to follow her out the door and away from this unexplainable room.

Chapter 12

The kitchen buzzed with activity. Flora snapped her fingers toward Prudence as we entered.

"You'll need to peel those much quicker," she instructed.

Sitting at the table with a pile of potatoes, Prudence pursed her lips together as I deposited the murky bucket onto the floor near the sink, the water sloshing to the sides.

"Still cleaning?" she asked.

"Yes, but a strange—"

Flora groaned. "And now you've spilled that disgusting mess on my clean kitchen floor."

My heart skipped. "I'm so sorry."

"Get the mop, Sister Hazel. You must anticipate these sorts of things without being asked. That's what makes a helpful wife." Flora made a show of stepping over the trickle of brown water on the floorboards to get to the sink. There was clearly no point in asking more about her moving the table.

As I cleaned up the mess, Abigail—Abby—pushed the back door open, her hands filled with carrots pulled fresh from the garden. In an instant, the air warmed around me. Flora stared down her nose at her.

"The children were supposed to do that, Sister Abby," she said.

Abby deposited the small bounty into the sink and shrugged. "Oh, I suppose I didn't hear you say that. Twice. I told them to go and play."

"You're spoiling them rotten!"

"They'll be fine for one dinner," Prudence said.

I only stood paralyzed with the mop, feeling more foolish each moment. But I couldn't let go of the thought: Why would Flora move a table? It was complete nonsense. I must have lost track of where I put it, that's all.

Flora snapped at me. "Are you done yet?"

"I—"

Abby scooped her arm through mine. "Never mind her. How are you doing, little Hazel?"

"Fine."

I allowed myself to be swept away to the table, leaving Flora grumbling behind us.

"And were you fine last night?" Abby asked. "It seemed you had a bad dream."

Guilt pulsed in my veins, certain that she could see straight through me. That she knew of my strange blood-soaked dream. I shifted back, more falling than sitting onto the bench.

"No, I only—that is, I have these—I'm fine."

Abby raised an eyebrow. "I heard your screaming."

"I . . . I didn't mean to . . ."

"It's quite all right, Sister Hazel. These things happen." Prudence spoke quietly, like I was a spooked horse. "Whatever it was, it was only a dream."

"There's no such thing as *only* in this house," Abby spat.

Prudence resumed her peeling. "Let's talk of better things, Sisters."

Abby's hollow laugh rumbled through the kitchen as she flicked stray peels off the tabletop. "Oh yes, better things for the poor cleaning mouse."

Prudence shot her a cautious look and the kitchen seemed to tighten with tension.

The problem was me; it had to be me. But perhaps she could assuage my sinful imagination.

"There's nothing strange about this house, right, Sister Abigail? I mean, Abby."

Abby stared over my shoulder at something behind me with a hard glare, then blinked out of her strange trance. "Oh yes, you should call me Abby." Her tone was off, as if weighed with a specific sadness. But just as fast as I thought it, a smile sliced across her face once more.

Despite everyone's insistence, calling her Abby felt wrong. She'd called herself Abigail first, though maybe she was only being formal. Still, the name Abby seemed too familiar, even as I craved a sense of closeness with her. Abby was far above my own station in beauty, age, and family position. And after that intrusive dream, it was probably best it continued that way. But still, she was entrancing somehow. Why had I dreamed of her?

"Speaking of help and scrubbing, were you able to get the stains out of your sheets yet?"

I swallowed a gasp. The blood. She knew about the horrible gore from the dream.

"Sister Abby, I don't think this is appropriate talk," Prudence said.

"Why not? We all had the marks on our own sheets after our wedding nights." Abby stabbed her knife through a potato.

A new mortification rose in my gut. She wasn't talking about the dream at all, but something far more horrifying than childish nightmares or imaginations.

"I've taken care of it," I said in a voice that barely sounded like my own. Why would she wish to discuss this, and in front of all the wives no less?

Abby laughed. "No need to look green about it, little Hazel. We're all women and wives. We can talk about it." She dropped her knife and grabbed my hand before I could react, then picked up Prudence's hand beside me and leaned in, giggling like we were a gaggle of schoolgirls sharing in a naughty secret. "Let's all share what our first nights with Jacob were like."

I tugged my hand back, but she held fast. Prudence squeaked. Abby's face was light and friendly, endearing even, but her words cut through, straight to the heart of things unspoken. Plural marriage thrived on realities unuttered and truths unquestioned. What was she doing?

"You're unbelievable, Abby," Flora said, dropping the washed carrots on the table with a thud. "Marriage and its sacred duties are between God, a man, and a woman."

"And a woman, and a woman, and a woman."

Prudence rubbed her hand down her protruding belly. "Perhaps we should change the subject."

I managed to retract my hand from Abby's grip. "Yes, it looks like we'll get some rain today."

But Abby was undeterred. "Adam and Eve were naked in the garden and not ashamed, Sister Flora."

"Oh yes, lots of rain, I imagine," said Prudence, louder, as if to drown them out.

"Must you always be so vulgar against our Father in Heaven?" asked Flora.

"I wonder if tomorrow will be sunny then." I kept my eyes on Prudence's pained expression, which matched my own.

"Must all you women have come to this damned house?" said Abby.

Silence collapsed around us. The air boiled heavier. The walls of the room rippled, or perhaps it was only my fears distorting my vision.

When no one responded, Abby stormed out of the room, leaving a swirl of accusations both spoken and not behind her.

"Don't worry about Abby," Prudence said in a low voice as she prodded me to resume peeling. "She can get into these moods, but she doesn't mean anything by it."

Flora scoffed. "Believe me, she means everything she says, always trying to see how she can mix up trouble. It's a good thing her parents passed on so they don't have to see it."

"That's a hideous thing to say, Sister Flora," Prudence said.

"Why? It's the simple truth. Though perhaps they didn't train her up right in the first place." Flora began work on the carrots.

"Abby's family is gone?" I asked.

"Her parents died crossing the plains when she was only a young girl," Prudence explained in a reverent tone. My heart tightened. Too many Saints laid buried in shallow graves along the trail to Utah, their loved ones forced to continue on to Zion without them after they'd been driven out by violence from the East.

Flora released a long breath that softened her face. "I was raised for the sacrifices of the gospel. My parents learned from the feet of Joseph Smith in Nauvoo. When I came of age, I knew I would one day be a plural wife and I prepared myself for it, but not everyone was given the same learning. This is why I try so hard to instruct you two."

Instruct me. I'd spent my entire life hunched over my scriptures until late at night, in stuffy Sunday school rooms memorizing lessons, on my knees in fervent prayer and fasting. But nothing could've prepared me for this life. My instinct was to give Flora a wide berth for fear of her disdain, but perhaps I shouldn't. Maybe I needed Flora's steady guidance to survive.

And then there was Abby. Mercurial and alluring. Angry, happy, wicked, daring, lovely Abby.

The kitchen door swung open wide once more. Jacob grinned in at us.

"When is dinner, my lovely wives?"

Chapter 13

The air in the dining room crackled with silent friction as I set to work. I approached the table with a stack of porcelain rattling slightly in my hands, my body on edge. Last night, Jacob had taken me to bed early and I'd fallen right to sleep after from exhaustion, so this was to be my first dinner with the family. I wanted it to go perfectly. Needed it.

The eldest girl, Esther, followed right behind me with an armful of forks and knives to set the table.

"Here, why don't you do the plates?" I suggested.

"Yes, Aunt Hazel." Esther was only ten and incredibly obedient already.

Jacob rose from his high-backed chair at the head of the long table. "Wait. Let me help you, Hazel dear."

My stomach fluttered as he snatched the forks from my hand.

"Oh no, Jacob. I can do it. You shouldn't mind yourself with such chores."

"Nonsense. I can set a table." With a gentle push, he moved me out of the way.

What was happening? I rarely saw my father do any kitchen

work; it wasn't his place. But Jacob seemed eager, teasing his daughter with a poke from a fork.

Jacob placed the utensil askew at the top of the plate.

"Father, that's not right," Esther said with an exasperated sigh.

"Are you sure?" he replied. At first, I thought he teased again, but his brow furrowed. "What about this?" He moved it to the bottom.

Esther rolled her eyes.

Jacob shrugged. "Well, I don't know these things."

"Then let us take care of it." I placed my hand on his to take the remaining forks. Heat ricocheted where we touched.

Jacob gave me a helpless look, then relinquished his claim. "I suppose you're right."

He sank back into his chair. "I should leave it to you women. You truly do know better than I at these things."

"Yes, I think that's for the best."

Men had their roles and we had ours. That was the way it should be . . . though setting the silverware had never appeared a hard task to me. I shook my head to throw away the thought.

Esther ran up the stairs to call her brothers as Flora and Prudence brought out platters of food. The rest of the children shuffled into the room on her returning heels and took their places at the table. I waited for them to converse or giggle, perhaps even fight over the best seats, but they were quiet. The only sound was the scraping of chairs. Prudence gave me a smile over the top of her son's head beside her, motioning for me to sit at the chair closest to me—the spot opposite the head of the table, where Jacob sat watching us all with a little smile. I hesitated, a voice in my head reminding me that I wasn't worthy of an end seat, but finally sat when I realized the rest of the family was staring up at me.

Jacob cleared his throat. "Nephi?"

Nephi, the eldest at twelve years, peered up from his lap.

"Please bless the food."

Every head bowed immediately. A few chairs squeaked as little bodies settled into them, but there were no grumbles of protest or squinting children spying on one another. As Nephi pronounced his supplication to the Lord on our behalf, no one whispered or giggled, as so often happened with children. The entire room felt wound tight by unseen cords.

Murmurs of "amen" scattered around the table when the prayer finished. I expected to see hands shooting out to claim their food quickly like my family, but instead we watched our patriarch as he served himself. All except for Abby, who watched the ceiling in a slouch like she pretended she wasn't here at all.

"What wonderful dinner, Flora," Jacob said. "How would we manage without you?"

Flora glowed. "Oh, the thanks should go to you for providing such a meal."

Abigail made no attempt to hide her eye roll.

"Yes, thank you, Jacob. What do we say, children, for this bounty?" Prudence asked.

A chorus of thanks echoed around the dining room.

Jacob settled back into his chair, a king fit for his kingdom. "Begin, family."

Again, I expected arms to grab for food, but instead, there was a slow and silent passing of plates and dishes. Even with many bodies at the table, there was hardly a sound as the meal began. The command and precision of the family was unlike I'd ever seen—nothing at all like the home I'd left behind. I wondered whether the silence grew from my strangeness, whether lightness would return to the table as they grew used to me. Or was I to endure these solemn meals forever?

My back prickled and I turned around. The windows behind me appeared to inspect me, and I shivered at the sense of being watched. I shook my head to force away the thought. Windows didn't watch.

Perhaps I could lift this somber mood.

I turned to Esther. "How were your lessons today?"

She creaked her head up from her plate. I waited with my pasted-on smile trying to ignore the confused glances turning my way. Embarrassment washed through me. I'd done something wrong.

Down the table, Jacob motioned to his daughter. "Answer the question, Esther."

"They were good, Aunt Hazel," she replied, then went back to picking at her food like a little bird.

"I'm glad to hear that," I said, my mouth barely moving. My head burned with more questions—what did she learn? How were the children taught in this home school? But the rule appeared to be silence at the table.

Edward's words from early this morning drifted back to me—*it likes it quiet*. What was *it*?

A cup slammed against the wooden table. Every face turned upward. Abby cast a daring look at Jacob. With a sigh, he met her gaze.

"Jacob, darling, don't you think we should give little Hazel a better welcome to our dinner table?" she said.

My chest buzzed with fear that this would only lead to more contention.

"She's been welcomed, haven't you, Hazel?" He looked between her and me like I was a coconspirator in some scheme he didn't follow.

"Oh yes, I'm fine." I shrank back against the hard wood of my chair.

Jacob gave me a handsome, lopsided grin that made my heart skip. Then he shifted back to Abby, who scoffed. "You know I don't ask for much as the head of this household but a simple, silent family meal after a long day of working to provide for you all."

"And you deserve it," Flora said.

The windows rattled. Esther yelped in surprise, knocking the contents of my cup onto my plate with her elbow. The water souped through the pile of potatoes and carrots. I stared at the congealing mess as I reminded myself to breathe.

Jacob's face dropped in disappointment. "Esther," he scolded. "Look what you've done to your aunt's food."

"I'm so sorry—"

"No, no, it's fine," I said. "The windows scared me too."

Jacob raised a brow as he appraised the pair of us. "It's simply the wind. She knows better than to cause problems during dinnertime. Up to your room, Esther."

"I'm sorry, Papa," she said as she rose. I caught her eye and offered a sympathetic smile, which she didn't return. Guilt twisted in my gut.

Jacob pressed his fingers to his temple. "As a matter of fact, children, you're all excused. I think that's enough excitement for one night and I've got a ghastly headache. Get to bed, please."

Without a voice of complaint, the children quickly shoveled their last bites into their mouths. They funneled through the kitchen door and back out again as if a trained little army depositing their plates. Prudence scooped up Edward and trailed behind Nephi as they scampered back out of the dining room, the echo of their footsteps disappearing before they even reached the hallway.

Flora shot me a look of disdain. I'd caused nothing but trouble at dinner. It was amazing they didn't simply toss me out the door and leave me to the elements. My heart beat back in a familiar pattern—*my fault, my fault, my fault.*

Abby's shrill voice cut through the thick air. "Must you be so cruel to our daughter?" she asked, shoving her plate across the table until it collided with Flora's with a clink.

"I'm teaching her, guiding her. Do you think God would allow rude behavior in His mansions?" Jacob said. "I will not lose my child to wickedness."

Flora stood to remove her and Abby's plates. "A firm hand is the way to lead a child to prosper," she agreed as she backed away into the kitchen.

"It was only an accident," I said.

Jacob sighed. "One day you will be blessed with our child and then you will see the hard choices we have to make as parents, Hazel."

For some reason, the thought didn't bring me any joy. I'd only ever imagined Elijah by my side with children, and I forced the invading images down deep in my mind.

"Well then." Abigail tossed her napkin down to walk out. "If you wish for a firm hand, Jacob, I'd avoid my bed for a while as I won't be supplying one. Though I doubt you'll prefer anyone but Hazel's hand for now," she said over her shoulder as she disappeared.

Jacob and I sat facing each other at opposite ends of the chasm of an empty table. The urge to jump up and run overcame me, but why, I wasn't entirely certain. My fingers slipped into my pocket and I remembered my chance for some hope.

"I should help Flora clean up," I said at last.

Jacob nodded, his gaze staring off into the expanse.

"And I have a letter for my family. Will you take it to town with you when you go back, Jacob?"

"Hmm?" He directed his attention back to me. "Oh yes, yes, that should be fine."

When I reached out to take his plate, he grabbed my wrist firmly. "You're a good wife, Hazel. Ignore Abby. God is pleased with you as a helpmeet for me."

My heartbeat raced. This was what I wanted—to please him and to please God. I did my duty, despite my many flaws. But nothing about this moment felt validating.

Jacob stood and pressed a kiss to my temple. "I will see you after you finish."

As he left, a draft sank its claws into me. Jumbled whispers fluttered around the empty room like someone unseen was speaking. I didn't dare take my eyes from the windows as I slowly backed into the kitchen.

Along the wall, a shadow flitted across the wallpaper like a snake. I startled, nearly dropping the dishes. But I blinked and the movement was gone.

Taking in a few breaths, I straightened cautiously. Walls didn't move or whisper. Houses didn't leer. All of this nonsense was in my mind.

CHAPTER 14

The next morning, Prudence placed a tray into my outstretched hands. Breakfast was another sober affair and while Flora furiously scrubbed the dishes, I prepared to bring a meal up to Abby, who was laid up sick in bed—a frequent occurrence according to Prudence. Doctors had been sent for in the past, but no one was ever certain what ailed her as she struggled to find the strength to leave the bed.

"I usually do it, but it's getting rather difficult to carry the tray," Prudence said, stroking her fingers down her stomach. The apron barely covered it anymore, and the sight brought a frustrating pang of envy.

Edward clung to her leg and eyed me suspiciously.

"You're still here," he said, his young tongue tripping over the words. He stared up at me, as though intent on dissecting and solving me. For only three, he had far more insight than my own siblings ever showed at this age.

"Where else would I be? Do you want to take me on another tour of the house?" I teased.

"Only if we go to the attic."

"There's an attic?"

Flora slammed the pot against the bottom of the sink. "Edward, mind your tongue and stop spreading nonsense," she scolded. He shrank back against his mother's leg.

"He's fine, Flora, only a child," Prudence said.

"You give him too much freedom. He needs to be taught," said Flora as she continued her washing, murmuring not so quietly about Prudence's deficiencies as a mother.

Prudence ignored her. "We don't have to be so old-fashioned. Children don't need to be perfectly quiet at all times to be well-behaved."

This wasn't the first argument I'd witnessed on the topic, but it was a fight I didn't dare to enter. I needed to do as I'd always been taught—be agreeable, sweet, and never contentious.

I rebalanced the tray on my arms and cleared my throat to change the subject.

"What if Abby is sleeping when I knock?" I asked.

"I should ask if you've been sleeping, Sister Hazel. Your eyes are nearly bloodshot."

Could she see through me, like her son did? Did she know of my tortuous nightmares splashed with blood and Abby? I held back an urge to spill everything out. "Oh no. It was a bit drafty last night, that's all. I'm fine."

Prudence considered me for a moment as if she didn't believe me. "If Abby is sleeping, simply leave the tray on her table. She'll be able to get it when she wakes."

I imagined myself sitting beside her bed watching her sleep the way I watched her in my dreams. My heart sputtered.

Flora clicked her tongue. "Well? What are you waiting for? She'll want her breakfast sometime this morning."

I hurried out the door. Fearful or not, it was my duty to care for Abby and I couldn't let my imagination get the better of me.

All too soon, I stood before Abby's door, my fist outstretched and ready to knock. She would be asleep, surely. I wouldn't have to speak to her. Confess to her.

My knock echoed loudly in the hallway, but no one responded.

I pushed it open and stepped inside despite the pounding in my chest.

Abby's room was silent. I watched her sleeping form on the bed, her chest slowly rising and falling, then rushed to place her tray on the side table. As I stepped back, I took a moment to glance around.

Her room was the mirror to my own at the other end of the hallway. A large canopy bed took up most of the space, and a shuttered window leaked tiny streaks of morning light. I didn't have to open it to know it offered a beautiful view of the surrounding valley, the same as mine.

Every piece of furniture in her room was abandoned to the dust. Her items lay strewn across the floor. Shoes cluttered in an uneven heap in the far corner. Her wardrobe was left open wide, dresses hanging over the tall door. Brushes, books, and cups cluttered the vanity.

The hair on the back of my neck prickled.

A sudden sense of dread clung to me. An unwelcome presence hovered nearby. Or perhaps, it was *I* who was unwelcome. This was Abby's domain and, just like in my dreams, I pried too much.

I stepped backward, praying silently that Abby would stay asleep and I wouldn't have to account for lingering.

Piano chords reverberated from above. My head shot up, tracing the sound. Stumbling back through the doorway, I shut the door harder than I intended, but I didn't wait to see if the noise woke Abby. A tugging sensation wrapped around me, bidding me follow.

Somewhere in this house, there was a piano, and I needed to know where.

As I moved briskly down the hallway, the music pounded louder. Notes danced up and down in a kind of jig, but the melody embedded within it was unmistakable—"Come, Come, Ye Saints."

Glancing back over my shoulder, I checked the hallway for others. Noise came from the designated classroom where the children were reading at Prudence's instruction, but the hallway remained empty. I turned the corner. The empty wall leered at me, the faint outline of the forgotten door almost glowing.

What if this was the attic?

This was madness and stupidity, chasing after unheard music, but I couldn't leave it be. Jacob swore to me there was no piano in the house, but I couldn't be going mad.

I knew I pushed toward a boundary I shouldn't cross, but for once, I didn't let my guilt stop me. I pulled the handle. The wall groaned and shuddered, but the door didn't open. Employing the other hand, I tugged it again with more force. It creaked open with a moan.

A passage with a wide set of stairs appeared.

And the prancing hymn played on, louder than before.

I picked up my skirts and started upward. Each step sagged beneath my weight. Musty air stung my nostrils as I climbed into the dark. I wished I'd brought a light, but I couldn't turn back now. The blackened walls thrummed around me. Every note of the song reverberated through my bones.

At the top of the staircase, a doorway streamed with muted sunlight. There *was* an attic. Holding my breath, I obeyed the beckoning sounds, the primeval need, the sinful curiosity, and stepped into the hidden room.

Light filtered in from two small windows, illuminating the filthy room. Fetid air potent enough to burn my throat choked me. A few pieces of discarded furniture sat covered in what must've once been crisp white sheets now stained dark with mildew. Several wooden crates stacked beside them like they were hastily placed.

The music stopped. Slowly, I spun around to take in the full room.

No one was up here.

In fact, it appeared no one had been up here in many years. There was nothing here of interest. Nor an answer. There wasn't even a piano. Frustration welled up and tears pricked my eyes.

Then a large wooden piece of furniture in the corner caught my eye. Despite its filthy surroundings, it was a lustrous brown.

I glided toward it, my shoes leaving a trail of footprints in the snow-like dust coating the floor. A long-neglected embroidered bench sat in front of it. Without thinking, I sat down, sending up a wave of dust. My fingers tracked the groove across the top of the box.

I slid my hands along the bottom and lifted the wooden lid. It moaned as it flipped open and revealed its long set of pearled keys. My heart jumped with the confirmation.

It was a small box piano.

The keyboard was beautiful ivory, untouched by the grime of the attic. It stood out from the deep walnut color of the instrument, in perfect contrast. Relief washed over me. It was real—the piano was real. But there was simply no way someone could've sat here and played it only moments before I came in without leaving a trace.

A hunger spread through me. My hands hovered over the keys, heat pulsing in my fingertips. The warmth climbed. I didn't know how or why, but I sensed the piano had been waiting for me. Invisible threads coaxed my fingers to the keys.

I blinked back unexpected tears. I could make music again. Possessiveness overcame me. This piano would be mine.

"What are you doing?" A serrated voice cut through my bliss.

Flora stood in the doorway, her arms crossed. Anger simmered in her eyes. Her face doused whatever euphoria had been growing inside me.

"I'm sorry. I only thought I heard something." Reluctantly, I reclosed the piano lid to show I was penitent, though of what transgression I wasn't entirely certain.

"Probably a rat. There's no reason to poke around a private attic."

"But this is my house too. Jacob said—"

"Jacob isn't here." Her scowl seemed to issue a challenge and I didn't dare to question her.

"It's only that—there's a piano. He said there wasn't a piano." I didn't add the words that punctured my thoughts—that he'd lied to me.

She glanced at the box piano, seemingly unimpressed. "He must not know it's up here. No one comes up here. There were so many things left over after the previous owner abandoned the house that it all got shoved wherever it could go."

"Are you certain?"

"Are you truly questioning your husband? You'll be as wicked as Abby if you aren't more careful."

The guilt was a physical blow. I recoiled and bowed my head, ready for confession, but a voice in my head stopped me. For once, the frantic one was drowned out. There *was* a piano. Perhaps Jacob didn't know about it, but still, didn't that make *him* wrong? I didn't know what to do with these thoughts.

"Forgive me, Sister Flora," I replied, though I wasn't certain I meant it.

Self-loathing and confusion pulsed in every step as I slipped past Flora and started down the dark staircase. There was a piano and someone had played it. I couldn't be going mad.

Chapter 15

Over the next weeks in the house, I slowly became accustomed to the rhythm of its days. Each week, I wrote a letter to my parents' home describing the small pieces of my new life. Writing it down made me feel a sense of control, as if writing down the mundane tasks would make the unexplainable of no consequence. I clung to the hope of those letters—both the falsehood that my new world was orderly and that words from my family would bolster me through it. Although Jacob had yet to return with a letter for me, I knew one would come. Eventually.

But despite what I wrote in my letters, the subtle worries, the strange movements just out of my eyesight, and the unexpected sounds moaning through empty rooms never became more familiar.

There's no such thing as only *in this house.*

Abby's words from weeks ago echoed in my ears as I reached up to take the dried linens from the clothesline. Picking up the basket, I bounded to the kitchen door, pushing it open with my hip as I stepped inside. Flora clicked her tongue from the table, where she sat peeling potatoes with Prudence.

"About time, Sister Hazel. I hope you weren't imagining things again."

Years of childhood accusations about my overactive imaginations and worries rose in her words.

"Forgive me. There were many items to bring in."

"There's no need to be upset, Sister Flora," Prudence said. "Be grateful the Lord has allowed us to live in such a way that we can share all our duties."

"Of course, I'm grateful," said Flora. "And need I remind you that *I* taught you all these duties?"

"Sister Emmeline says—"

"Don't spout your suffragist nonsense in my kitchen, Prudence."

The door slammed shut behind me, rattling the line of plates on the top shelf. It must've been caught by the wind. But that didn't stop my heart from pounding.

"Never mind," Flora continued. "We must not have contention in our home, Prudence. You know it's important to have a pure heart while you're with child, or the babe may be afflicted with a wicked spirit when they are born."

"Yes, we wouldn't want that." Prudence motioned me farther inside.

"And it'd do you good to take note of that as well, Hazel. It's my job to instruct you in these things, after all. Heaven knows Abby won't do it, so you should thank me. Your eternal soul is at stake."

Flora flicked her potato peels with extra vigor.

Prudence gave me an eye roll and I bit my tongue to keep from laughing.

"Thank you, Sister Flora," I repeated, as if I were a child in Sunday school again. I rested my basket on the back of a chair beside them.

"I'm surprised you're not with child yet," she continued. "Are you certain you're counting properly?"

My stomach instantly turned.

"I bled only last week," I confessed, warmth rolling up my spine.

"It's your duty to be fruitful, and multiply and replenish the earth."

"Yes, I'm aware." Could I do nothing right here?

The door rattled in its jamb, as if it too sensed the tension blooming.

"I'm sure it's not for lack of trying," Prudence said, mortifying me further. "I'm certain Jacob loves you very much."

"Love has nothing to do with it." Peels flew right and left across the table as Flora went on. "You young wives are all so obsessed with your husband loving you. Why, I don't care one bit if Jacob loves me. I shout hallelujah that I've got a man from the Lord at all! I'm a mother and I do my duty to God's kingdom. That's all that matters, not love."

It felt as if I sat across from Elder Crowther once more, being told my calling mattered more than my feelings—as if Elijah and his affections were only trivialities, a kind of counterfeit happiness compared to the Principle's true joy. Good Mormon women didn't need love for contentment—they needed obedience and sacrifice.

"I should finish this laundry," I said, not daring to meet either of their gazes. I knew Prudence's held quiet sympathy and Flora's unwavering faith. Neither would be a balm at this moment. "I'll return shortly to help with dinner."

I left the kitchen quickly. More than ever, I wished for my piano and a place to find some solace. But I hadn't dared to reexplore the attic. My fingers twitched on the edges of the basket. Perhaps it was time to bring the matter up with Jacob again. He'd been so busy of late that I'd hardly seen him outside of the two dedicated nights each week he spent in my bed. Some nights we spoke at length, others he took carnal pleasure without pretense. Some he simply slipped into bed and nodded off quietly, probably too exhausted from his duties to even notice me. I tried not to think about what he did the nights I slept alone.

The sound of hushed voices slowed my feet. Around the corner of the parlor, Jacob and Abby leaned together in rapt conversation. I stopped, uncertain of what to do. They blocked the only path to the stairs.

". . . Hazel . . ."

I heard my name and froze. Staying out of sight, I leaned against the doorway. The wood paneling shook against my back. I held my breath as I listened in to the conversation.

"Abby, you must calm down," Jacob hissed.

I couldn't see them, but I could imagine well his furrowed brow.

"Calm down?" Abby replied, her tone laced with ice. "It's only getting worse and you tell me to calm down?"

"You're having one of your hysterical episodes. You shouldn't be around others. I'm concerned for you."

Her laugh was biting.

"You weren't so concerned last night when my mouth was on you."

I clenched my teeth to keep from gagging. The squeak of the shifting floorboards suggested Jacob didn't find it amusing either.

"Get back to your room, Abby."

"Not until you admit that it's worse, ever since you brought home your latest pet."

Me. I'd made whatever was troubling Abby worse. I gripped the basket tighter.

"I won't engage with this nonsense. The problem isn't me, Abby, it's you. You need to help yourself—What? What are you staring at?"

"You know perfectly well what it is," she responded, her tone deadened.

"I don't. Your episode is overtaking you. Let's get you back to bed."

A cry rasped in Abby's throat.

"Would that I could gouge out your eyes, husband."

Jacob's reply was muffled, though I just made out the words, "Even in my blindness, you'd still be mine."

Their steps echoed away. How could Abby speak in such a way to her husband? Our husband. But if Abby dared to say such things to him, could there be a reason for her sickness? A loose edge of the wicker basket pressed painfully into my skin and cut off the terrible thought before it took further root.

CHAPTER 16

The bed sagged as Jacob rolled over beside me, flopping his arm across my waist. Streaks of early morning sun sliced the room in a haze. Although my body ached with exhaustion, my mind raced, recalling the strange conversation I'd eavesdropped on yesterday. I pushed to sit up, but Jacob's arm weighed me down.

"Shh, don't get up just yet, my Hazel," he slurred.

My body tensed beneath his touch, unsure of what it wanted.

"It's morning already and there's many chores to be done."

His fingers stroked down my side and over my bottom. I exhaled as quietly as I could. No desire stoked awake. Seeds of fear rooted inside me. *Mine.* I was Jacob's for this life and throughout eternity. This should be safety and real love.

But Elijah . . .

Memory and longing flooded through me as Jacob continued his exploration of my skin. The thought of Elijah's hands on me stirred my heart and body. The imagined feel of his weight pressed against me, his kisses and hands trailing down my skin flushed heat through me—along with the heart-tearing memory of his rejection.

Once more, I hummed with the need to express these feelings by pouring them into music. I'd been doing my best to suppress it, but it'd only grown stronger.

"Jacob?" I asked tentatively, rolling onto my back.

His fingers danced around the buttons on my nightdress. "Yes?" His mimicking, slow tone must've been playful teasing of my timidness.

"I was only wondering if you've had a chance to look for my piano?"

He un-threaded and re-threaded my top button as if debating his answer. Fear choked me. Was it too late to take the question back? I must've come off as too demanding.

"Not yet, my dearest," he said at last. "The mine has been quite busy of late, and most of my time in town is taken up by meetings with Elder Crowther and other men."

"Right, yes, of course." I almost wished he would undo the buttons and take me just so I could show my compliance, that I wasn't a burden. "I understand completely."

"Soon," he whispered, resuming his exploration of my thighs beneath the sheets.

But I didn't react. Why did his delay in retrieving a piano hurt me so? Our marriage could still only be counted in weeks; it wasn't as if he'd been promising for years. Selfish, that's what I was. The Devil clawed my lungs, threatening panic. *I was fine, this was fine, everything was fine*, I repeated again and again in my head. My husband was an important man. Besides, he'd been using his extra time in town to hand-deliver my letters as he promised.

Jacob's hands stopped their wandering and he sighed. "Now what are you thinking?"

I almost didn't answer. Hadn't I already asked enough this morning?

"I was wondering if my letter last week got delivered," I said quietly.

"Yes, I left it with your father. He said he would write back soon. I think he's rather busy with the newspaper right now."

Another trip, another time he returned empty-handed.

"This is the fifth letter with no response."

"I wouldn't worry so much about them, Hazel. If there was any true urgency, they would contact you."

I waited for a sense of relief to sink in, but none came. "It's been so long and I've heard nothing. How could they not want to write me?"

"To be honest, my dear, it's not unusual."

My ribs cracked with the weight of such a thought. "It's not?"

"You're no longer part of their family. You're part of mine. I'm your priesthood leader now, not your father. I'm sure they think of you often, but you're not theirs anymore." His fingers stopped on my neck, almost too tight.

It wasn't fair. Right. Kind. His words were true, but why did they have to be? If plural marriage was the only way to find happiness, then why did I never feel content? Why did it seem that every desire and thought of my own was wrong?

As if he could sense my bitter thoughts, Jacob went on in a softer tone. "But *I* care about you, Hazel. I'm your family now. And I can't say I dislike having you all to myself."

His lips brushed against mine in a rough kiss.

As his weight dropped over me, I let the kiss grow. He was my husband. I loved him. But a static fizzed in the air around us, bubbling and frothing with frustration to match my own. The walls creaked like they heard my questions, my pain.

The nib of my pen tapped against the surface of my vanity as I stared at my sealed letter addressed to Ammon. It felt like an act of defiance after my conversation with Jacob this morning, but I needed to make one more effort to reach out to my family. I had to know if what he said was true. Were they truly so uninterested in me now that I'd married? Did I ever cross their mind or at least their prayers?

Is this what happened to women once they married—swallowed up in their husband until they meant nothing to anyone outside of him?

But of course, I hadn't asked Ammon any of that directly. I simply inquired about his sweetheart and the state of the apple trees out back he worked so hard to care for. I avoided any mentions of the unseen pianist or the strangeness of the manor. How does one put such madness onto paper? Instead, I silently pleaded between the lines for any grasp of where I stood with the family and how their life went on without me.

I placed the letter to the side and pulled out a fresh sheet of paper. There was one last one I needed to write. One I'd held off for too long. One that threatened to rip the flesh from my body and strip me into nothing but chattering bones.

Elijah.

I couldn't keep pretending that he was allowed to live in my mind as he once did—the young man who carved the darkest desires inside me. Now he had to be relegated to an entombed piece of my past. The words of this letter would seal off the cavities he'd whittled into me.

Elijah didn't want me, I reminded myself. So why could I not banish him completely? Anger and longing seethed together. I worried I would never want to be rid of him.

At last, I dipped my pen and began. The ink bled into my skin as I wrote of my misery at his actions, at my decision to marry and follow God's command. Part of me hoped each word would cut through Elijah, yet another wished there was a way to offer my pain for his.

My heart begged for relief. I needed to purge myself of all memories of him.

Do you remember the time Aunt Emma threatened me with a paddle for taking a sweet from little Ammon, and you took the blame and punishment for my actions? You shouldn't have. I don't know if I ever thanked you. Or the

> *time Sally made fun of my penmanship at school and I climbed up a tree to cry? You sat on the bottom branch and listened to my sobs for hours to just be with me. ~~I think that was the moment I loved you.~~*

A tear splotched onto the page. And then another. This was a death by a thousand cuts.

> *You used to tell me we could go anywhere in the world together. That we'd see the jungles of Africa and the crashing waves of the Sandwich Islands. You used to listen to my stories of places I'd imagined in my head and promise you'd find such a world for me to explore. When did you stop sharing those visions with me?*
>
> *You never mocked my questions or my panics. You always told me to trust myself more. ~~I wish I still had you here to remind me of that.~~ You told me we were going to share everything together, only the two of us, and no one else.*

Once the words started, they didn't stop. My pen moved quicker across the page, turning my sentences almost illegible.

> *You used to make so angry too. I recall the time you insisted that you knew the correct quotation of scripture and I didn't. I wanted to push you off a pew and give you a swift kick for good measure. (I was correct, by the way. I looked it up after Sunday school.) Or the time you led me to believe there was a monster in the back field. I've still never forgiven you for that fright when you jumped from the bushes.*
>
> *Or the time you danced with Lucille all night when you were supposed to be my partner.*
>
> *Or the way you stared at me the entire night from across*

the dance hall like I was a flame you couldn't stop coming to even though you swore you were infatuated with Lucille and her pretty face. But later as we walked home you admitted my face was the last thing you saw when you fell asleep at night. ~~You're still the last one I see.~~

And now I must remove you from my mind completely. As if I could. As if I could simply bury away all the ways you annoyed me, adored me, angered me, absolved me. As if I could cleanse my soul of the parts of me that belong to you and be done with it. ~~As if I could ever stop loving you.~~

I tossed the pen across the vanity and buried my face in my hands as it rolled off the edge and tumbled to the floor. My words didn't eradicate my wicked desires as I hoped or provide any solace. My grief didn't subside. The past didn't change.

I would never send this letter. I should burn it. Wiping my tears from my cheeks, I walked to the fireplace and dropped the unaddressed letter onto the charred logs. But I didn't bend to light it. Burning it would be like burning a piece of me—our memories, our future. It was all too final. I dropped to my knees, the soot biting at my nose, and placed the folded letter beneath the top log. Perhaps one day I'd be brave enough to light it, to truly extract him from me and be a perfect wife. But for now, Elijah stayed as he'd always been—tucked away in the fleshy tables of my heart.

I turned away from the hidden evidence and scooped up my letter to Ammon, straightening my hair in the vanity mirror. I'd leave this letter on Jacob's desk for his next trip into town and surely, it would receive a reply. My ever-dutiful brother would write back to me.

"Or maybe, he'll ask me to come back for an extended stay," I said aloud. "I could get away from here."

The thought made my heart flutter. Even a week away from the weight of this suffocating house would be a heaven. I imagined myself walking arm in arm with Ammon down the street without a word of complaint for his company, sitting with Mother in the parlor at the piano, even cooking with Aunt Emma. Why was it humanity didn't know the joys they had until they were torn away?

A ripple moved across the vanity mirror, distorting my image. I gasped, dropping the letter to the floor. But in a blink, the mirage was gone.

Cautiously, I bent over to retrieve the letter. As my fingers brushed the floor, the boards shivered against them. I tugged the letter tight to my chest.

"Are you mad at me?" I spoke in a low voice, my eyes darting around. "Does this house hate me?"

Behind me, the door of the armoire groaned open. I spun around on my heel.

"Are you upset I dream of leaving you?"

The only response was the wild thrashing of my own heart.

I crept backward to the door, not daring to take my eyes off the room. My hand found the doorknob without looking and I shoved myself into the hall, slamming the door like it could close off the frenzy in my mind.

The hallway greeted me with empty silence. I took the stairs two at a time, each step bounced with the erratic rhythm of my pulse.

A shadow shifted across the wall too quickly to catch its origin. I pulsed on the balls of my feet, glued to the floorboards.

A crackle whispered above me.

Dropping my head back, I followed the sound. It only hissed louder. The ceiling fissured in jagged lines away from the chandelier in the center. It spread at a supernatural speed as if invisible fingernails scratched the cracks into the surface.

I jumped back, my heart racing.

"Are you dancing, little Hazel?"

My attention snapped to the stairway. Abby, still dressed in her nightgown, gripped the banister as she peered down at me.

"No, I . . ." I pointed upward. "It's the ceiling. Just . . . just look!"

She tilted her head up, shifting it shoulder to shoulder as she took in the broken ceiling.

"The house is old," she said.

"But that can't be safe."

"And is that such a bad thing?" she asked.

The letter crunched in my hands. Did Abby mean to suggest harm?

Flora crept up behind her, half hidden in the darkness of the hallway. "What have you done now, Sister Hazel? Why is it you're always causing trouble? Wives are to be helpmeets, not difficulties—"

Abby cut her off. "Oh, shut up, Flora. You're insufferable."

Anxious voices shouted in my head, hating me. I caused this—all of this—somehow. The contention, the broken ceiling, the undeniable tug of the Devil on my chest. I was trouble. Difficult. Wrong.

And only minutes earlier I'd carried on a conversation with the house as if it could hear me. Sense me. This peculiar house. This unsettlingly silent, decaying house.

Every shudder of the walls, creak of the floor, flutter of the air. When I swore the room breathed with me or the armoire heard my mutterings. Walls slithered. Floorboards rattled. Windows leered.

What did any of it mean?

"I'm sorry," I squeaked, panic overtaking me. I couldn't breathe and I stumbled back.

"Hazel, are you all right?" Abby asked.

I couldn't respond, only gasped.

"Hazel!"

Footsteps echoed down the stairs, though they were somehow also far away. I felt two hands clasp me from behind. Abby held me against her chest. My body went boneless and I let her tug me as a ragdoll. She directed me into the parlor, where she forced me into a chair.

"What is happening?" she asked, tracing me up and down.

"I'm fine," I lied.

She clicked her tongue. "You're obviously not. You're acting as if you can't breathe."

"Do you—Sister Abby, do you—" I struggled for words. "Do you think the house is trying to harm me?"

"What do you mean? It's only a cracked ceiling."

"This house it's . . . it's wild. Unnatural. And I think it's after me. I think it wants—something."

"It's a *house*," Abby said.

"But I've upset the balance somehow. Ruined it with my presence. That must be it. Flora was right. I did something wrong. I always do. I'm broken and wicked and the house knows it and I deserve to be punished."

Everyone—every *thing*—wanted me gone.

"What makes you think that would solve anything in this damn place?" Abby said.

"Perhaps it's like an atonement. Someone must be sacrificed to appease the balance of God's nature."

I didn't know why I thought of that teaching of Brother Brigham—that some sins were so heinous they could only be forgiven through shedding one's blood unto death and pouring it onto the earth. The house seemed to bring out all the darkest pieces of my lifelong fears.

The Devil grasped my chest with his claws. I needed to force more air into my lungs, but even as I gulped, I couldn't catch my breath. Part of me wished to curl up on the spot and sob, while another pumped adrenaline through my legs begging me to run as far as I could.

"That's the most ridiculous thing I've ever heard," Abby said, her face creasing with fear.

My fit was surely terrifying her, but I couldn't stop it.

"Hazel!" Prudence called as she waddled into the parlor. "Flora told me something was wrong. Are you all right? Are you hurt?"

Tears cascaded down my face. "The house is—it—"

"It's falling apart is what it is," Jacob interjected as he strode through the door with Flora on his heels. "It's simply an old ceiling. No need to overreact."

His face reflected disgust as he surveyed me. I couldn't breathe. Hadn't he said my struggles endeared me to him? I must be imagining it. My vision was blurry.

Prudence leaned in, stealing my frantic attention. "You're perfectly safe, Hazel." She tugged me against her chest, gripping me tight.

I sank into her embrace with hiccups of sobs. Prudence didn't say a word, only gently stroked my back. Her touch was warm and soothing. She didn't chide me for my panic, for losing my sensibilities.

I lost track of time in our awkward, trembling embrace, but as my breathing once again slowed, the strange thoughts that seemed so solid only minutes ago melted away.

Jacob squatted down, blocking out Prudence. "At last," he said only in a whisper. "I thought you'd be cured of this sin by now, Hazel. Has my love not been enough for you?" His expression sagged with hurt.

I'd hurt him. Guilt replaced my temporary calm.

"And as I said before," he continued loudly, "there's nothing to fear in this house."

Abby stifled a laugh. "Of all your lies, that might be the most egregious, husband."

Jacob stood slowly. "Abby—"

"I'm sorry, Jacob. Family," I said, hoping to interrupt whatever dispute brewed between them.

Prudence squeezed my hand, redirecting my attention. "Not

every little thing we do is an offense, Sister Hazel. We're here to help you."

I looked up at the four faces before me. Prudence with her patient smile. Flora with her not-so-patient raised brow. Jacob with the pain I'd caused him. And Abby with her unreadable expression, appearing as if she couldn't decide if she should laugh or scold.

Not one brought me the reassurance I longed for deep within.

Chapter 17

It wasn't my night, thankfully. I wasn't ready to face Jacob after what I'd done to him with my panic. After praying on my knees for what felt like hours for forgiveness and a revelatory sign from the Lord of what to do, I climbed into the bed and tucked the covers tight around me. It seemed He held no answers to the mysteries in this house either.

Silence. All I desired now was silence. Silence from others and from my own mind that hummed without end imagining terrors and accidents, and a never-ending litany of sins that weighed me down. I closed my eyes, desperate for sleep.

At once, the room warmed, the air cocooning around me. I sank in my bed, now gently rocking as if lulling me to sleep. My breathing slowed.

From the top of the stairs, I stared down at the entry glowing golden in the fading sunlight. An unknown odor hit my nostrils, sickening my stomach. This world wasn't as it should've been.

An invisible tug drew me down the staircase. A curious sensation pierced through me—there was something here I needed to find.

I reached the bottom step. The stench of wrongness grew stronger. On the floor below, splotches of color covered the floorboards as if a clumsy person had dropped paint across it. I squatted to get a closer look. Each blemish was dark crimson. I skimmed my fingers across the top of the red stains and my hands drew back sticky and wet. A rusted tang hit my tongue and I gagged.

Blood.

It dripped down my fingers and across my palm, sizzling with heat as it spread. This blood was fresh.

Leaning over, I heaved but nothing came up. Droplets of blood slid down my arm in streaks.

What had happened here?

A trail of red gore smeared across the entry and disappeared through the doorway. Fear pulsed through my veins. Coming face-to-face with whatever caused this horror scene wouldn't be wise. But my body moved as if pulled by strings and I shakingly got to my feet.

I followed the scarlet path, my feet sliding more than stepping. I rubbed my hands together trying to clear the blood, but the evidence of this nightmare stayed put. The blood on the floor streaked through the parlor and snaked into the dining room.

The door to Jacob's study was propped open. Crimson ran in a stream across the threshold.

It took a moment for my eyes to adjust to the darkness, and a moment longer to realize what I saw. I froze.

A pair of boots slick with blood protruded from the doorway.

I screamed, but the sound died in my throat. Panic rose. Invisible hands shoved me forward.

This couldn't be what I thought it was.

"Help!" I mouthed, my throat not emitting a sound. Dropping to my knees, I fell over the body to examine them for injury, perhaps to aid them. I gasped.

Abby.

Her green eyes stared up at me, wide and glassy. Fiery curls surrounded her head but did little to mask the blood oozing from the back of it. I reached out but stopped short of touching her. What had happened to her? How had she gotten to this room?

I needed to help her, but I also knew it was too late.

Abby was dead.

Blood pooled where I sat, the hem and knees of my nightgown soaking up the liquid, staining the crisp white red.

I scrambled back from the body, but the blood spread wider. The fabric of my nightgown clung to my legs, heavy with the gore. I pressed my back against the wall, but I couldn't escape. Blood filled the study, lapping at the legs of the broad desk.

I prayed to disappear on the spot. To wake up from this nightmare. The red sea covered my feet now, inching its way up my ankles. What if I drowned in it before I woke up? My hands searched desperately for the doorframe but found no purchase.

Above me, the bookshelf quivered and a book dropped to the floor.

The chaos stilled. Curiosity overtook me and I bent to retrieve the book. Miraculously, the blood dripped off the cover leaving no stain as I lifted it. It was a black book of scripture. It slid from my hands and sank back into the muck, now up to my knees.

I looked down at Abby, her body almost entirely consumed by the rising tide. She leered up through a final patch in the bloodbath like she saw me. My stomach heaved again. My sister wife was dead.

And it didn't appear the cause was natural.

A hand grabbed me from behind and shook me.

"Hazel, wake up!"

I screamed as I spun around. Jacob stood in front of me, his face barely visible in the low light of the lamp in his hand. The rest of the room was bathed in darkness.

I held up my hands to my face. No blood.

"What happened—"

"You were sleepwalking, Hazel," Jacob said. "You were screaming."

"Dreaming, I was dreaming."

I looked behind him to find an empty floor. There was no sign of Abby or her death, no mark left behind by a sea of gore or trail of crimson, only the same peculiar study I'd seen weeks ago.

"Why were you in my study?" Jacob leaned in closer until his face was only inches from mine, his tone irritated.

"I don't know."

"Since this is my room, I can only imagine you were looking for me. Though there's no need to scream if you want me so badly."

He chuckled, slithering his hand to my waist. But, as before, my body didn't warm to his touch.

"I didn't know where I was."

"Will you tell me what you saw?"

Jacob's face shifted in the shadows. Despite the natural urge to obey, I couldn't form the words on my tongue. I couldn't tell him.

"It was nothing," I said, tugging out of his grip. "It was only a silly dream. I hardly remember it."

Though he held on to his smile, something I'd never seen before smoldered in his eyes.

Jacob studied me as I wobbled back against the wall, searching for my footing. I became too conscious of the loud tick of the clock on the shelf.

"Sometimes the Lord speaks to us in dreams," said Jacob.

My uneven breath caught in my throat. Could this have been some kind of prophetic vision? Was I being warned of blood to come?

"No, I'm sure it was nothing," I insisted, though I didn't believe my own words. That nightmare was most certainly something. Something important. "I'm sorry for waking you," I added.

"I wasn't sleeping. Abby . . ." He trailed off.

Heat spiked up my spine at her name.

Jacob's voice hinted with an invitation. "I was coming down to read my scriptures when I heard you."

But I didn't want to think about Abby or scriptures, or anything else. I slipped toward the door.

"I apologize for interrupting you, but thank you for waking me. I'll go up to bed now."

Jacob caught my hand once more.

"I'll walk you." His voice was breathy and low.

"Oh no, I'm fine. Fully awake now."

I edged into the doorway, but he didn't drop my hand. An invisible current rushed between us. *Let go, let go, let go*, I begged silently.

"Very well, Hazel. Good night." With a tug, he drew me against him and pressed his lips to mine. He tasted of salty sweat and forbidden drink.

"Good night," I said when he broke away.

I stumbled back out the door and broke into a run, not stopping until I threw the lock closed on my own door and slid to the floor.

I didn't understand what that nightmare meant to tell me. Perhaps it was better I never found out.

Chapter 18

I volunteered to take Abby her tray in the morning. She'd been laid up in bed for over a week now. My chest hummed with worry. I needed to make sure she was all right—alive and whole. Despite trying to keep the nightmare from my mind, I couldn't shake the feeling that she may be in some kind of danger. That we all might be in danger.

The kitchen door flung open, and I nearly dropped the tray. Abby stood in the doorway, inspecting us. Her face flushed vibrant pink, and her dress was impeccable. She even bounced a little on the balls of her feet. Nothing about her smiling demeanor appeared out of place, as if she'd never been ill at all.

"Well, good morning to you all too," Abby said with a huff. She eyed the tray. "No need for that today. It's such a lovely morning."

She flopped into a chair at the table and plucked up a piece of bread.

"Oh, of course, Your Majesty. Heaven forbid you tell us when you've miraculously risen from your sick bed," said Flora.

"Don't be so dramatic, Sister Flora."

Prudence replaced the plate she'd been assembling. "Glad to

see you're well, Sister Abby," she said. "Did Jacob anoint and minister to you?"

Men could pronounce a blessing of healing on others by virtue of their priesthood. Faith and the power of God wielded in men's hands would heal us.

"I don't need Jacob's blessing when I'm perfectly fine."

From the stove, Flora grumbled. "Perfectly fine."

"Glad to hear you're doing well," I said.

"Thank you, Hazel." Abby clapped her hands. "Well, we mustn't keep the children waiting for their lesson today. Prudence, you'll come with me, and, Hazel, you can help Flora finish tidying up from breakfast."

"And as always we must bow to your whims?" Flora said.

"No, as always we see to our duties," Abby replied, her voice soft as silk. "Unless, of course, you think you know better than God in heaven?" She raised an eyebrow, daring Flora.

Flora opened her mouth as if to say something further, then promptly closed it. Satisfied with her victory, Abby steered Prudence by the shoulders back out the kitchen door.

I stood, my fingers dancing through the loose thread on my bodice. Their footsteps disappeared, leaving only the sounds of the sloshing water in the basin and Flora's scrubbing behind.

I knew I needed Flora to teach me the intricacies of running a household and being a successful plural wife, but I would have given anything at this moment to be anywhere else in the house.

"Don't just stand there," Flora snapped. "Fetch a towel and dry these dishes."

I opened the nearest cupboard to comply and drew back the requested cloth.

"It's little wonder how this house would function without me. This is *my kitchen*, you know, despite Abby's attitude," Flora went on beside me.

From the prickle on the back of my neck, I wondered if something unseen listened in to our conversation.

With stiff arms, I took the first wet dish from her hands. "You must struggle with Sister Abby frequently," I said, immediately regretting continuing this conversation.

"Well, I'm the one sacrificing time with my children to mind the kitchen. Heaven knows what goes on in that schoolroom when I'm not around." Flora's words were strong, but her shoulders drooped lower.

"I imagine that must be difficult. It seems that you and Sister Abby don't get on."

"That's putting it mildly. She has no respect for my position in this household." Her rag scrubbed faster against the dish in her hand. "She's only brought Jacob two children yet expects me to show *her* deference."

I resisted the urge to scowl. Her words reminded me of Aunt Emma and her large brood, which was constantly maneuvered as a wedge between my parents.

"She can rile me as she wishes, but at least *I* am fulfilling my duty in Zion, though it may kill me."

Flora tossed her rag to the bottom of the basin and let out a long exhale. She leaned over the edge of the sink. Unspoken sorrows wafted off her. Even if I could offer words of solace, there was no balm for the hidden grief of plural marriage that we all buried within our hearts.

But still a part of me urged to try to lessen her burden.

"I've been doing my best to follow your instructions, Sister Flora."

She straightened up and pushed her glasses up the bridge of her nose. "Have you been snooping around the house again?"

"No, I promise."

"Then why did I see you standing before the attic door again yesterday when you were supposed to be doing the mending?"

I nearly dropped the wet dish in my hands. Flora watched me. But why? She wanted to train me, yes, but how could following my every move be needed?

"Are you the one always spying on me with that light?" I asked, unable to hold in the question.

"A light? I don't know what you're talking about."

"I've just seen this—"

She cut me off. "You saw nothing."

I gave her a confused look and she sighed. For the first time, Flora appeared despondently human—battered and thrown against the rocks of life.

"Sister Hazel, listen to me very clearly," she said. "You might have thought you saw something, as I did once, but such things are tricks of the Devil and not real."

My heart thudded out of control. What precisely had she seen? My tongue tied, unable to voice the dozens of questions dancing in my head.

She spoke deliberately, sincerely. "You're young, so very young, and you're easily mistaken and confused, as I once was. You can't possibly understand all it entails to be a wife, let alone a plural wife. This Principle is our test of faith and I fear you will fail. I must help you."

Since I was a child, my mind repeated over and over that I was doomed to fail. It echoed day and night that I always lacked—too sinful, too idle, too distant, too shy, too useless. I was never enough.

She drew a step closer. "I wish this household would realize that I would do anything, anything, to save you all. Even if it meant great sacrifice."

"But what kind of sacrifice would be required to save us?" I asked breathlessly, though I wished to ask, *Save us from what?*

Music swelled from above in response.

Why should we mourn or think our lot is hard?

"The music . . ." I whispered.

'Tis not so; all is right . . .

I raked the beams of the ceiling with my eyes. Flora gradually tipped her head back, mimicking me.

Why should we think to earn a great reward . . .

The hymn rattled through the walls, piercing my skin. I exchanged a look with Flora.

If we now shun the fight?

"Flora," I whispered. "Do you hear it too?"

I said a silent prayer—a fervent pleading that I wasn't mad, that I wasn't alone. That Flora would confess more.

"Hear what?"

My face fell. "The . . . the music."

Her voice once more turned cold. "There's no music, silly girl."

My heart sank. I was alone in this madness.

The attic door creaked open much easier than before. I climbed up the passage, making certain this time to close the door behind me, obeying the siren call drawing me in. I needed one moment of solace and quiet contemplation, perhaps to at last hear the word of God telling me what was true.

Prudence and Abby had taken the children out for a walk, and Flora toiled in the small garden among her cooking herbs, leaving the house empty. I was supposed to be cleaning, but this was perhaps my only chance.

In the mildewed attic all was the same as before, even my trail of footprints lay undisturbed. Untucking the bench, I gathered my skirts and sat down at the box piano. My fingers pried under the wooden lid and it lifted with a creak. My hands stretched out above the keys, poised and ready.

I glanced once more over my shoulder. I was alone. Warmth started in my toes, rising as floodwater. I gasped in relief as my hands settled onto the keys, a displaced part of me honed and ready.

The first few notes were soft. I struck the keys with resolution, craving each stroke of the ivory against my fingertips. I closed my eyes. The notes grew bolder, inflating that sore part of my soul with hope. A tear trickled down my cheek. Here was my respite. Here was my God.

Hymn after hymn poured from my hands. The notes were slightly sour from lack of tuning and the keys stiff. But the music was a cloud elevating me above this sordid plane.

Was all this madness in my head? Mother taught me as a child that Satan desired to have me, to sift me as wheat as the scripture said. I'd prayed and fasted my whole life for this burden of a worrying mind to be removed from me, but it never gave way. Places I'd never been and stories that existed only in my head were as much a part of my reality as my own body. This affliction was my greatest weakness, my place for refining. For who would want me if I couldn't give them perfection?

I opened my eyes. Tears dripped onto the keyboard below in a light fall of rain. If only flowers would grow from them.

A light flashed. My hands froze mid-chorus. Had the sun suddenly emerged from behind a dark cloud? I shifted my gaze to the window.

My mouth dropped open in a scream.

Abby stared back at me. All around her a light glowed—a dull white that outlined her vividly but lacked brightness. Her hair was undone, her curls surrounding her head in a fiery headdress. Her faded white dress was nearly worn through and splotched with dark stains. Her eyes were heavy, drooped with a universe of sorrows.

I blinked again and she was gone.

My hands slammed into the keys, sounding a loud, discordant jumble of notes. I shoved away from the piano and shot up to my feet, knocking over the bench. Then I turned and ran from the attic as fast as my legs could carry me.

Chapter 19

I paced back and forth across my room. I'd missed dinner and the day had given way to night, but I couldn't settle.

Abby. Abby. Abby.

I swore I saw her in the attic, but then again, how could I have? Nothing made sense.

I should've told Jacob about my fears, shown him the piano right away that he didn't know about. But what if he dismissed me or gave me that look of disgust again? I wasn't certain I could bear disappointing him once more with my failures. Deep in my belly I knew the inescapable truth that my husband was all I ultimately had; my claim on him in this life and the next would exalt and save me. What were temporary pianos and ghosts compared to an eternity of hellfire?

No, I couldn't do it. I couldn't ask him about the piano or what I saw. I couldn't risk the consequences that could literally stretch into eternity.

The door pushed open. I glanced up expecting to see Prudence with a tray insisting I eat, but instead Jacob stood in the doorway. I'd forgotten it was my night. Gooseflesh pimpled up my arms as we stared at each other.

"You seem troubled, my dearest," he said.

The room rattled as he shut the door. A frantic hive of bees awoke in my chest.

"I'm fine, simply not tired," I lied.

Jacob crossed the room to the bed, still studying me. The mattress groaned beneath him.

"Prudence said you were out of sorts and didn't come to dinner."

"I wasn't hungry."

Jacob drew his hand into his coat pocket.

"I've brought something to help, Hazel." He held up a black book like a beacon. "The word of the Lord is what you need. And a generous husband," he added with a chuckle.

I recognized that book. The last time I saw this book it was sinking into the mire of blood surrounding Abby's body.

"Kneel, Hazel," Jacob commanded, licking his lips. "For prayer."

I obeyed, unable to tear my eyes from his book. "Are these your scriptures, Jacob?"

"Yes. I've had it since I was called into the mission field years ago."

He flipped open the front cover to reveal his name etched in looping browning scrawl. Then, he closed his eyes and bent his head to pray.

I couldn't understand the words of the prayer; each supplication sounded as if coming from too far away.

The book of scriptures Jacob now held was the same as in the nightmare and, as that first day when I ran my fingers along his bookshelf, alive with lightning.

I cautiously cracked my eyes open as Jacob continued his oration to God. The black book of scripture filled my entire vision. I could almost see the phantom blood seeping off the cover.

Could this book be the clue to who wished Abby harm?

"In the name of thy son, Jesus Christ, amen."

"Amen," I murmured, unaware of the words I sealed my own lips to. I didn't rise.

His fingers gripped the bottom of my chin and he lifted my face to meet his. There was no indication of a secret in his unusually darkened eyes, but there was another gleam to them: lust.

"Perhaps we could return to the scriptures later tonight, my darling." His voice was soothing, slow. With a light touch, his thumb stroked across my jawline.

"Say you will always be mine, Hazel." His fingers pressed harder into my skin, digging against my bones.

"I will," I whispered back, my tongue fat and uncooperative.

"Say you love me."

"I love you."

My vision blurred as he pressed his mouth to my lips, to my neck, as his hands wandered down my chest to grab at my breasts.

I closed my eyes and willed myself to disappear. Each kiss, each touch wasn't my own. My phantom limbs moved, drawing into the heat of Jacob's body, but my head spun elsewhere.

The house. The book. The blood. *Abby.*

I matched his moans and pressed my hands into the sweating flesh of his back as he moved over me. But deep within, I didn't feel desire. I felt myself floating farther away, watching myself from outside of my own body.

The house. The book. The blood. *Abby.*

Jacob's fingers stroked my arm, but I stared up at the cold ceiling. His words slurred with sleep.

"You're turning into a good wife, my Hazel. God is pleased."

For the first time, I distrusted how much I craved that approval, how my pulse raced with excitement at the pronouncement.

"I believe you might have earned your piano," he continued softly.

I swallowed a surprised cry—a strange mixture of elation and confusion.

Though he bordered on sleep, I could sense the anticipation of my response in his breathing.

Knowing just what he wanted, I whispered, "Thank you." Why did it feel like jagged glass coming out of my throat?

Jacob nodded and closed his eyes. "I have one in the attic I could bring down for you. It would be wonderful to hear your beautiful music through the house. You could play for me every night."

My mind screamed.

I have a piano in the attic.

But Jacob said there wasn't a piano. He swore he knew nothing of the music I heard. Either he hadn't been telling me the truth, or he'd had been watching me far more closely than I'd realized. I held in my hands proof of a deceit but didn't know what to do with it. In all my years of instruction from home and church, no one had ever offered the possibility that husbands and priesthood holders could openly lie to their wives.

I glanced back over at Jacob, unsure if I was ready to accuse or accept, but he'd succumbed to sleep. The conversation was resolutely over, leaving me unmoored. His low, even breaths held no comfort for me in the darkness as they had before.

I twisted out of his embrace. The bed shuddered as I escaped it, and I ran my hand along the floor to retrieve my nightgown. I stalked to the window while throwing the gown back over my head. My hands gripped the windowsill and I leaned my head against the glass. Even the usually brilliant stars were dull.

Another light flickered at the corner of my eye. A faint luster grew slowly in the room, gathering strength bit by bit. I spun around, holding the sill behind me for support.

The apparition of Abby stared back at me. Her despondent face matched mine—twin reflections of shame and terror. I knew I should scream or command the vision to leave, but I couldn't muster the strength. Perhaps I needed to offer her my hand, to see if she was from heaven or hell, as the prophet Joseph taught.

"What do you want from me?" I whispered.

The visitor glanced at Jacob's sleeping form.

"What does that mean?"

She lifted her eyes to the ceiling. Another hymn swelled through the night air, filling the room until it threatened to choke me with its mournful chords.

Then in a blink, the vision was gone and the room again empty.

I sank to the floor, cradling my legs against my chest, unable to drag myself back to the bed to lay beside him. Instead, I closed my eyes and prayed for the oblivion of sleep on the hard floor.

Chapter 20

"Now, children, what is the most important rule?" Jacob asked as our cart approached the center of the city.

"Don't talk to gentiles about Mother or our aunts," the eldest, Nephi, immediately replied. He scratched at his dark blond hair before throwing me a careful look. His eyes—Abby's eyes—stared back at me. I offered an encouraging smile, although my insides twisted into knots.

"Quite right. We don't know which men out there could be informants."

Threats from the federal government kept most plural families in isolation these days, rarely coming out into public altogether for fear of detection and possible prosecution, especially after the recent passing of the federal Edmunds Anti-Polygamy Act.

The Sabbath morning sun beat down on us as we traveled. I was surprised to be woken early by Jacob that morning, who declared it the perfect day to travel into town for church for the first time since our wedding.

Prudence was far too close to her confinement to travel in a bumpy cart, and so I assumed care of her Edward. Flora protested that her cooking duties couldn't be neglected and stayed back with a frown creasing her forehead. Abby simply laughed and shut herself back in her room.

Edward glanced up from my lap. "Are you okay, Aunt Hazel?"

"Oh yes." I painted on a smile for the child I'd grown so fond of. "I simply didn't sleep so well."

His eyes brightened. "Did she keep you up too?"

"Are you eager to attend Sacrament meeting?" Jacob asked loudly, interrupting us.

I forced my gaze from Edward to Jacob. Snatches of memories of his fingers branding me the night before burned like scar tissue.

"Yes, I'm always eager to worship the Lord." I knew my words were thick with lies. I couldn't muster the desire to praise God today. I felt only the unbearable need to leave that damned house.

"My righteous Hazel. You've blessed me greater than any woman. Our Lord is too good to me," Jacob said.

I grasped Edward tight against me. "Yes, we're truly blessed."

The enormous, silvered dome of the Tabernacle stood out against the farmlands surrounding it as we approached. Chisels and hammers usually echoed through this square as workers built the Temple, but today was a day of rest. This square was the literal heart of the city, and it would continue to grow as a beacon and as a fierce warning to the incoming gentiles that this Territory was built on the sweat and faith of the Mormons.

Jacob ushered us into one of the large wood doors of the Tabernacle. The hall was instantly quiet, save the few whispers of the members finding seats bouncing off the massive domed ceiling. Long rows of brown pews filled the Tabernacle, and painted columns stretched upward along the round walls to hold up the curved balcony. Without any windows, the only light was that of the hanging lamps and my eyes took a moment to adjust.

We settled into our hard seats, the children reverently folding their arms as they eyed their father's serious face. They reminded me of my own siblings when we attended Sacrament services here more times than I could count. Many parents would leave their children at home, but my father loved to parade his into the Tabernacle, wiggly bodies, frustrating fights, and all.

Sadness wrapped around me as I peered through the gathering congregation of faithful Saints in their Sunday best, wondering if my family would be among them. As difficult as they'd been at times, I missed my siblings. I missed their pleadings for piggy-back rides and more songs on the piano to dance to. Heat warmed in my cheeks in a mix of joy and shame. I'd forgotten too much of a life I used to hold close.

And it seemed they'd forgotten me too, letter after unanswered letter.

Even if they were here today, I wasn't certain they'd even want to see me.

I tried to redirect my focus and lessen the sting. The colossal mahogany and gold organ pipes along the front wall filled me with longing. My fingers itched at my side, almost feeling the mighty pulse of keys and stops beneath them. But that dream was long gone.

Soon, the Sacrament services began. I shifted in my seat as the prayer was spoken and trays of bread began circulating down the aisles. The speaker at the pulpit was a man I recognized but couldn't place. His long beard, clean suit, and air of authority as he lectured signaled his importance in the church, but his words flew in and out of my ears without my truly hearing them. The trays continued their way around, the speaker breaking only when it was time to bless the Sacrament water, then continuing on with his words.

He slammed his fist against the pulpit and I startled. I needed to refocus on the words of the Lord. The speaker went on about the truths of polygamy as God's will through His prophets and my heart heaved.

"Plural marriage or damnation," he said. "That was the teaching of Brigham Young."

If these men spoke directly for God, why was it He could speak of nothing else?

I chastised myself, though an ever-growing part of me wished I would stop.

As the Sacrament goblets finished their rounds, the speaker began his conclusion. Worry swirled in my chest. I didn't want this meeting to end. I didn't want to return home to all the strange visions and blood-soaked nightmares. If only the all-knowing God would tell me what it all meant.

The first notes of the organ startled me from my thoughts. I hadn't noticed the chorister rise for the final hymn. The beginning notes of "Come, Come, Ye Saints" sounded dark and distant, like the stops were set in an odd pattern.

But the organ bench was empty.

No one else in the congregation startled or pulled out a hymnbook. The speaker continued his final testimony. I glanced around. It seemed only I heard the music. It pierced through my skin to sink into my marrow.

Come, come, ye Saints, no toil nor labor fear
But with joy wend your way . . .

The ghosts of Manwaring Manor had followed me to the Tabernacle. The house's claws stretched out across the valley and grasped around me. God didn't care for my struggles and He offered me no balm. But the house—the specter, the breathing walls—they knew me. They saw me and they answered.

Chapter 21

Our wagon rolled down the dirt street toward an unoccupied park to lunch and prepare for the journey home. Only thinking of home filled me with dread. Once more, I wished I could see my family, but I knew they didn't want to see me. I belonged to Jacob's family now, not theirs, and their silence spoke volumes.

Even though the meal prepared should have been delicious after a long morning, I barely tasted it. I twitched at the slightest groan of the branches above in the breeze, unable to keep my thoughts off the memory of the Tabernacle and the echo of the hymn rattling through me.

I watched the rest of the family as if through a window. From the outside, it was picturesque. The girls sang and played a jumping game while the older boys wrestled, with the littlest trying their hardest to tag along and join in. Jacob himself even rolled up the sleeves of his fresh white shirt and joined in the tumble, staining the back of his shirt green.

"I better be careful," Jacob teased as he plopped an apple slice into his mouth. "People may see my green gown and it'll cause a scandal."

It was only a joke, but didn't he see this wasn't the time? Our house was a nightmare, our lives a game with an unknown force pulling the strings. He'd gifted me a piano he swore he didn't know of, so what else could be hiding in his house?

Was Abby in danger, as the nightmares seemed to prophecy? Or was I?

I pushed off the picnic blanket Flora had so neatly packed for our lunch, desperate for distance. I would never be able to escape this life, my wedding covenant made that certain, but perhaps I could have a single moment of solace.

I stumbled to a bench at the far end of the park. My legs sank onto the wooded seat, which had warmed beneath the rays of the summer sun, and I dropped my head into my hands to stare at the grass between my feet.

Two feet stepped into view. "Hazel?"

Slowly, I drew back to sitting. His voice, *that* hesitant voice cut through me.

Elijah.

Elijah. He'd returned home!

He stood before me alive, solid, real—not a phantom, memory, or daydream. His dark brown curls were longer than I'd seen them over two years ago, framing his face. His delicate features always reminded me of a painting by some Renaissance master. And his eyes. His eyes were the same honeyed brown that I saw every night before I closed my own to sleep. His gray suit was threadbare and hung off his already slender form like it was meant for another man, or he'd lost weight too fast recently. But he was whole and the same as ever. He studied me cautiously, his smile small as he took me in.

Elijah. Here.

I could scarcely breathe for the shock of it. His presence stirred thrill and fury within me.

"I thought I saw you in the Tabernacle," he said at last, rubbing the back of his neck.

"Did you follow me here?" I asked curtly, wincing at my own tone. Though it was probably earned unconscious ire. If this false man hadn't thrown me over without explanation, this wouldn't be my life. I wouldn't be trapped in this nightmare of secrets and lies.

"I only wanted to inquire and see how you were doing. Perhaps speak to you some."

"Why?" I ignored the prick in the corners of my eyes. "What would we speak of?"

"Well, I mean, my father told me of your choice to marry—"

I scoffed. *Was it truly a choice?* I'd never thought of such before.

Elijah bit his lip, trying again. "I wrote you—"

"You don't need to lie to me," I said, swallowing down the burning hurt. "I've received not a word from you since before my marriage."

He appeared stung. "What?"

Out of the corner of my vision, I noticed Jacob shifting up from the picnic. He stared right at me. My heart ticked with fear.

"Yes, thank you, Brother. I'm doing fine this Sabbath," I said, my voice probably much too loud to be convincing.

"What? Hazel, please, we need to talk. I don't understand—"

Jacob began a steady walk toward us.

"There's nothing to understand or discuss," I hissed between my teeth, keeping a false smile plastered on.

Elijah's face fell with a melancholy that shredded through me. That wicked part of me wished to reach out and clasp him against me so he'd never make such a face again. "If that's what you truly want," he said.

It wasn't at all what I wanted. But Jacob was approaching quickly and I couldn't risk him suspecting anything untoward. My panic struggled to stay contained in my chest.

"I'm glad to hear you enjoyed today's sermon as well." Then lower, I added, "You must go now. My husband is coming. This isn't proper."

He blinked as if he'd suddenly understood where he was. "Ah, yes. Forgive me, Hazel," he said, taking a step back.

"Sister Manwaring," I replied, the words scratching my throat.

Silence sliced between us like a knife. Too many thoughts left unsaid, too many wants left unfulfilled. Jacob was close enough now that he could surely hear us. My heart scattered in my chest, the panic lingering right on the edges of my strength.

"Good day, Brother."

"Good day . . . Sister Manwaring."

Without a glance back, Elijah swiveled on his heel and stalked away, his shoulders hunched. My feet itched to run after him. To throw myself into his arms. But hadn't he brought this on himself when he broke our vows and dashed my world to pieces months ago?

"Who was that?" Jacob's voice cut through my thoughts.

"No one. Only a man who'd lost his way."

Jacob turned to watch Elijah fade into the distance. His face didn't betray any anger, but it certainly didn't hold any amusement. Would he yell or threaten me for speaking to a strange man?

"What are you doing out here all alone, my darling?" His tone was as silk, but his neck was splotched with red as he sat down beside me.

"I've only stopped to think, Jacob," I said.

We sat in silence watching the children twirl and jump in the distance. Then he slid his arm around my shoulder locking me in place against his side. I held my breath without meaning to.

"Did you see the boys and I brought the piano downstairs this morning?" he asked. "It was quite a struggle, but surely you appreciate that."

I nodded. The piano in the parlor this morning should have been a respite from the uncontrollable whirlwind around me. But seeing it only reminded me of Jacob's strange behavior. Had he lied to deceive me? Perhaps he'd meant it to be a surprise for me and I'd ruined it by snooping. Despite being outside, there wasn't enough air around us. What if I simply misunderstood everything—stupid, stupid me!

Someone cleared their throat.

"Mr. Manwaring, is that you?"

My breath caught as we both turned as one toward the newcomer.

"Or do you insist on Brother Manwaring like the rest of the Mormons?"

The graveled voice belonged to a lanky man certainly not dressed in his Sunday best. His hair was shorn tight against his head almost to balding, and his eyes flitted up and down us like we were specimens from a circus. It was clear from his speech and the reek of tobacco on his person that he was a gentile.

"Either is quite fine, sir. I admit you look familiar, but I've forgotten your name or the consequence of our introduction." Jacob's tone hardened over.

The stranger stuck out his hand. "Reginald, John Reginald. We spoke at your mine a few weeks ago."

"Oh yes, Mr. Reginald. From the mining company back East. I trust your visit to our Territory is still pleasant?"

"Mighty interesting, that I will say." Mr. Reginald's eyes raked over me as his hands sunk back into his pockets. I angled closer to Jacob on instinct, suddenly feeling naked and exposed before this unknown visitor.

"We're a peculiar people, Mr. Reginald," he said.

The man licked his lips. "And this pretty young thing is your wife?"

Jacob's hand tightened possessively on my shoulder. "This is Hazel, my wife. Hazel, may I introduce you to Mr. Reginald."

"Pleased to meet you, sir. I hope you enjoy your stay in Utah."

"Oh yes, you Mormons sure are fascinating. Tell me, Manwaring, this one your only wife?"

Jacob sprang up.

"Why do I get the impression mining isn't your only profession, Mr. Reginald?" He towered over the man, having at least six inches on him.

Mr. Reginald only laughed, not appearing the least bit intimidated. "Supposing it might not be. Your other wives are here?"

"My *wife* is here, as you've seen. Now I must ask you to leave us. It's growing late and we need to collect the children."

Jacob pulled me onto my feet. I didn't know what else to do but cling to his hand. All thoughts from before—Elijah, the piano—fled my mind. This was the greatest fear now—discovery.

"All those your children, ma'am?"

My throat grew dry.

"I beg your pardon, sir, we aren't yet that acquainted. I must bid you good day."

There was no greater fear instilled in me by Mormonism than this—that covert authorities from the East would come and imprison us for living in what they called bigamy.

"Good day, Mr. Reginald," Jacob spoke with finality.

"Good day, Mr. Manwaring. Be sure to give your best to your other women. Wouldn't want them to feel left out. Oh, and Manwaring, I'm sure I'll be seeing you again, so be sure to bring the right wife back when we do."

Jacob froze and my heart skidded into my throat. The threat may have been veiled, but it was certain. Mr. Reginald wasn't a miner at all.

"Jacob—"

"Fetch the children, Hazel. We're leaving. Now."

Chapter 22

We'd barely stopped the wagon when Flora flew down the porch steps, her face dour. The sky had clouded over on our ride home, the threat of rain thick in the muggy desert air. Outlined by the blackening storm, the gables of the house grew more forbidding.

"Finally! Jacob, we need to send for the midwife," she said.

Abby stalked down the steps behind her with a face as solid as stone.

All remaining thoughts of Elijah and our miserable encounter dissipated instantly. I remembered all too well the pains of Aunt Emma as she delivered her recent baby, her screams shattering through the house. My muscles tightened in anticipation of Prudence's cries.

"Are you certain?" Jacob said, his tone impatient.

"Yes. Now, please, go and fetch her."

Without waiting for his confirmation of her commands, Flora disappeared back inside the house.

Jacob scrubbed his face, then handed the reins of the wagon over to Nephi. "Take the horse and fetch the midwife." He turned to the other boys. "Put the cart away before the storm gets stronger and then get up to your rooms. Abby, make certain Flora doesn't smother poor Prudence."

The heavens ripped open, sending large drops of rain cascading down.

"Of course. We wouldn't want anyone to harm the mother of your child," Abby replied.

Jacob gave her a long look and I was certain he would scold her, but he finally waved his hand and the family broke off to their tasks, running to avoid the downpour. I handed Edward over to Esther and turned to follow Abby.

Jacob extended his arm to stop me. "Come with me, Hazel. I need your help."

I nodded but hesitated watching Abby's skirts slip through the doorway. A flash of lightning cracked the sky.

Jacob tugged my arm again. "Hazel, come."

Inside, Manwaring Manor was in commotion as I'd never before witnessed. Children's footsteps raced down the hallway, doors clattering behind them. Faint screams from above penetrated the air. The walls wheezed in a frantic rhythm as if unsure of how to handle the magnitude of life rebelling against the house's usual static.

Drawing up after Jacob, I took the stairs two at a time to keep up with his pace. He didn't even pause at Prudence's door as he hastened to the end of the hallway. Instead, he pulled me into his bedroom and slammed the door shut. The house hissed in response.

This room was the smallest of them all, used as more of a storage closet to hold his clothes and private things. I'd never been admitted inside before. He went straight for the drawers and ripped one open, rifling through the pile of clothes inside.

"What are you looking for?"

"Fetch the bag from the shelf," he said without peering up.

"A bag?"

"My large traveling bag, top shelf."

My blood pumped at a ferocious rate.

"Are we leaving?"

Jacob didn't respond. Mechanically, I pushed onto my toes to fetch the bag peeking over the top shelf. A cloud of dust descended around me as I tugged it down.

"Where are we going, Jacob? And why now?"

He took the bag I extended out to him and thrust it open to stuff clothes inside.

"Prudence is in labor! Please tell me what is happening," I pleaded.

"On the bottom shelf there's a brown box. Grab it for me." He extended out his hand expectantly.

Biting my lip, I followed his directions and bent over searching the shelf for the brown wooden box tucked up in the corner. I pried the lid open. Inside the carved box were two large stacks of paper money and a jumble of various colored coins. I slammed it shut again and handed it over, the money jingling with my trembling movements.

I swallowed past the barbs in my throat and repeated, "Where are we going, Jacob?"

"We aren't going anywhere, darling. I'm going." He shoved the box into his bag.

"*You're* going? But where? Why?"

"I have to keep myself from jail. It'll ruin us." He straightened up and clasped the bag shut, then peered around the room as if looking for what else he may have forgotten.

"Jail?" I croaked out.

"Come now, Hazel. You're smarter than this. You must've noticed that Mr. Reginald isn't a miner. He's a federal agent."

"I understand that, but what does that have to do with leaving right now?"

"You heard his threats. I've been marked. All he needs to do is find this house and he'll have the evidence he needs to turn me in to the marshals for bigamy."

Bigamy. One of the twin relics of barbarism, as the Republicans declared it. I'd studied the Edmunds Act—a hideous law created by Congress to punish our polygamous practices—when it passed only months ago and everyone knew the guilty sentence of Brother Reynolds at the Supreme Court.

"You don't know that. They need more proof than cohabitation to arrest you. Just because this new law has been announced doesn't mean—"

"Oh, Hazel, how naïve you are." His voice laced with a mixture of pity and frustration as his hand slipped up my cheek, dragging me closer. "You don't know that things have changed. The damned government's started sending enforcers now. A man from the mine was found out only last week and carted off."

I'd once prided myself on being at the forefront of news in the Territory as the daughter of a newspaper man, but of course, I'd been isolated out here for months. The entire Territory could've disappeared and I would never have known.

"It's all still new, Jacob. We're so far out here from the city, he may never find us."

"I know these kinds of men better than you and they will stop at nothing to destroy Zion and our way of life. I can't risk it." His cold fingers caressed my skin, sending ice through my veins.

"But must you leave tonight? Perhaps we can discuss another plan of action. Prudence is delivering your child!"

"It's regrettable, but it must be so. I know you'll take care of her." He drew his hand back, leaving an uneven wake between us as he moved away. "Reginald will only be around a few months and then he'll move on. I know his type. I'll speak to the Brethren and follow their examples. When it's safe, I'll return."

"What about the mine?"

"The foreman can run it well enough through my correspondence."

He had an answer for everything. I knew I needed to listen and obey, to cease my arguments, but my body tightened, pulling back as a quiver on a bow.

I stepped forward and blocked his path, mustering every ounce of my courage.

"How can you leave your wife in her greatest hour of toil? And what of the rest of us? Your children? This doesn't feel right, Jacob. Are you simply trying to save your own skin?"

Down the hall, Prudence's screams reverberated louder. More doors slammed and footsteps clicked with sharp, echoing tones. The household was finally breaking through the long silence, roaring and straining to be known. The house allowed the anguish of its occupants to at last be heard. It was almost buoying, a kind of rebellion feeding my fortitude to question him.

A wide, uneven smirk split Jacob's face. It wasn't handsome or alluring like his usual smiles but reminded me of a creature in a forest before it consumed its prey. He stepped forward, discarding his bag as he closed the space between us.

"Save my own skin? Is that what you truly think of me, wife? I do this—I do everything—for my family. For the eternal Principle that created this family. For my God and His kingdom. Do you truly dare to question my judgment?"

"No." I shrank back though my body screamed at me. "But perhaps if you leave, we should all return to our own families for a time." I knew from watching my own mother the afflictions of a woman in polygamy left alone without her husband. Surely, he didn't want that for us.

I couldn't help thinking too of my bloody nightmare, imprinted forever in my mind. Would Jacob's absence lead to its fruition, for Abby or any of us?

"You would have my family leave me?" he asked.

"No, but why should we suffer here without you to protect us?"

A flash filled the room and the window rattled with a strike of lightning.

Jacob's lips twisted up. "Do you know what I found, Hazel?"

Silence beat between us as the rain pelted against the windowpane.

"I don't know, but—"

"I found a letter. Hidden in the logs of the fireplace, addressed to a certain young man."

My letter to Elijah. Color drained from my face.

"But . . . but you had no right to my things!"

"I have a right to *everything*. How else can I protect and guide you? I'm your husband and your head. But you were writing love letters to another man!"

I backed up until I hit the wall. He pinned me against it, arms outstretched on either side of my shoulders.

"Jacob, I—It wasn't as it looked, I swear—"

"It wasn't? *'As if I could ever stop loving you*,'" he quoted. "You were supposed to forsake him for *me*."

"I did. Jacob, I swear I did."

"It grieves me that you would make such a sinful choice. That you would spit in the face of our sacred covenants! What have I done to deserve such mistreatment?"

Jacob's fingers shot out to grip my neck. I floundered, helpless against his strength.

"Listen to me, Hazel. I'm your husband. You've sworn before God that you will be *mine* for eternity. Your body, your soul, and your salvation are in *my* hands."

His breath burned against my skin. His words etched into me.

"You've been taught the fate of a damned soul. I do all this to save you from that terrible hell because I care for you. You can't be saved without my priesthood.

"So you see you must remain here with all of the family. It's the only way for you stay in control of your wild emotions that would condemn you if I let you roam free. It's for you! All of this is for you and my family to keep you safe!"

Still holding my neck with one hand, he slammed his other fist into the wall, narrowly missing my ear. I felt the walls shudder in response.

"And if you so much as murmur a word about leaving this house to the others for any reason, I will take your letter straight to Elder Crowther. What do you think the Brethren will do to an adulterous woman?"

I couldn't speak. Such accusations were destruction—in this

life and the next. I would be thrown out of the church, society, and damned for eternity. Certain leaders even taught a blood atonement must be made for the most wicked of sins—a death at knifepoint, shedding your blood onto the ground as a sacrificial offering to save your soul from eternal perdition. Could such a thing happen to me?

I opened my mouth to say that I hadn't done anything to amount to true adultery, that he was mistaken. That it hadn't been a love letter, but an exorcism. But what would my protests matter in opposition to a man's word? His evidence would always count more than mine.

Jacob let out a long exhale, softening. "I know you're scared, Hazel. I know you fear me leaving, but I must do what I can to save this family. Would you destroy us all with your selfish fears? Where is your faith?"

Shame potent and hot coursed through me. It flooded my gut, rising until it choked my throat more than his tightening grip. Jacob leaned closer until his lips hovered directly over mine.

"I said, where is your faith, Hazel?"

"With God," I whispered. "With you, my husband."

His lips crushed against mine. Hard and hungry, claiming me, owning me. His teeth caught my bottom lip and bit down. The rusted taste of blood hit my tongue.

The wall moved against my fingers and Prudence's cries again split the air. My heart pounded against its cage for release from its prison.

Jacob drew back, his eyes shining with desire and fury. I shrank back, praying I could somehow dissolve into the wallpaper and hide away forever. My husband acted now like stranger to me, so unlike the amiable man I knew. That I loved. I hadn't known he was capable of such anger. It was terrifying to behold.

He backed up, each step slower than the one before until he reached the door.

"I have the letter in my possession, Hazel, and I can bring you before Elder Crowther at any time. Do you understand? You will stay here, and you will wait for me to return. You will chase off any marshals that come by and protect us. Is that clear?"

I nodded, and he disappeared out the doorway.

Panic fully overcame me; I could not stave it off any longer. As I struggled to breathe, all sorts of profane and shameful thoughts flooded through me. This was all my fault—my secret longings for another, my lack of faith and trust in my husband. I was the vilest of sinners drowning in an ocean of my own making.

Within the hour, the midwife arrived. Jacob slipped away into the falling night with only a short goodbye to his family. The children pressed their faces to the nursery window, watching him vanish into the darkness while we wives travailed with Prudence. I held her hand close to my chest as she delivered her child—stillborn.

The house descended back into its oppressive silence. Only the muffled cries of a mother's loss broke through.

Chapter 23

Two months later

The porch steps sagged beneath my weight. Though the late-September air danced with a light breeze, sticky heat leftover from summer clung to my skin. I had been fetching water and should've gone inside long ago, but I simply couldn't bring myself to take the final steps. The sweat dripping down the back of my neck was better than the stifling, helpless quiet inside the house.

Two months had slipped away. Weeks of ghostly lights appearing throughout the house while I tried with all my strength to ignore them, and then finding myself once more staring at the piano, fervent whispers tingling up my spine. I tried to play for solace, but it seemed Jacob's lies stained the keys. No joy came from the songs I managed to pluck out. Days of hard work to live off meager resources and nights of twisted dreams that left me itching to run out into the wilderness and never return.

Regret weighed on me as I stared down the drive, the buckets of water beside me, sentinels to my vigil. If only I'd never written that letter to Elijah. Perhaps then Jacob wouldn't have felt the need to keep me controlled—or keep all of us tucked away in this haunted house. I'd sinned in my wish to write Elijah, to somehow touch him even from afar. But even now, I couldn't drive him from my secret longings.

As I predicted, life had only become more difficult since Jacob's sudden departure, a daily struggle for survival and unity. If only I could tell my sister wives to leave, instead of working against them to keep us trapped here, alone and struggling. If only I wasn't so imprisoned by my fears.

I pressed my palms into my eyes. This was my burden to carry alone, and I loathed it. The others didn't know—and never could know—that Jacob had written once, to me.

I'd burned it as instructed, but I read it enough times first to brand it into my mind.

Dear Hazel,

I'm well and hidden, but the time is not yet prudent for me to return. I fear it will be some time. Continue to watch for Mr. Reginald and turn him away. Be assured I'm in frequent contact with Elder Crowther, and your letter is kept safely in my pocket. Remember always what I said. Remember that without me, you have nothing but disgrace. You have nowhere to go and even if you did, remember that God will be your final judge. Do you think you can pass under His all-seeing eye and not be punished? The pains of a damned soul are far worse than you could imagine. Keep the family as they are at Manwaring Manor until I return and your letter will be destroyed. Most of all, remember that if you go or lead your sisters astray, their blood will be on your hands.

Your husband,

Jacob

Their blood.

I rubbed my hands on my skirt absent-mindedly. What did Jacob mean by that? He was still my husband, and I wanted so much to imagine him as being guided by his fears and not truly dangerous. But the feeling of his hand clasped around my neck was hard to forget. I knew he wasn't the same man I thought I loved.

The clap of horseshoes cut through the cottonwood trees. I watched the dirt path, waiting. Could it be Jacob? What would happen after he returned to us?

A horse came into sight around the overgrown trees, its rider tall in their seat. I could see even from a distance it wasn't Jacob, but that didn't assuage my nerves. The rider drew closer and I slowly rose.

Mr. Reginald had returned.

"Hello there, Sister Manwaring," he called as he tugged his horse to a stop. His smile reminded me of a jack-o'-lantern with spindly teeth.

"Good day, Mr. Reginald. You're back again, I see." I forced my tone to stay even and uninterested. "I'll stop you before you even dismount. My husband isn't here, so you'll forgive me for asking you to leave."

"He's away on business a lot for a mine owner."

"He has other duties as well, to the church."

This informant wouldn't get what he wanted from me. I would protect this family, as strange and miserable as it was.

"It's so hot out here. Perhaps I could step inside and catch my breath?"

"I can offer you some of the water I just fetched, but it wouldn't be proper to allow you inside. I'm a woman alone in this house and wouldn't dare allow a strange man to join me. Surely you understand."

He sucked in and spit onto the ground. "You sure you're all alone here? Don't make a lot of sense to leave such a pretty young bride. If I were your husband, I'd never let you out of the bedroom."

"Get out," I commanded. "Go now or I'll fetch the gun my husband left me for protection."

For a moment, I thought he'd call my bluff. He shifted his glare up to the gables, his eyes widening. The horse neighed loudly and startled back.

Mr. Reginald fought to stay in his saddle.

I twisted around just as the curtains shifted in the window.

His horse reared.

At least my strange ghosts had their uses.

"This isn't over, Manwaring. Don't think I'll give up. Next time, I'll be back with far more men and your damned husband will have to give up his harem." He spit once more, then urged his horse on.

As the click of horse hooves hurried away, any sense of confidence I'd had deflated within me. What would happen when he came back with more men? I couldn't hold them all off. Even if they didn't find Jacob hiding inside as they thought, they'd find the rest of the wives. Jacob would be found out and a ransom placed on his head. He wasn't wrong that him in jail would ruin us, leaving us wives to fend for ourselves without an income or aid all the way out here. And his punishment would only allow his anger against me to stew. . . .

I raced up the steps to the front door and slammed it behind me. I did not want to think on the misery that would rain down if I failed to keep us hidden.

That evening, the fire in the bricked hearth crackled and spat sparks onto the kitchen floor. No one seated at the table made any move to clean the residue left behind. The taste of ash hung in the air. With the children tucked into bed, the only other noise was the howl of the growing wind.

I sat beside Prudence, who kept her eyes on the whorled grains of the table. She'd been little more than a ghost since we buried her baby girl beneath the large tree out back. Across the table, Flora kept her fingers busy with mending a child's shirt. Abby—who called this meeting of the wives—pressed her palms into the table as she waited expectantly.

"Well?" she finally said. "What are we going to do?"

"Do about what, Sister Abby?" said Flora.

"Our lack of husband and food."

"We don't lack anything. He's still my husband, and the good Lord always provides," Flora replied with astounding calm.

We weren't starving—not yet at least—but rations were growing small. Soon, we'd be left without enough to feed the children. My ears echoed again with the rattle of coins as I handed Jacob the box during his packing. If only I'd been wise enough to realize that he'd taken it all, that he'd be gone for so long that his own children would suffer.

Abby snorted. "I'll be sure to tell your children such when they go to bed crying for food."

"Oh, ye of little faith—"

"Faith doesn't fill my belly."

I agreed with Abby but pressed my lips together tight. I couldn't risk sparking greater contention. But what if the nightmares were a warning of our demise by starvation?

It'd been a long two months without Jacob. At first, we'd managed quietly as if nothing had changed. But as days slipped into weeks and then months, we struggled to keep the tentative harmony of our home.

"We could visit the bishop's storehouse," Prudence suggested.

I nodded at her encouragingly. "That may be necessary. I can help Nephi drive the cart into town and—"

"Don't be ridiculous. The bishop's storehouse is for the poor and needy," Flora said, shoving her needle into her mending.

"*We* are the poor and needy," Abby grumbled.

"I doubt the bishop will see it that way," Flora said sharply. "Surely, there's somewhere we haven't looked, some place we haven't scoured—"

"We've torn the house apart, Sister Flora," I said. "I've searched every crevice for coin."

"Don't tell me you actually thought Jacob was wealthy?" Abby said with a small laugh. "It's all long gone in speculations and bad investments."

Elder Crowther, my father, myself—we all believed in Jacob's great wealth. This battered house stood in warning when I first arrived, but I ignored what was plain before me. My husband didn't have all that he boasted he did. The truth sunk into my gut with the weight of a brick.

"Then we'll think of something else," I said.

We had to stay here, but we also had to live. Flora appeared resigned to fate, buoyed by her unending faith, and I couldn't yet decipher Prudence's thoughts beneath the hard shell she'd retracted into months ago. But our survival depended on us staying here together. Abby and Prudence had no one to return to even if we could split apart.

The thread of an idea glimmered in my mind. I allowed myself to tug at it, watching it unravel as the fire popped again.

"Then we must take up an occupation for ourselves to bring in money," I pronounced, lifting my chin.

"What kind of occupation? None of us have great talents for dressmaking or farming, and we're far too secluded on the edge of town to run a proper laundry." Abby's voice was soft but questioning. My nerves were as unstable as ever around her.

"When I was a child, my father went on a mission and my mother was left with few resources. She took up boarders at our home to earn enough for us to live." Many plural wives took on boarders to supplement meager incomes from husbands stretched too thin with many wives and children to care for.

I glanced around the table weighing the other wives' reactions. Beside me, Prudence nodded, and Abby raised a thoughtful eyebrow, but Flora thumped her sewing to the table.

"Boarders? You mean you wish to bring strangers into our home? Strange *men*?" Flora's eyes were wide and accusatory as if I'd just proposed our demise.

"'I was a stranger and ye took me in,' Sister Flora," Abby quoted from the Bible. "I think little Hazel is onto something, Sisters.

We have plenty of rooms and a kitchen large enough to host more. We're close to the mouth of the canyon, so miners traveling from their families would find it ideal."

"And the presence of good Mormon men might help protect us when Mr. Reginald comes back," I said.

Flora rolled her needle between her fingers. "I suppose I could cook enough to feed a few extra mouths, but we can't run faster than we can walk. Start small. One or two boarders that we can trust."

Abby clapped her hands. "Well, it's settled then. I'll take care of finding our first boarder. Sister Hazel, can you clean out the rooms?"

"Certainly," I replied, trying not to be reminded of her cruel nickname that still haunted me: Cinderella.

Prudence shifted in her seat, still not fully meeting our gazes. "But what about when Jacob returns? Will he be displeased with our industry and lack of trust in him?"

I sensed an unspoken fear behind her question but didn't dare to pry further, not when she was so unlike her cheerful self.

"Industry is the way of Zion. He'll be proud of our work when he returns." It wasn't a lie, but the words tasted sour in my mouth. I honestly didn't know how he'd react as I knew less of him than I once imagined. The man I thought was sweet and charming, who kissed me with passion and called me his dearest, had a darker side laced with half-truths and threats. I tried not to think on it, but I didn't know my husband at all.

Abby rose to leave the kitchen. "*If* he returns, it'll probably be with another wife on his arm."

Chapter 24

I dragged myself to bed far too late. My fingers and knees ached from scrubbing for hours as I cleaned every inch of the spare bedrooms. Shame clung to me for my idle thoughts throughout the day that continued to return to Elijah, wherever he was now after our unhappy meeting months ago. Maybe Jacob was right, after all; that I needed to be controlled even more to save myself from carnal sins.

My eyes closed as soon as I sank into the pillow. The house creaked as it settled. It was odd how comforting its moans had become to me, like it mirrored back my own anxious thoughts.

A dull light illuminated my room. I must've forgotten to turn out the lamp before I crawled into bed. With a small groan, I forced myself up to sitting again. It took a moment for the obvious to sink in—the lamp was already extinguished.

But the light continued from out of the corner of my eye. I turned and my stomach flipped.

The specter had returned.

She hovered at the edge of the room, her naked feet floating above the floor. Her edges jagged and flickering with a glow of white light. Once more, the ghost appeared as Abby, like a vision dragged from a nightmare.

I hadn't seen this spirit since that night before Jacob left, which I'd buried away as the feverish output of my troubled mind. But I had seen its light throughout the house, which I quickly ran from and tried to forget. Perhaps the strain of the last two months finally brought the collapse of my senses and now she was back in full form.

"Surely, this is a dream." I squeezed my eyes shut, then open again, but nothing around me changed. I pinched the skin of my arm between my fingernails, drawing real pain.

I was awake.

My heart beat louder, thumping out of time against my ribs.

"Abby?" I whispered to the spirit.

Her presence was real and yet her body was not. I had the distinct impression that if I reached out, my hand would pass straight through her like wisps of a cloud. She *did* look like Abby—but she was not. The specter shared the same oval face, fiery hair, and piercing eyes. The same porcelain skin and perfect nose. But a different constellation of light freckles crossed her cheeks. Her eyes were slightly farther apart. This ghostly version was a clever counterfeit.

A cunning trick of the house.

But what was it trying to tell me through this manifestation?

A sad sort of smile lingered on her lips. It was oddly disarming. The light she bathed in was inviting, enticing even. I wanted to trust her.

"I saw you before, with the piano and Jacob. But I don't understand why you're here."

Her face drooped into a frown, pain deadening her eyes. She didn't even open her mouth to respond. I felt that she wouldn't—or perhaps couldn't—answer me in words.

She floated toward me.

I grabbed the blanket tighter, balling up on the bed and pressing into the headboard. She eyed my movement and stopped before she reached my bed.

"Is there something you want from me?" I tried to keep my voice calm.

The apparition's light brightened. An affirmation.

My head swam. There was a ghost in my room—one that looked painfully like Abby—and she desired something from me.

"But how can I help?"

She beckoned me toward her.

A trickle of sweat dripped down my back as panic started within me. Should I follow her? What if this was a deception of the Devil?

But deep within me, a voice cried out for answers to mysteries always lingering: Why was this house so silent, so sentient? Why had Jacob lied about the piano? What did my blood-filled nightmares mean for Abby, or for any of us?

This Abby now before me was terrifying, but she could also be an answer.

I slid to the edge of the bed and stood.

Her feet sank into the floor until her toes glided only inches above the floorboards. The specter now stood eye to eye with me. Her light made me blink, but I couldn't look away.

Before I could inquire for more information as to where we were going, she stepped back and sank through the solid door.

I startled. The air rushed around me with a chill. This was my last chance to climb back into bed and forget the entire madness. But something thrummed in my veins—a spot of courage, or maybe simply desperation. My life in this house was too shrouded in confusion, and perhaps ghostly light would provide some illumination.

Holding my breath, I pushed open the door to follow.

She waited at the top of the stairs. Even though the hallway was drenched in darkness, I didn't require a lamp. The specter's unearthly glow reflected off the fading papered walls enough to illuminate the space surrounding us.

She trailed down the stairs, her feet never touching the steps. My shadow was a black splotch against the stairwell wall as I descended. No shadows mirrored the apparition.

We padded across the entry in silence. Downstairs, the larger rooms swallowed our bubble of light, making me feel even smaller. We moved quickly through the parlor, my eyes tracing the dark outline of the piano with a mixture of longing and revulsion. My marriage had taken so much from me, even my music. I turned back to my companion, who suddenly stopped outside Jacob's study.

Cold wrapped around me. Memories of that horrifying nightmare and sea of blood flashed in my head.

The ghost disappeared through the study door, leaving me in the gloom of the lightless dining room. My hand reached for the door handle but hesitated. What if the nightmare were to play out in reality now?

The floor shifted beneath me. With a gasp, I tripped into the door and fell into the study. Straightening up, I braced myself. But the room was empty except for its usual furniture and the incandescent figure hovering now against the desk. The study air crackled. Shadows flickered at the edges of her light. Book spines dripped with sputtering light, elongating the titles until they seemed to bleed.

"What are we doing in here?" I asked, finding my voice.

She moved to the bookshelf on my left and looked up at the line of books on the high shelf.

"We're looking for a book?"

She motioned more precisely to a black textured spine, wedged against the side of the shelf at the end.

My heart jumped into my throat. I recognized that book.

"Why do we need Jacob's scriptures?" I couldn't hide the quiver in my words as memories of his hands branding me that night assaulted my body.

Gesturing again, her eyes grew wider, her face more fiery.

I wanted to shrink back but instead swallowed past the gravel filling my throat. I couldn't stop the barrage of anxious thoughts, but deep within, the voice pleading with me to keep going marshalled through them all.

I stretched up and pulled the volume from its place. The room settled into a distinct hush as I brought it down. It weighed far more than I expected, as if carrying the weight of all my fears. Dropping to the floor, I knelt and placed the book before me. She sunk down with me.

I waited, wondering if another manifestation would reveal itself. The walls shivered and pulsed around our huddled cocoon of light, but nothing happened.

I looked to her.

But she made no indication of a clue. She was a completely different woman than the Abby I knew in the light of day, who spoke her mind no matter how scandalous. This Abby was painfully quiet, but with so many frustrations brimming just beneath her surface.

Returning my attention to the book, I flipped open the cover. My finger traced down the inside cover, revealing Jacob's name, signed in browning ink. My mind jumped back to that night in my bedroom, the time I'd last seen her. Before Jacob prayed, he had showed me this stamp of ownership.

My heart thudded. "You want Jacob?"

Her expression turned grim.

"He'll be home soon," I said.

Her face darkened as a storm cloud.

I glided my fingertips over the thin paper, pieces sliding together in my head.

"Unless you're . . ." I exhaled. "You're worried about him returning?"

She seemed to coil up within herself, dragging her light tighter around her.

"You're afraid of him? But Abby always seems so confident around Jacob." What if the first wife and I weren't so different deep within us, with unspoken worries about our husband?

Her face twisted in fury, sending her light cracking across the page.

Fear coursed through my veins, but I tried my best to ignore it and stay planted.

I picked up the book and it parted naturally to where a folded sheet of paper marked a passage. With trembling fingers, I lifted the note and unfolded it. It was in Jacob's looping writing, the same as his letter. I quickly read through the message.

It wasn't much of anything. Jacob's note detailed instructions for how to give a priesthood blessing to the sick and infirm. Such ordinances were common for healing ailments of the body and spirit. It appeared he'd written this short list of directions to remind himself, probably when he was on his mission and learning the ways of the priesthood Brethren.

I glanced back up at the specter, her visage remained stony and unanimated.

I skimmed the note again. Dark splotches blurred down the edges of the page. I brought the note closer to my nose to decipher it. In the bottom corner of the page, Jacob had scrawled an additional sentence: *What you bind on earth is bound in heaven*.

A spark tingled in my fingertips. Binding. We were all bound to Jacob by virtue of our marriages, even after death.

"'What you bind on earth is bound in heaven,'" I repeated.

The room plummeted into sudden darkness.

The visiting spirit was gone, leaving me alone.

"Hazel!"

A faint glow lit the doorway. Flora held aloft a lamp that cast dark shadows across her hardened features. She stared down at me with an expression as rigid and solemn as if I'd spoken out of turn in Sunday school.

"What are you doing, Sister Hazel?" She lifted her lamp higher, stretching the shadows around her into a forest of darkness.

"I—" My throat shut up tight. There was no way to explain myself. I slammed the book shut.

"Well?" Flora demanded. "It's the middle of the night and I find you reading in the pitch-black in Jacob's private study? Have you gone mad?"

Nothing could be said to make sense of or remedy this situation. I knew she'd never believe me.

"I was dreaming," I lied. "Sleepwalking. It happened once before. I'm sorry for disturbing you."

She stepped closer, and without asking permission, snatched the book from my hands.

"You shouldn't be nosing around Jacob's private things," she scolded.

"But I was reading it."

Her brow furrowed as she studied the cover.

"*This* book?" she said to herself.

I jumped up. "You've seen this book before?"

"Yes." She shook her head and straightened over me. I shrank back on impulse. "Of course, I've seen this book. These sacred scriptures belong to my husband."

My mouth was suddenly too dry. Why wouldn't Flora say more?

"You're tired and it's unbecoming to wander around in the middle of the night. You can do better. Now, go back to bed." Flora pointed to the door like I was a child to be scolded. "Good night, Sister Hazel."

The fight flickered out in my chest, and worry took its place. I brushed past her out the door and slipped into the parlor. Everything appeared the same—mismatched furniture and sense of disarray. But inside me, worlds had shifted. Abby's specter was real, and there was something she needed me to know.

"Move, Hazel," Flora commanded.

I didn't wait to be told twice and scurried down the hallway to the stairs.

"What's happening?" The real Abby called from above.

I startled back, nearly falling into Flora.

Atop the stairs, Abby watched us. With her hair undone and her crisp white nightgown, she looked not unlike the ghost herself.

Flora let out an exaggerated sigh. "Sister Hazel was wandering around Jacob's private study in the middle of the night."

"I was only sleepwalking," I said.

"And carrying on a conversation with the air," Flora said.

Abby's gaze flicked to me. She studied me up and down, her face cinched tight and unreadable in the dim light.

We reached the top of the stairs and, with one last look of frustration, Flora turned on her heel down the hallway, carrying the light away with her. Abby and I remained in silence.

"Good night then," I said at last.

Abby reached for my arm, pinching my skin.

Instinctively, I tried to pull away, but her grip held strong.

"Who were you speaking to in the study?" she hissed, her eyes growing round in the moonlight.

"Th-The Lord, Sister Abby," I quickly lied once more. "I was communing with Him."

Her fingers tightened, digging into my flesh beneath my sleeve. "Whatever for?"

"I don't know," I confessed.

"He's never listened to me," she said.

I noticed the fear shining in her eyes. I tugged my arm back and she released it, staring down the stairs as if watching for something. I followed her gaze. The entry below was empty and quiet, but a strange tang hit my tongue.

My pulse raced. I needed to get out of this hallway.

"Perhaps try again." Old, rote answers from my Sunday school days slipped out. "Have more faith. Pray more. Study your scriptures and the words of the prophets."

"I wonder . . ." Her words drifted off as if she'd long forgotten me.

Without another word, I slid through my doorway and turned the lock. I collapsed back into my bed and threw the blanket over my head like it would protect me from the encroaching darkness.

Chapter 25

For days afterward we spun in a strange dance, Flora, Abby and I tiptoeing around one another, uncertain of what to say, what to confess, what to accuse. My nighttime visitor didn't return to my bedside, but the dreams revived in the brightest hues. When I closed my eyes, I saw my world stained with blood and lust without explanation.

Still, we settled back into the uneasy equilibrium demanded by a household in crisis.

After dinner, I stood by the sink drying dishes while Flora fretted about our woes.

"If this boarder plan doesn't work, I will take my children to my father's farm. And then what would you all do without me?"

"Leave? But you don't need to leave, Sister Flora." The words of Jacob's letter burned bright in my mind.

"Why not?"

"Because I need your help." I spoke as fast as the words would come out. "I still need you to teach me."

It wasn't a complete lie, at least.

She gave me a satisfactory nod. "Yes, you truly do. I'm glad to see I'm finally appreciated." And on she went with a list of things I needed to improve on.

I let out a deep breath behind the dish I held. Hopefully her pride was assuaged enough to drop thoughts of leaving. Not that I particularly wanted her to stay if I had the choice.

The door burst open, rattling the line of saucers along the shelf, and Abby floated into the kitchen. My heartbeat quickened. This was the first time the three of us had been together alone since that night on the stairs.

"We've done it, Sisters. Our first boarder arrives tonight after he finishes his day's work. And he already paid for the month in full!" Abby rapped the table in a celebratory gesture.

"Who is it?" Flora asked, her fingers scrubbing the pot in the sink with extra vigor.

"A young man, newly returned from a mission. He's taken up work with a nearby farmer," Abby said.

"Is he respectable?"

"As respectable as any man can be."

"I merely worry about the influence on our children—"

"That he'll corrupt them?" Abby said. "I don't think we need a boarder to do that."

"A priesthood man will be good to have in our house," I said, hoping to further appease Flora's doubts. "He can give a level of protection. Mr. Reginald was back recently."

Flora grumbled beneath her breath.

Abby pressed on. "You'll hardly even see the man aside from mealtimes, most likely."

"Have you told Sister Prudence the good news?" I asked.

After dinner, Prudence had thrown off her mask of a smile that she reserved for the children and disappeared up to her room, even as I had begged her to stay and sit with me a while.

"I haven't. The poor thing keeps slipping off."

"She's sulking," Flora said.

I gripped the dish in my hands tighter. "She's mourning."

Silence billowed over us. Only the fire popped and crackled in the hearth as if on command. Not even Flora dared to speak, but the water sloshing over the side of the sink betrayed her thoughts. The walls surrounding me inched tighter, suffocating the remaining air.

I needed to get out of this stifling kitchen.

As I placed the last plate on the shelf above, I glanced over at the empty woodpile by the fireplace. My feet decided before my head. I untied my apron and crossed to the back door.

"I'll fetch more wood before night falls," I said.

The early October sky was already pinkening on the edges as the sun began its descent. We would need more kindling for the cold night and morning ahead as the weather shifted again. Though I hated the brutal feel of the axe in my hand, I'd learned the necessary skill after Jacob's departure and preferred it to another minute in the kitchen.

"Let one of the boys do it," Flora said as I pulled my coat off the row of hooks.

"It's all right. Let them rest after a long day. I'd like the chance to be outdoors."

Before either could protest, I disappeared into the hazy twilight. The crisp air nipped at my face and sunk into my skin, a welcome balm. A breeze rippled through the trees, swaying their branches in a dance with the leaves in their fall colors of red and orange. I breathed it all in.

For as long as I could remember, I'd loved dusk. There was something magical about this time of day. It became a physical place to me as a child, somewhere I could crawl into and hide away from the never-ending worries and panics that besieged me throughout the day. Back home, I'd play the piano and disappear into selfish thoughts I otherwise never allowed myself to have, and found a space free of guilt, panics, and the all-seeing eye of the church.

I'd lost that time and beautiful place since my marriage. Now I longed for it more than ever.

I crossed the yard to the wood pile, soaking in this fleeting moment of freedom. Too soon, I'd be called back to my life, and to the choices that weighed too heavily in my chest.

Large logs lined up beside a heavy stump with the axe protruding out. My muscles hurt simply from looking at it, but I didn't shy away from my task. Any excuse to stay away a little longer.

I set to work, my breathing growing heavy as I forced the axe above my head and slashed it back down again into the logs. Splinters flew like tiny knives. As I worked more vigorously, my mind settled into thoughts of another dusk years ago:

Elijah's mouth pressed against mine while we hid among the trees of the orchard.

It wasn't only the rush of love that I remembered, but the way I felt truly alive for the first time in my life that evening. Like I could create my own world on my convictions and desires, not simply the one prescribed for me as the only path. That I could be unburdened of the expectations to be perfect in order to be accepted, that I could allow every messy piece of myself to simply exist without the pressure to refine it. Elijah was more than the man I loved—he was part of the world I selfishly wanted to build for myself. One that set me free.

My mind went quiet as I savored the memory.

The axe thudded against the stump, sending a shock up my arms. I tossed the last split log onto my pile and eased up, each bone in my back cracking. The sun dipped out of sight, leaving only a golden dusting of light across the sky. My window of liberty was closing quickly. Glancing up at the gables, I watched the house shiver and expand.

Resigned, I adjusted my coat and readied to return inside. I bent down and piled the wood into my arms. Across the yard, the kitchen door watched me, ready to swallow me back into its depths.

Leaves crunched behind me.

"Hazel? Is that you?"

I froze. That voice. A sound my soul craved but had forced down deep to try to forget. The Devil himself come to torture me.

"Hazel, it's me."

I turned around slowly, my armful of wood suddenly heavier. My breath caught in my throat.

"Elijah," I said. "You can't be here. You're . . . you're not real."

He laughed awkwardly, scratching at the back of his neck. Even after all these years, it still held a thrill like music. "But I'm here, alive and whole as you can see."

"I can't trust everything I see."

"I'm glad you haven't lost your imagination."

A boyish grin cut across his handsome face, even as his cheeks pinkened. He dared a step closer, snapping a fallen twig beneath his boot heel as he tugged his hat from his head, revealing his untamed hair. He quickly brushed it back, shifting between his feet.

I studied him in silence, uncertain of what to say next.

He was here. This was real.

"But you can't be here."

"I've been desperate to see you." His tone was laced with sadness.

"Don't you remember what happened at the park months ago? Haven't you already done enough to hurt me?"

I hated how I meant for my words to sting him.

"I hope you'll let me explain," he said softly, gripping his hat tighter against his chest.

"I don't know if I want to hear it."

I held the rough wood closer to my chest. Splinters drove into my soft flesh, but I only clutched it tighter, welcoming the pain as a reminder that all of this around me was real and I couldn't give in to the urge to bury myself in his arms.

"You need to leave, please." I glanced back up at the looming house, at the many windows anyone—or any ghost—could peer out of. "Before someone else sees you."

"Can I help you with those?"

"No, Elijah. You need to go. We're expecting someone."

"Yes, the boarder," Elijah said.

I frowned. "How did you know that?"

He replaced his hat, rubbing his hand on the back of his neck. "Because I'm him."

I dropped the logs, which cascaded to the ground. My legs threatened to crumble.

Elijah was the new boarder?

I stood a moment, stupefied. When I made no move to regather my fallen logs, he sprang forward to collect them. His hand brushed against my boot.

"No, no, stop!" I shouted, my voice shaking as I leapt back. He couldn't come this close to me, he couldn't touch me—he couldn't be here at all.

"What's wrong?"

I dropped to the ground, snatching up the last pieces of wood. "You're here as a boarder. And this is my husband's house." Jacob wanted to keep me here to control my wild emotions, yet somehow, they still found me here in the worst possible way.

Elijah recoiled, still holding his bundle. Guilt rippled through me at the way his face fell.

"I know." His voice was clipped, but it wasn't harsh.

I almost wished he would rage like a tyrant against me. That would've been easier to take than watching him kneel as though groveling at my feet.

The autumn breeze picked up and misplaced strands of my hair streaked across my face. He knelt so close to me. Warmth shot through my body and pooled in my center. Only one small movement and I'd be touching him. I blinked back a rush of tears and forced myself to lean away.

"Then why are you here, Elijah?" His name was a sweet poison on my tongue.

Elijah rose steadily with the bundle of wood. "I needed a room. I found work at a nearby farm."

"Is that truly all?"

This was akin to torture. The man I once loved—still loved—had to come to plague me before I could bury him away in the past for good. He'd broken my heart and then dared to come to my house of tarnished rot. Nothing good would come of this.

Elijah's face softened, the corners of his lips upturning. "Would it be truly so terrible if I came to see you as well?"

The hole I'd clumsily stitched up in my heart ripped open. Fresh lifeblood spooled out into my chest threatening to drown me. The overgrown ground beneath me was no longer so solid.

Elijah rejected me. His rejection and his father's commands had brought me to this dreadful place. Now he came to be close to me—to be something I would always see but never touch. To plant roots in places within me that I'd forced to lay barren. Elijah was a temptation that would damn me.

And this house—this godforsaken manor—sent ghostly visitors with demands and no explanation. It brought nightmares of blood and held too many secrets. I couldn't shake its grasp on me.

I controlled nothing of my own life.

Perhaps that nightmare was a twisted prediction of my own demise. In my mind, I saw myself prostrate on the floor of Jacob's study in place of Abby's body, sinking into a sea of crimson gore.

Elijah snapped his fingers. My face shot up from the pile of browning leaves I'd been staring at. He had remembered my mother's old trick to ground me back in the present.

"You came to see me? After all you've done?" I choked out.

Anger coiled within me. He understood nothing of the games he played at, what was at stake if I stepped out of line. I reached out and grabbed the logs from his arms, my hands brushing up against his chest as I wrestled the bundle away. Heat drew up my arms at his touch.

"Still as sharp-tongued as ever, I see." Only Elijah ever saw the truest depths of me, not just the quiet mask I wore. "Are you sure I can't carry those to the house for you?"

"Yes, very certain. I'm grateful to see you're well, but you'll have to tell Sister Abby you changed your mind about boarding. I can call on you the next time I come into town at my mother's house and you can give me your excuses for your behavior then."

Elijah ran his long fingers through his tousled hair. My own fingers itched, recalling how those curls felt in my hands.

"But my job is out here and I've already paid for the month, Hazel. I understand you're in need of the money too. Please don't ask me to go back on my word and make the other women suffer."

More frustration mounted within me. The children needed to eat. I wouldn't deny them and my sister wives the opportunity for needed income, and he knew he could press this to his advantage.

I almost wished I could finally bring myself to hate him.

"And you'll behave yourself properly? You must understand this situation is dangerous for me."

"Of course, Hazel. I'd never do anything to cause you harm."

I drew in a slow breath, then lifted my chin. "In that case, let's agree to keep our distance and never speak to the others of our . . . our friendship."

"If that is what you want, Hazel." Sadness darkened his voice, but he offered a small smile.

"Now please go around to the front of the house to greet Sister Abby, as is proper."

I hurried away without another glance back, though in my mind I could see almost perfectly how he looked staring after me, his beautiful face a mixture of confusion and satisfaction.

I glanced up at the highest window. A bright face stared back at me from behind the curtains. My chest cinched tight. Abby's specter watched, her eyes burning, and then she was gone.

* * *

Abby's voice echoed through the house as I deposited the pile of chopped wood by the fireplace. Elijah laughed and my skin tingled as I pressed my back against the wall of the parlor and waited for them to move farther into the house. The only way I would survive this complication would be to avoid him as much as possible.

Chapter 26

Elijah. Elijah. Elijah.

He etched his name into my skin as we moved together, our bodies climbing with sticky heat. My hands mussed his hair. His lips roved down my body. We laid together in a bower of towering prairie grass. Warm sun blazed overhead, the sky painted azure and with streaks of sugar-white clouds I could taste on my tongue as I gasped. Elijah's finger stroked downward, making me moan.

"Say that you're mine, Hazel," he whispered into the crook of my neck, his voice thick with longing.

I arched into him, savoring the touch of our skin pressing together. "Elijah—"

"Say it, please. I love you."

I kissed the edge of his mouth. "I love you."

The vision shifted around us. I was in my room on the bed alone again, but the core of me continued to burn with unsatisfied want. I rolled my head to the side searching for Elijah, needing his embrace once more.

But instead of finding Elijah, Abby sat at the table staring back at me. I shot up at once, embarrassed by my compromising position. She didn't say a word, though, only studied me with frantic eyes like she craved something unspoken from me.

A drop hit the top of my head. Tilting my head, I looked up at the ceiling. Another drip landed on my nose. The blood returned with a storm of force, raining from above. Abby sat steadfast, her eyes boring holes into me. Crimson seeped down her face, but she made no move to wipe it away. The unholy rain pelted my naked skin until I was quickly coated. I screamed, an animalistic, shattering cry that I didn't know I was capable of producing.

"Stop screaming, you child," Flora scolded. "Good wives don't complain."

Her words echoed off the walls, though I couldn't see her. She commanded silence over and over, but the storm never ceased. The blood filled my throat.

I awoke screaming into my pillow, my body drenched in sweat. For days, my dreams had been a torturous mix of Elijah and Abby, a confusing jumble of desire and blood. I tossed and turned all night, praying the nightmares would cease, only to be thrown headfirst into another.

It seemed the last bits of the fabric of my reality were disintegrating—my nightmares, Elijah's unseen presence in the house, Abby's specter, and the ever-present threats of hunger and Jacob's wrathful return. This morning, in an attempt to regain some semblance of control, I focused on scrubbing the parlor until my fingers turned raw. I ran my rag, blackened with dirt, along the top shelf of books and it shuddered in reply.

I made my way through the doorway to the dining room. I'd add these rags into the growing pile of laundry and pretend this was all perfectly normal. That I wasn't slowly losing my mind to panics and imagined horrors. I remained so lost in my own thoughts I didn't notice Abby lurking in the doorway of Jacob's study.

"Hazel! Come and help me."

I startled. "Oh, Abby, I didn't see you there. Are you—"

The rest of my sentence caught in my throat.

Abby wore only her chemise, the long cream sleeves and high collar of her garments exposed beneath it. She didn't appear bothered by my intrusion on her state of undress but waved me into the room.

"I was too anxious to get started and didn't bother to dress. I barely slept anyway," she said at my staring. "Come, now."

I set my rags down and followed her in.

"Grab every journal you can find," she instructed as she reached up onto her toes to pull a slender volume from the top shelf.

"What for?"

"Study." She gave me an expectant look over her shoulder. "Well?"

I moved forward, running my hands along the lower shelves. We worked in silence for several minutes, stacking the few journals we could find onto the desk. But what was Abby intending to study in Jacob's private journals?

Seemingly satisfied with our findings, she dropped into the chair, releasing a tiny puff of dust into the air. She grabbed the top journal and flipped it open.

"Is that all you need?" I asked, tentatively.

Abby laughed, ignoring my question. "So many notes on Brother Brigham! You'd have thought he was his scribe. Jacob wrote down every word he heard the man say."

I shifted between my feet, somehow certain the eyes of Brigham Young's portrait on the wall bore into me.

"If that's all, then I'll—"

"Look at this, Hazel," she said as I shuffled toward the door. "'*There was never a time when man did not exist, and there will never be a time when he will cease to exist.*' He certainly thinks a lot of men."

"What are you looking for?" I asked, panic stirring within me.

"'*I could find more girls who would choose me for a husband than any of the young men.*' And he certainly thinks a lot of himself."

"Sister Abby," I pleaded.

At last, she looked at me.

"I'm studying the words of the Lord through the prophet, as you suggested on the night of your little sleepwalking excursion."

I'd never seen Abby so much as pick up a book of scripture, and that night had been days ago. I wondered what could be driving her to such sudden spirituality. Though it was simple to say the Holy Spirit had moved her as I'd been taught in church, the way she peered at the words as if she would devour them from desperation unsettled me.

I recalled the fear in her eyes as she told me I saw nothing that night. Perhaps it wasn't religion at all. Perhaps we both felt unmentionable things in this strange house, things that also kept her up at night.

Abby settled back into the chair, a queen on her throne.

"I simply need to find the answer to end this torment. Have we not been promised the words of God would deliver us?"

"Yes, of course," I said.

"Then why are you staring at me so peculiarly? Everything can be made right once more. At last, I'll have peace, even in this godforsaken house."

I nodded, stepping back to the door as quickly as I could. If Abby wished to become a gospel scholar suddenly, then so be it. Nothing she did surprised me anymore.

"Here's an interesting one," she said. She leaned closer to the journal and flattened out a newspaper clipping. "Sermon, 1857 . . . '*this is loving our neighbors as ourselves; if he needs help, help him . . .*' "

I slipped toward the door, ready to leave Abby to her strange education.

"*. . . and if he wants salvation and it is necessary to spill his blood on the earth in order that he might be saved, spill it.*' "

Her words were little more than a whisper. A cold shiver ran down my spine. The strange and nearly forgotten doctrine of salvation through sacrificial death—Brigham's blood atonement. I left as fast as I could from the study.

Chapter 27

That evening, Esther's legs shifted against my knees as she squirmed in front of me. "You're certain you'll tie them extra tight?" she asked.

I spoke around the pin in my mouth.

"Of course, but you'll need to please stop wiggling so much," I said.

Obediently, she straightened up, her eyes catching mine in the nursery mirror as I twisted the strip of rag around a section of her damp hair. I pinned the end up at the top of her head to match the other sections.

"There. You'll have the loveliest curls tomorrow."

She bounced on her heels as she turned her head to get a better look at my handiwork in the mirror.

"Oh, thank you, Aunt Hazel!"

I smiled. "Now be sure to say your prayers before you fall asleep, Esther. I'm needed in the kitchen."

"Yes, Aunt Hazel. Good night."

I left the room with her staring at her face in the mirror, no doubt the rush of youth and imaginations of grandeur dancing in her head. An ache settled in my heart as I hurried down the stairs once more, but whether it was for sweet Esther or my own loss of innocence, I couldn't say. One day she'd be a wife the same as me, her duties before God and husband already determined. The sacrifice of her youthful dreams laid on the altar of marriage.

I shook my head and hurried downstairs to the kitchen, flinging the sad thoughts from my mind.

"Forgive me, I was helping Esther . . ."

My voice trailed off as I swung the door open and froze in the doorway. Flora wasn't there, but the room wasn't empty.

Elijah.

My heart did a somersault.

All at once, the chilled kitchen felt entirely too small. He smiled as he stood from the table, nearly knocking the bench over in his haste. His awkward politeness was disarming.

Since his surprise arrival, I had kept my vow to avoid him. His work kept him away for long hours, leaving at sunrise and returning only for the evening meal. Although we'd exchanged pleasantries in the company of the family, until now, we'd never been alone.

"Good evening, Sister Manwaring," he said calmly, as though he didn't also sense the current surging between us, threatening to burn away the very air. "I missed dinner and so I made myself a plate. I hope that's all right."

"Of course, Brother Crowther. We're meant to feed you. Please, sit down."

The kitchen returned to silence, but my heart thumped loud enough that I was sure he would hear it. A buzzing worry pricked at me, but I couldn't command my body to leave.

"I should go."

"Please stay," he said. "I would appreciate some company. I feel like I've been alone for days."

His sincere expression stopped me.

"All right, I can stay for a bit."

My answer won me a crooked smile that made my heart patter faster.

"Wonderful. And besides, I'll need to make sure you get the plate back safely."

I sat down across from him at the table.

"Why, were you planning to steal it?"

"No, but I get the impression that the tall Sister doesn't appreciate anyone messing with her kitchen."

"Oh yes, Sister Flora. Best to avoid her ire."

"Like you avoided Sister Emma's ire?"

I resisted the urge to stick out my tongue. "I was always civil."

"Do you remember the time you—"

"Put a spider in her soup? Yes, but in my defense—"

"She never noticed it," he said.

A familiar sense of happiness rose within me. One I hadn't felt in years.

"And you're one to talk. You're the one who—"

"Put sand in Father's sandwich to see what would happen. I remember the thrashing I received quite well," he said with a groan. "I still maintain—"

"That it was my idea? I'll never admit to such malfeasance."

Laughter bubbled from our lips like we were once again two naughty schoolchildren exchanging secrets. The kitchen swelled with our mirth.

But as our laughter died out, we watched each other closely. Seconds ticked by as hours. Being alone with him felt dangerous, like getting too close to a raging fire. But right now, I wanted to be consumed.

His fork scraped across the empty plate.

"Anything else I should know about this house?"

I opened my mouth, but my tongue grew thick, unable to form words. While part of me wished I could pour out and tell him everything about this haunted home, another part of me held back. I thought of my letter, tucked away in Jacob's pocket. This was still his house.

"There's nothing to know," I said, my voice rising in pitch.

"This is our husband's home and we all work together. And my sister wives don't know you're Elder Crowther's son, or that we know each other. We must keep it that way."

"Yes," he said with a bitterness I could taste. "How could I forget you're now a plural wife. Especially when you were so against it before."

He'd crossed a line, knowing right where to stab.

"And what's wrong with that? You no longer wished for our union, so I found comfort elsewhere."

"I never said that," he said with frustration, his fingers turning white as they gripped the edge of the table. "And I certainly never wanted you to marry a stranger as his plural wife."

"Jacob's wife. I'm Jacob Manwaring's wife."

"A stranger," Elijah repeated. "His fifth wife. Why did you choose Manwaring?"

Jagged heat rose between us. Elijah had no idea how much I adored him, craved him. How much I suffered for my sin of forbidden love. The man I'd tried so hard to forget was here demanding my attention and answers I didn't have to give. Elijah had chosen his duty over me, and I'd done the same.

I ignored his ignorance of my situation.

"I'm his *fourth* wife. And your father is why. *He* contrived this match. *He* told me it was my calling to obey, and I did so. Because of *you*, Elijah. Because you didn't want me."

I let my held-back vexations burst forth as a dam breaking.

"He told me that this was what God wanted. That my obedience was expected for my own salvation, so certainly, I had to comply."

The echoes of my confessions—both spoken and unspoken—danced around the kitchen. Tears pressed against my eyes, but I refused to let them fall. I'd cried far too many tears already over this tragedy I couldn't alter.

"I'm sorry, Hazel." Elijah's voice quivered like he strained to hold in his true emotions. "But he was wrong. About *everything*."

"He's an apostle of the Lord. How can you question him?" I said.

His gaze burrowed into me. "Why are you so upset that I do?"

"Because I gave up everything, changed the course of my entire life, based solely on his word," I nearly shouted back. I couldn't control the rage boiling inside me, though I knew it wasn't all meant for him. "I refuse to believe that after all this—this madness I've suffered here, that everything has been for naught."

"I'm sorry, Hazel, I truly am. I'd give anything to go back and stop this. I wrote you letters—"

I cut him off. "It doesn't matter. There's nothing we can change." Every moment of this conversation slashed into me. I couldn't bear more of his arguments against my choices—if they'd truly been that at all. It was useless to argue or to wish for what might've been. This was my reality, unable to be molded or reshaped to my longings. As firm and immutable as the words of prophets and patriarchs.

Then why was I so upset?

"You shouldn't have come here," I said. "You spurned me, and you should've forgotten me."

Elijah rose from his chair. "I didn't. That would be impossible, Hazel."

Slowly, he walked around the table. I tracked every step with a beat of hunger growling in my chest. I'd built a wall of stone around myself the day he discarded me, and now my heart cried out for it to crumble to the ground.

He knelt before me. Heat as palpable as fire flamed around us. One night years ago, we drew this close beneath an apple tree and promised ourselves to each other with passionate, burning kisses. Now the temptation stung fresh again.

"After our entire childhood together, how could you honestly believe that I would leave you? That I would stay away from you when my heart is just as much yours as it is mine?" He reached out his fingers, gently stroking them across my cheek.

I closed my eyes to savor the sensation pulsing through me. I wanted more. He'd stoked the fire and it threatened to grow to a blaze. A wicked, sinful blaze. When I looked to him, his eyes flicked across my face, then down to my lips. Every breath he let out, I drew in.

Chapter 28

The windows rattled in warning. The back door screeched open, dousing us in cold night wind. Elijah jumped to his feet.

Prudence stood in the darkened doorway.

"Oh, forgive me for startling you!"

Her voice was hoarse, as if she'd been shouting. Or sobbing.

Though being interrupted by Prudence was surely better than by Flora, my heart still jumped. "There's nothing to startle. It's only dinner."

"Sister Hazel has been keeping me company, making sure I returned her plate," Elijah said. Scooping up the empty dinner plate, he walked to the sink.

"I can do that, Brother Crowther."

I nearly ran to take the plate before he could wash it himself. Glancing over my shoulder, I watched Prudence sit stiffly down at the table, her back to us.

She hadn't seen anything—not that there was anything to see. Elijah and I would never—we weren't . . .

I bit the inside of my cheek to awaken my senses. To feel the pain I deserved.

"What are you doing?" I whispered.

Elijah's tone remained cool, unlike mine, though quiet so as not to be overheard. "Cleaning my dish. And we shouldn't part on such terms."

"Please, no, Elijah." I couldn't rip myself open for him after the burden of all that'd just transpired.

"You have to let me explain."

"There's nothing to explain."

"But there are concerns you must know," he pleaded.

"I don't want to hear it, it's too late. Please, just stop."

He bit his lip and stepped back from the sink. "Very well, Sister Manwaring. Good night."

I finished scrubbing the dish as he retreated with a soft farewell to Prudence. Once I knew he was gone, I turned back to the table.

"What were you doing outside in the dark, Prudence?" I asked.

"Only wandering near where we b-buried her."

"Wandering? In the darkness? Prudence, that isn't safe."

"It matters little," she said.

My hands stilled in the sink. "Why wouldn't it matter?"

"I don't matter."

Her chilling words were only a whisper, so quiet I wasn't sure they were meant for me.

"You missed dinner. Why don't you eat? I'm sure that will help calm your . . . wandering." I took a piece of bread from beneath the cloth on the shelf.

She stared back at me but made no response. The fire crackled in the hearth but did little to chase out the coldness of the room.

"Please, you must eat something, Prudence." I tried again with a smile. "For Edward."

The mention of her son was the only thing that seemed to pull her from these spells lately. Her eyes refocused and a hint of shock lit her expression, as if she had only just realized where she was and that I was beside her offering food.

"Of course, Sister Hazel. How silly of me." She took the piece of bread and after an excruciatingly long minute, began to eat it.

"Perhaps you can tell me now why you feel the need to wander."

"No, no," she protested. "I don't want to bother you with such a trivial thing."

"It isn't trivial at all to mourn for those we've lost."

"But I've sinned, Sister Hazel. I've loved my baby more than I've loved God. Every moment I should be joyfully serving and continuing on, I think of her loss and I'm pulled down into such despair. If I was a good woman, I wouldn't let the past consume me so. I would praise God and be happy. I need to stop these feelings and simply be content."

Prudence's head drooped in shame.

Her words hurt. I knew that burn of shame well. We were commanded by the Brethren to not love the things of this life more than God's will. Sometimes that meant our fine possessions, others it meant the bodies of our children. The faithful pioneers who first came to the Salt Lake Valley wept, then dried their tears and left their loved ones buried on the trail behind. Everything, *everything*, needed to go onto the altar of sacrifice. And then we needed to be joyful in our obedience.

Like scales dropped from my eyes, I took in Prudence and her suffering. What if it wasn't supposed to be like this? What if we deserved more as women—as humans—to feel the depths of life and not call it a sin? What if we were allowed to explore the multitudes of ourselves and not hide away the most jagged pieces?

Was all this sorrow and struggle truly worth it? It terrified me to even allow the question within my own mind, but I didn't silence it.

I reached across the table and took her hand. "Just focus on getting better. Edward will need you. I need you."

For the first time in a long time, she smiled.

"And how have you been, Hazel?" she asked.

A hum started in my chest; one I'd been burying for days. Inexplicable tears burst in my eyes and I fought to blink them back. The panic was sudden and overwhelming.

"I—" My voice cracked. I was unable to go on.

"Oh dear, I've been so caught up in myself I haven't been helping you at all." Prudence reached back across the table to grab my hand. "What's wrong?"

I simply shook my head, uncertain where to begin or what to confess.

"You've been holding us together, Hazel. Ever since Jacob left." Her tone was thoughtful, as if she'd only just realized her own meaning as she spoke.

"I have to. I have to keep us here. Together." My words came out so strangled, I wasn't certain she heard them.

Prudence studied my face as if contemplating something.

"And you need help with that. *We* need help."

My shoulders shook, but perhaps it seemed I nodded, for Prudence whispered, "Yes," in agreement. She squeezed my hands. "Breathe, Hazel, breathe."

She made a pantomime of drawing air into her lungs, encouraging me to mimic her. Minutes ticked by and eventually, my breathing returned to almost normal and my tears ceased.

I pulled my hands back across the table to my lap. "Thank you."

"Of course. Let's go up to bed. I'm certain you need your rest." The bench scraped across the floor as she stood.

"I need a moment. I'll follow you up shortly."

"Very well. Good night."

"Good night," I called after her as she left.

The silence of the kitchen fluttered around me. The wicked panic had subsided, but I couldn't shake the revolting taste coating my tongue. Something was still not settled. A question played in the reaches of my mind, but I could not grasp it. As if it agreed with me, the chair nearest me shook against the floorboards.

"It's fine," I scolded. "There's no reason to be worried."

A wail splintered through the chimney with a gust of wind.

"Stop it," I said. "Nothing is wrong."

But the sickening reaction in my stomach belied my words.

I needed to finish my duties and leave this suffocating kitchen. I grabbed the fireplace stoker with whitened knuckles. As I bent to separate the final coals of the fire for the night, Elijah's words came back to me.

My heart is just as much yours as it is mine.

It didn't add up. If he cared for me, why did he tell his father he didn't want me? Dropping the stoker back onto the hearth with a clang, I turned on my heel and ran out of the kitchen. All I wanted was escape—from Elijah, from Jacob's looming threat, from everything.

Chapter 29

Back in my room, cold autumn air seeped in through a crack in the window. My curtains were drawn, but streaks of moonlight trickled in. The mattress creaked beneath my weight as I shifted in another failed attempt to get comfortable. It had to have been near midnight and I couldn't sleep.

Every worry and fear I'd tried to suppress paraded through my mind in a sickening cycle.

In the darkness of my unhallowed room, each one rattled through me.

Abby's specter. What did she want from me that no others could give her?

The blood. Did my nightmares mean that death was coming for Abby? For us?

Elijah. If I heard his pleadings, would the frail pieces of my resolve against him and my treacherous longings finally collapse?

Jacob. Was he truly so vicious and would follow through on his threats to destroy my standing and salvation?

I rolled over, gripping the blanket around my head.

If only I knew where Jacob was now and how close he was to Elder Crowther.

What if Abby's flippant words weeks ago in the kitchen held more truth than they seemed to at first? Jacob could be hidden up somewhere with another wife—a new wife. Perhaps the thought of his shifting attention should've brought me relief, but it only drowned me in more misery.

This was the dark underbelly of plural marriage—women abandoned and left destitute by the men eternally yoked to them. Mothers forced to learn how to survive alone and feed their children, never knowing when their husband might return. Women left in far-flung towns with little more than what they could carry, and a promise he'd return. And then the vicious cycle turned over again. Men had the right to find a new wife while their other women languished alone.

The sour taste of bile scorched the back of my throat.

Just as I thought I'd succumb to this eternal wretchedness, a door slammed down the hall. I sat up. A chain of rattling windows moved down the length of the house, each one louder as it approached. My own window shook with such a fury I thought it'd shatter into a million shards.

The sinister movements of the house seemed to press down on me, suffocating me. I couldn't be here a moment longer tonight. My feet caught on the blanket in my hurry to get out of this strange room, and I fell to the floor. I pushed up from the floorboards onto my knees, looking around the darkness. This room held too many secrets.

I grabbed the lamp from the table as I flew to the door. I slipped into the hallway, my heart crashing against the walls of my chest as I tore down the stairs. Every step pounded with growing fear that the house tried to swallow me into its depths.

Once in the parlor, I stumbled across the threshold, catching myself with my palm against the doorway. I leaned over, bent in the middle, until my dizziness settled. The piano loomed before me. I pitched myself toward the instrument as if grabbing a rescue line and collapsed onto the bench. I hadn't found the strength to play in months.

I placed the light onto the top of the piano. Menacing shadows coated the walls, leering over me. This house—this cursed house—with its secrets and its perpetual veil of silence. No home should feel like it has rejected its occupants. This mansion was built to display its owner's opulent wealth—a beacon of fortitude and riches in the vast desert that only the Mormons were desperate enough to try to tame. But like the vines climbing the house and cracking its foundation, this place sought to be reclaimed by its wilderness and bury us along with it.

Come, come, ye Saints . . .

I startled as music rose from the piano. My fingers didn't move at all and neither did the keys, but the sound was unmistakable. An otherworldly hymn played for a piece of hell on earth. Even my music betrayed me.

I steadied in my seat, allowing the mysterious chords to wrap their tentacles around me. I closed my eyes.

No toil nor labor fear . . .

Beneath my breath, I sang the next line to the invisible chorus: "'But with joy wend your way.'" Joy. What joy was there in this place?

Though hard to you this journey may appear . . .

"'Grace shall be as your day,'" I sang.

'Tis better far for us to strive . . .

"'Our useless cares from us to drive.'"

Do this, and joy your hearts will swell . . .

"'All is well!'" I sang along with the unseen musician. "'All is well!'"

I didn't move as the music dripped away. The walls were shrinking in closer. This house was my home and my marriage bed—and it would be my grave.

"Sister Hazel?"

I flinched at Abby's intrusion but didn't move from the piano. My fingers shook and plucked the keys one by one.

"What in heaven's name are you doing?" Abby said as she approached. I noticed she hadn't yet undressed from the day. In her arm, she carried more of Jacob's journals. Her own lamp sparred with the light from mine.

"Up late studying?" I asked, watching the twin flames dance.

"Not that I need to explain myself to you, but yes. I feel I'm getting closer to answers and relief."

I stopped playing and shifted toward her, taking her in as if it were the first time. Abby had always done and said whatever she wanted. It was her right as the first wife, I'd supposed. But perhaps it was simply *her*. Abby in all her magnetic strangeness.

"What relief are you searching for?"

Abby had everything—charm, beauty, power, and the ability to not care about anything. I couldn't imagine there was much she needed succor for.

She dropped the journals onto the nearest table. Beneath her breath, she hummed the same haunting hymn.

"You know, I used to be quite the dancer before I married," Abby said. "Jacob would take me every Saturday night to the social hall and we'd dance until our feet hurt. His hands always wandered to places they shouldn't have on the ride home.

"Then the next morning he'd come to drive me to church, and he'd chide me for the entire ride about my sins. *Abby, you ensnared me with your beauty. Abby, you shouldn't have made me touch you. Abby, your sins are a stain on me.*" She let out a hollow laugh. "The horror I would feel! I'd lay prostrate on my floor begging for God's forgiveness for such wickedness. For daring to have a body. Only to find myself kneeling before Jacob the next Saturday night. *Abby, oh Abby, just trust me.*"

I sat paralyzed on the piano bench, listening to Abby's confessions.

"Again and again, week after week. Oh, I loved him. And his wicked fingers. *It's your fault, Abby*, he always reminded me. My sins. Never his. But it never is for men, is it?"

No, perhaps it wasn't, I was learning.

"He was the first to call me Abby, you know. I liked being his little pet, someone special to a godly man, even if I hated the butchering of my mother's namesake." She paused, probably remembering her lost mother whose name she apparently carried. "But Jacob insisted on keeping the nickname, said it endeared me to him. Now it grates on my ears."

"So you're seeking relief from Jacob?" I said. "Surely, he has enough wives now to divide his attentions."

"Oh, little Hazel." Abby collapsed onto the chair closest to the piano. "If only you knew the stories we carry."

"I suppose you could tell me." Part of me screamed for her to keep them to herself, though, unable to bear any more burdens in my fragile mind.

Abby yawned and stretched out as if settling in for a long night. "Come, Hazel, let's lighten the mood. Play another duet for me."

"I wouldn't want to wake the house . . ." My words faded away. *Duet.*

"You can hear it too, can't you, Abby?"

She pressed her lips together tight.

"The music, Abby. You said 'duet.' I know you hear it too."

I struck my fingers into the keyboard, creating a dissonant chord.

"Tell me the truth, please." I spun to face her. My desperation for my own solace was a heat, smoldering as an engine. "What do you know about the music?"

For one fleeting moment, the entire room disappeared. Only Abby and I remained. We stood as if at opposite ends of a tunnel, studying each other. The light around us focused into a pinprick, illuminating only her distant face. Whispers swaddled us.

Her face hardened. "It's nothing but a reminder of the things I cannot change."

"What is it you wish to change?"

Judging by the grief shattering across her expression, it seemed something too heavy to speak of. Part of me cried for retreat, feeling shame over dragging up things that only brought my sister wife torture. But another part needed and begged for more. For answers.

Abby's words came out jagged. "Do you know who this piano belonged to?"

"Sister Flora said the previous owner."

"If only. There used to be another."

Another? Another what?

Fifth, Elijah had said. I swallowed.

"Another . . . wife?" My voice was only a squeak.

She held unnaturally still except for the quiver of her chin.

"Yes. Her name was Sariah. She was his second wife."

Was. My pulse skipped. "What happened to her?"

"She disappeared many years ago. No one has seen her since."

"Disappeared? How could she simply disappear?" I asked. Panic clung to me with sharpened claws.

Abby stared off into the distance as if she saw something I could not. Pain etched into the lines on her face, grooves too deep to be forgotten.

"As I said, you know nothing of what we carry," she replied.

But now I carried this knowledge too, and it was heavier than I imagined.

Another wife. I *was* the fifth wife. But no one had told me. No whispers, no photographs, no mentions. Elder Crowther had told me Jacob had three wives. But Elijah knew. Did that mean Elder Crowther had known?

Pieces of a puzzle fit together in my mind. The evidence of the other wife had been here all along, unnoticed or unsaid. Fragments of clues scattered throughout the house: my room with its heavy furniture, chosen and painted with care by someone else, and the piano tucked away in the attic to be forgotten.

"Do Flora and Prudence know? Was I the only one?" A slap of

betrayal hit me. They all could've been conspiring, holding this vital piece of information away from me.

Abby blinked hard. "No, they've been kept from it as well. Though I doubt they don't suspect something amiss in this abnormal house."

At least I wasn't alone in the darkness I'd been kept in. The thought brought only a measure of relief too small to cover my swelling pain.

I opened my mouth to say something, anything in response, but my throat was too tight with oncoming tears. Abby shot up from her chair, collecting her books and light. A sudden desperation to hold her here, to hear more, loosened my tongue.

"Do you mean we should be afraid?" I asked.

Once more, her face was as stone. She rounded over me and I gasped from the sudden coldness overtaking her.

"You should always be wary in this house. Hasn't that been made abundantly clear? Don't think that what happened here won't happen again, little Hazel."

The curtains billowed angrily and our lamplight flickered, almost extinguishing.

"This house is a cage for Jacob's prizes. We are nothing more than goods to be collected and discarded at his whim."

Jacob's angry words as he pinned me against the wall seared in my memory. I tried to take in more air and fight off the piercing panic still holding fast.

"This strange house, and its hauntings. This house that won't let us live," Abby continued, lifting her eyes to the ceiling as though addressing the manor itself. "But with my help, these wrongs will be righted and we will have peace."

"Whose wrongs?" I said, though my lungs clenched tighter, fearing the answer. If this place was a prison, then Jacob was its jailer.

Abby only shook her head without confirming my unease. "Heed my words, little mouse."

Before I could respond or plead for more understanding, she walked into the darkness with purpose. Only her cautionary words lingered, carved into me as if with a knife. But as she disappeared, she softly sung the words to the final verse of the hymn:

"'*And should we die before our journey's through, Happy day! All is well!*'"

Chapter 30

As the sun rose, I paced my room after a sleepless night. Every time I grew close to sleep, the conversation with Abby would play again in my head, and all thoughts of exhaustion would flee. It seemed the floorboards were deep with mud, for each length of the room my feet trudged slower, matching the paralyzed state of my mind.

I couldn't go forward—I had no true answers. But I couldn't stay put—I'd been deceived and was possibly in more danger than I realized.

I needed to find an outlet for these raging nerves.

Throwing on the first dress I could find, I didn't bother to study my surely haggard reflection in the mirror. What did any of it matter, how I looked now that the truths of my world slipped away from me?

I marched into the hallway to find Prudence. Perhaps at least comforting her this morning would bring me purpose and distraction.

But Prudence was nowhere to be found.

I searched the house room by room but couldn't find her. When I checked in on the children, I found Edward with his siblings playing a game of jacks, but there was no sign of Prudence. A sickness churned in the pit of my stomach at the memory of her melancholic wandering the night before. My feet quickened to the kitchen as I prayed silently that her condition hadn't overtaken her.

I pushed the door open with a loud clatter. Abby sat silently at the table while Flora chided her about something. I avoided her gaze as I shuffled in, the memory of her warning too fresh and painful in my mind. The morning fire had long since extinguished in the hearth, but the taste of soot hung in the air.

"Does anyone know where Prudence is?" I asked.

Flora scoffed. "In bed, probably. This time of grieving needs to end. Her duties as a wife are being neglected and her idleness is sin." She kneaded the mound of dough in front of her with extra vigor.

"I checked her bed. She's not there or with the children, or anywhere else that I can find."

"Maybe she went to town for one of her rowdy women's meetings," Flora said. "My son told me a horse was missing from the carriage house this morning."

"Without telling us or asking for help? She shouldn't be out in her state."

Abby's chair scraped across the floorboards. "I think we should be worried, Sister Flora. She has been strange of late. We must do what we can to find her."

Worry hung in Abby's expression. Was she also thinking of the missing second wife?

"I won't waste more time on her deficiencies," Flora replied, her tone so bitter I could almost taste it.

"Deficiencies?" I was no longer concerned one bit for her ire. "Your determination to earn your way into heaven isn't much of a virtue when it lacks any bit of charity."

Flora pushed her glasses up the bridge of her nose with clear surprise. But my outburst felt good; too good to give into the immediate guilt that I should beg her pardon for rudeness. Maybe I didn't want to beg anything of her anymore in this house built on falsehoods and terrors.

But before either of us could say more, Abby stepped between us in what appeared to be an unheard of act of peacemaking. This day was full of amazements.

"We don't have time for this," Abby said. "There are real problems here, Sister Flora. I insist you help us."

Flora threw the ball of dough onto the table, sending up a spray of flour. "Of course, you care for Prudence and her problems. But what of my problems, Sister Abby? *I* am the one with the most children, *I* am the one who runs this kitchen, *I* am feeling the absence of our husband most keenly, and you care nothing about what I've been saying to you all morning."

"You truly think you've suffered so greatly in this house? Being able to waltz around with unchecked superiority and zealotry?" Abby's words were ice.

I froze, staring between the two of them.

"As the mother with the most children and the most righteous, I should run this household, not you. I have the faith and fortitude. I've proven that time and time again," Flora said. "So help me, Abby, if you don't take my needs seriously, I will leave, and you will starve."

"No one needs to leave," I said forcefully. "We don't need to do anything drastic."

Abby ignored me.

"Then do it, Sister Flora. Leave! Take your precious children and go. Nothing is stopping you but your own pride." She extended her hand to the door, beckoning her to follow through on her threat.

I swallowed. I'd started this fight and now it was out of hand.

"We just need to find Prudence—"

Flora cut me off. "Fine. I will leave today. I will find a way to write to Jacob and tell him we are at my father's farm, and I will demand my own household as is my right as his most important wife."

Panic shattered in my chest. Everything was unraveling and I couldn't take hold fast enough to keep it together.

"But what of Prudence?" I said.

For a single moment, Flora's face softened. Then as fast as it happened, she hardened back into her usual demeanor.

"She probably went for a ride and will wander back in with her spirit of the Devil at lunch, demanding to be pitied. Your worries are wasted on her childish behavior, while you should be concerned with greater things. Have you listened to nothing I have taught you since you arrived? It is our faithful works that will save us, and this household has drained the last of mine."

"How can you be so unfeeling?" I spit out each word. "How can you speak of us so coldly? Where is your care in all your lectures and demands?"

"Is that truly what you think of me, Hazel? That I'm cold?"

A slow beat passed between us, the air thickening with the current of a gathering lightning storm.

"Did you know that ever since the loss of her child I've come to her room every night to pray with her? That even when she wouldn't permit my entrance, I would kneel down at her door in supplication for her soul?" Flora said.

I shrank back in shame.

"Did you ever think that striving to fortify her *is* loving?" Flora fixed her gaze on me. "We're all together in this refiner's fire of plural marriage. We're all struggling and it's by design. This is all a test to prove our faithfulness. God will separate the wheat from the chaff, Sister, and burn the unworthy with His mighty power."

She spoke with the passion of one of the Brethren delivering a Sunday sermon.

"If I didn't love her, I wouldn't bother with her at all. I have been doing what I can to strengthen Prudence precisely because I care for her. That's why I refuse to coddle her, or you. I care enough to cut you down, to aid you to work hard and to suffer for righteousness' sake. I want the best for our family.

"And you," she continued. "You've done nothing but skirt

around the house with your head in a cloud and no more conviction than a leaf being blown in a new direction with every breeze. One day you will stand for judgment, and if you remain as you are now, you will be found wanting."

Her words were a sword cutting straight into my core, through every layer I buried myself in day after day. They struck exactly where I'd always been weakest, the horrible truth that simmered within my soul. For as long as I could remember, I lived in constant fear of discovery that I wasn't the flawless Mormon woman I should be. But the truth I couldn't escape was that I was seen in all my faults and shame. My entire life I'd clung on to the rules and obedience because deep down I thought they would save me and make me acceptable. Make me worthy of love. But in the end, I still hadn't been enough.

I made no attempt to respond, only wrapped my arms around my waist to hold myself in. I was in danger of spilling out across the floor—every blight and wicked imagination spread out for all to see.

Abby slammed the table, breaking through the quiet.

"Get out, Sister Flora. Just go! Leave us to our sinful ways then in this burning hell. God knows I would leave it if I could. Take your children, take the food, take every damn thing you want. You've already taken my husband, the same as all the others."

Her words brought my disordered thoughts to an abrupt stop. All the others—the missing second wife, Sariah, included. But Flora didn't know; she might never know if she left. Was that a kindness or a deception? I couldn't form the words to ask.

"And there will be more, mark my words, and they will only get younger. You think you're important now, just wait, Sister. Plural marriage isn't the refiner's fire to press us into diamonds. It's the hellish lie that crushes us into powder beneath men's feet."

I reached for Abby's hand as she stalked to the door.

"Wait, please. Sister Abby, we can't let her leave us," I pleaded.

She glared at Flora over my shoulder, who appeared too stunned or angry to speak for once.

"And why not?"

Was it wise to confess Jacob's letter now, with all the secrets Abby still held so close to her chest?

"Please, you alone know what Jacob's capable of," was all I could think of to say to beg her to say what she knew of Jacob's true character and Sariah's disappearance.

Instead, Abby tugged her hand from mine. "Indeed, I do, little Hazel."

The door slammed as she left the room. A plate slipped from its precarious perch on the lopsided shelves and smashed to the floor. I held my breath, feeling as if I were the plate—shattered.

With a shake of her head, Flora undid her apron and tossed it to me. Then, without so much as a backward glance, she disappeared out the kitchen door. I heard her voice calling through the quiet halls for her children to pack their things.

Part of me wished to follow her, to reconcile, but my feet stayed planted in place. I'd failed. Like the tick of the clock in the parlor that pounded directly in my ears, I knew I was running out of time. Jacob would return and then I'd know true hell.

Chapter 31

Sitting on the porch as the midday sun blazed in the autumn sky, my heart sank with the last shards of my hope. Prudence hadn't returned from wherever she'd wandered, and now Flora was gone. She'd ridden away in the cart with her children only minutes ago—or was it hours? I couldn't be certain how long I wallowed here, frozen in my fears.

Each creak of the house reminded me of our isolation. With the nearest neighbors at least a mile away, we were alone on the edges of the valley that cradled God's people. It was only when I came out here on the fringes of the Mormon world that I finally saw the cracks fissuring in my world's façade.

Jacob's face loomed behind my closed eyes. I could almost feel the press of his hand into my throat from the night he fled, the sour taste of his breath on my cheek as he swore to damn me if I disobeyed.

Would he even bother to send word to Elder Crowther to ruin me, or simply drive his own knife through me to save the trouble?

Despite the warmth of the day, cold fused up my spine and through my limbs.

Once, Sariah had sat on his porch, eaten at his table, warmed his bed. And now, she was nothing but a concealed memory. Did her family still search for her, mourn her? Maybe like me, they'd never written, as good as dead once wed. Maybe when Jacob returned and meted out his judgments, my family wouldn't miss me either.

Had Sariah defied Jacob or loved another as I so sinfully did? Did her insolence drive her to run away? Perhaps her husband was her executioner. Or perhaps she'd wandered off as Prudence, lost in her own tortured mind.

The only one who might know what truly happened to her refused to tell me. Maybe Abby was every bit the tormenter Flora thought she was.

The wind whistled through the gables above, drawing me out of my own head.

I could stay here all day, weighed down by my fears. But I needed to keep going. I didn't know what time I had left, and Prudence still needed to be found.

The rotting wood sagged beneath my feet as I stood. I needed to make sure that Edward was fed and cared for, and then to seek help in searching for Prudence. I couldn't yet give up on her safe return.

Hooves pounded the ground and I jolted upright. At the end of the drive, a single rider appeared. Their horse was steady, racing toward the blighted house with surprising speed. My fingers twisted together tightly. Was it Prudence?

The outline of a man blurred against the cloudless sky as the horse drew closer. Oh no, was it Jacob? Each crack of its feet battered my head. The rider reached the porch, pulling back on the reins.

I let out a grateful gasp.

It wasn't Jacob, but Elijah. My knees gave way and I sank back onto the porch steps. I wasn't certain when I'd started crying.

Elijah sprang from his horse and dropped in front of me, his face etched with concern. "Hazel, what's wrong? What's happened?"

I shook my head. I felt ripped open, ready to bleed out on the untamed land. "Flora and her children are gone. I couldn't do what he told me. I couldn't keep us together. Now I'll be punished."

"What do you mean?" His eyes flashed with confusion.

"And Prudence is also gone," I continued. "But I don't know where she's gone to. She could be hurt, lying in a ditch somewhere. She's not herself."

"Hazel," he said softly. "Slow down. Breathe."

His hands grabbed my arms to steady me. They were warm, so welcoming.

"I have to find her. I have to do at least one thing right today!"

"Then let me help you."

"Help me?" Heavens, I wanted to hit him. Or kiss him. "How can you help me when you do nothing but torture me?" I screeched.

Elijah's face fell. "I promise that was never my intention."

I wrestled from his grip though I loathed moving farther away from him. "You dared to come here, invading my home like a knight come back from a quest with dreams of courtly love—as though you hadn't turned your back on all we planned. But you don't understand the agony it puts me through!"

The words were spilling out too fast to recall them. I was almost shouting now as I backed toward the front door to put some space between us.

"You're oblivious to the fight I put up against the things I see in my head—positively wicked, lustful things."

Elijah's chin lifted. His expression smoldered. Suddenly, he jumped up, crossing the porch in only two strides. He stopped just as his body grazed against mine. I pressed myself into the door.

"You truly think I don't fight the same demons? That I don't still love you with all my soul?" he said, his chest heaving as if unable to catch his breath.

I couldn't find mine either.

We both waited, paralyzed by unspoken longings and broken vows.

On instinct, I tilted my head up and he lowered his. Our mouths stopped just far away enough to speak without touching.

"Let me help you find Sister Prudence. Let me make up for my failures," Elijah said.

I needed to dismiss him, once and for all. I knew it. But I couldn't.

"Very well." I searched for the doorknob behind me. "And then you are never to speak of love to me again."

He said nothing, but his lips nearly brushed against mine, sending a shiver through me.

The knob twisted in my hand and I fell backward through the doorway.

Abby sat on the stairs, not unlike the first night I met her. She eyed Elijah, who hung back leaning against the far wall of the entry.

"It'll be better if I help you search for her," she said. "I know the land better."

A part of my heart sunk, but I knew it was for the best. I shouldn't be alone with Elijah ever again. Not even on a search as important as this. I glanced his way and his serious expression seemed to agree.

"Yes, you're right. But we can't leave the house unguarded, not with the children alone while federal marshals are still looking for Jacob," I said, wishing I could tear my face away from Elijah's.

Thankfully, he was the first to look away and shifted toward Abby on the stairs.

"I'll stay here to protect them should anything happen. And if Prudence returns, I can be here to help her, in case she's harmed in any way."

"Thank you." Abby's voice didn't sound the least bit encouraged, though. "We'll start on the drive and head down to the road."

As she rose, a voice called from the top of the stairs.

"What's happening? The house is being loud," Edward said from between his siblings, who all stood at the top step looking down on us with questioning faces.

Esther tugged his arm. "Hush now, it's only the wind coming through an open window."

"A wind that moans like the dead," Nephi murmured.

His sister glared at him over Edward's head. I winced at his choice of words.

"We need to leave for a bit and you'll stay here," Abby said to the children. "Don't leave the house. Brother Elijah will be here."

Nephi studied our boarder with curiosity. "Do we have to do chores?"

Elijah stepped away from the wall, a smile brimming on his lips. Lips I'd been far too close to only moments ago. A sickening ache dug into my very core. I was well and truly damned.

"I think we can hold off on those for a bit, Sister Abby?"

Abby nodded her consent.

He stopped at the bottom of the stairs, looking up at the cautious trio of children. "I've a special game we can play instead. Have you ever ridden a flying carpet?"

Esther and Nephi exchanged a glance, probably silently weighing together whether they would give credence to such silly talk at their old ages of ten and twelve. Edward, however, didn't hesitate.

"Please, I want to ride!" Edward squealed.

"Excellent." Elijah rubbed his hands together. "Let's retrieve the magic carpet from its hiding place."

Esther giggled and bound down the steps after Edward, while Nephi trailed behind, probably pretending he wasn't as interested as he truly was. Warmth moved through me watching the children light up with possibility and mischief for what may have been the first time since I arrived.

Touching my elbow as he passed, Elijah leaned in to speak softly. "I'll keep them distracted so they won't worry about Prudence. Good luck."

He swore to me he'd never speak of love again, but didn't he realize that every small tenderness spoke it in volumes? I slipped out the door after Abby before I would say something I regretted.

Chapter 32

Abby and I wandered the road for hours calling for Prudence and searching among the brush and scattered trees. There was no sign of her but a trail of horseshoe prints leading down the road.

"Those could belong to anyone's horse," I said to Abby for possibly the dozenth time, as if stating it over and over would bring us comfort.

She wrung her hands. "I don't think there's much else we can do here, Hazel. The sun is beginning to set and we need to get back to the house before nightfall. Come."

We turned to walk back up the road to Manwaring Manor, defeat tangled between us. Dirt and gravel crunched beneath our footsteps, each one somehow louder and more final. Prudence was truly missing.

I couldn't help the fear that this was somehow my fault. If only I'd been kinder or better, or more able to help her in her sadness. *Do more, you're failing*, my head always repeated.

"We should have told her," I said quietly when we finally rounded the turn of shriveled cottonwood trees leading to the drive. "We should have told her about Sariah."

Abby stiffened beside me but didn't break her pace. "And what good would that have done?"

"I don't know, perhaps warned her of dangerous things to come."

"Whoever said dangerous things are coming?"

I stopped short, tugging Abby back by her skirt. She rounded on me and I expected her usual haughty glare, but extreme exhaustion clung on her face. It was as if she'd finally given up some terrible fight.

"Sister Abby, please, you must tell me what happened to Sariah. Did Jacob . . ." I struggled to form the words. "Did Jacob harm her?"

I wasn't certain if I wanted her to refute me or confirm my worst fears. I peeked over the house just twisting into view around the bend. Its dark gables peered through the cluster of empty tree branches like half a dozen eyes, waiting and watching.

Abby scrubbed her face and sighed into her hands, calling back my attention.

"Jacob brought us here to be his dutiful wives. To build his kingdom, where we live to serve and pleasure him. Bear his children so he can see his increase, and obey his word so he can play at being a god. Oh, he acts as charming as any gentleman, but it only serves to cover the falsehoods within him. So truly, little Hazel, who hasn't he harmed?"

I gaped at her speech. She tore her skirt from my grip and marched on, disappearing between the trees. But I couldn't bring myself to move.

I squeezed my eyes shut, praying to block out the images barraging me. Jacob's fingers around my throat, his threatening words sharp in my ears. His deep kisses on my mouth and his strokes up my thighs. The soft lilt of his voice as he sang our favorite hymn: *And should we die before our journey's through . . .*

Picking up my dress, I ran as fast as I could after Abby. I'd distrusted him for his threats, his abandonment, but still I hadn't allowed myself to honestly believe what I knew deep in my sinews. Abby hadn't said it either, but she didn't have to.

If it wasn't for Jacob, Sariah would never have disappeared.

Sariah might have run—or she might be dead.

I fought to keep the worry down where I didn't have to acknowledge it: the suspicion that we all might be next.

Abby set to work at making dinner with the help of her daughter. I scrubbed up Edward and left him in the care of Nephi, then walked slowly across the house to join them in the kitchen. The house felt empty without Flora and Prudence, too big around me.

As I entered the dining room, the air shifted. I wrapped my arms across my chest as sudden cold bit through the air. A rusted taste descended on my tongue when I opened my mouth in surprise.

Light gathered near the study door. I braced myself. The specter hovered once more before me. I choked back a sob.

"What do you want?" I asked Abby's mirage.

She bade me follow her.

A thought unwound in my mind. If Abby wouldn't share the past's secrets, perhaps her double would.

"Do you know what happened to Sariah, Jacob's other wife?"

She dimmed. Her face broke into almost a snarl, but I didn't startle back. Carefully, I approached the study door.

"Please, I need to know."

The apparition stayed silent as the grave, her vexed expression hard to best.

I reached out to grab her as I had Abby earlier, but she was nothing but a wisp. "Tell me something, anything, I beg of you!"

Her light brightened some and she slid into the closed door of the study. Sucking in a deep inhale, I followed after her.

The study was as I'd left it that night before. Glancing up at the line of books, I saw that Flora had indeed replaced the black book onto the shelf. Part of me wanted to rifle through it once more, but somehow I knew that there was nothing more to find.

It was only one more fractured clue hiding in plain sight throughout the house to torment me.

She looked toward Jacob's desk, then as I drew closer, a gentle glow outlined the bottom drawer. My head hummed. I'd never dared to dig through its contents before. Twisting back over my shoulder at the door to be certain I was alone, I ripped the drawer open, startling the objects inside.

I moved without thinking, for too much worry would only stop me. Most of the items tucked inside were papers. Deeds, pay stubs for workers, another map of the canyon. I shifted these onto the desk without glancing at them closer. Beneath them lay a large stack of envelopes.

The specter's eyes widened when I looked to her. I retrieved the envelope on top, sliding my fingers along its edges. I gasped. All thoughts of Sariah and her secrets flew from my mind.

My name. The letter was addressed to me. I ran my thumb across the tight loops of *Hazel Russon*, penned in Elijah's hand.

I stumbled back. The return address was my father's, but the writing was so distinctly Elijah's—the loop of the letter *a*, the sideways cross on the *z*. Hadn't he spoken of writing to me all those months ago after the Tabernacle? But why were they hidden away?

Slowly, I turned one of the envelopes over. The seal was broken. Reality shifted in my mind as I pieced it together.

I grabbed the next letter from the pile. *Hazel Manwaring.* And then the third. *Hazel Manwaring.* Each one bore my father's return address but a different script—Mother, Father, Ammon, even Aunt Emma. There was an entire pile of letters here in this drawer, all addressed to me!

I flipped another over, grinding my teeth. The seal was also broken.

I slammed the drawer shut with my knee, not wanting to see more, and screamed into my fists, the letters clenched tight within them, absorbing my sorrows. I looked up to plead with the ghost, but she only dimmed, her face long and mournful.

"I didn't know . . . all this time . . ." I bit my cheek to keep from screaming once more. "Why would Jacob do this?"

The light snuffed out, leaving the study in only the faint glow of the finishing sunset.

"Hazel, were you shouting?"

I swung around to see Elijah leaning in the doorway, out of breath as if he'd run here. I unclenched my hand and held out the envelope bearing his writing.

"My letter?" Confusion hitched in his voice. "I thought you said you never received it."

He took a step inside and grasped the shaking letter from my hand.

"I didn't," I said. "The seal is broken, but I've never read it, nor even knew of its existence."

Elijah's voice shook. "He took it. He took it from you!"

"Would you deliver a letter from your wife's former sweetheart to her?" I hated that I defended Jacob, even now. But the burn of fear, of uncertainty, was instinct.

"How would he have even known it was from me? I took care to address it from your father's house. Unless . . . Hazel, no. He's been hiding all your letters?"

Behind us, the tall windows of the study rattled. Books tumbled from the highest shelves in a jumbled cascade of crashes. Elijah jumped, but I didn't move.

"They're all here. At least, I assume so." I felt like a statue, wrenched to the floor. Perhaps I'd stay here forever until I dissolved into bits of dust and bone. "He must have had a reason for it."

"A reason?" Elijah nearly shouted. He grabbed my shoulders. "Hazel, what has happened to you?"

"Aunt Hazel!" Nephi called from the dining room. "It's time for dinner!"

Without thinking, I pushed Elijah away and toward the door. "Get out. Go to dinner."

"You need to take and read your letters," he protested.

I grabbed the front of his shirt, fisting the starch beige fabric. "My entire world is already coming undone, Elijah. Do you think I can stand to let the last threads of it rip away from me?"

I shoved him away, tears dripping down my cheeks. I couldn't . . . I simply couldn't. Shoving the letters into my pocket, I fled from the study. I doubted I would possess the strength to read them, though. Each broken seal was a damning testimony to my doomed fate. It didn't matter what more I learned or horrors I uncovered—I was Jacob's for time and all eternity.

Chapter 33

After tucking Edward into bed, I undressed for the night but didn't crawl into bed as my limbs begged to. The moon rose full and pale over the valley from my window, illuminating the twisted cottonwood trees at the end of the drive bowing in the desert wind. My heart scraped empty.

Abby told me again and again that there was nothing to be done now, not tonight. Prudence must've ridden into town and stayed too long, requiring her to find lodging for the night. We'd searched everywhere and now we needed to wait for daybreak. She'd turned in early so she could resume the search at first light.

But I couldn't sit still. If I didn't move, I'd think. And if I thought, I'd admit that my husband had read and hidden my letters. That he had something to do with Sariah's disappearance. And that I had no inkling of what fresh terrors awaited me day after day in Manwaring Manor.

I simply had to keep searching and keep my body occupied so I wouldn't dwell on my entrapment. I had to find Prudence.

Not taking the time to redress, I shoved my feet into my waiting boots and threw open my door without bothering to retie them.

"Hazel?"

I froze at the top of the stairs at the sound of his voice behind me.

"Go to bed, Elijah," I pleaded.

"Where are you going?" he asked.

"I need to keep searching."

I didn't look behind me as I whisked down the stairs and across the house, but I knew he followed close behind. In the kitchen, I peered through the darkness, but the room was empty. My final hope that Prudence had returned for a late supper died. I crossed the room and grabbed a shawl from a peg. Wrapping it around me, I turned the handle of the back door. A swift burst of cold air hit my face. Gooseflesh pimpled my arms, but I didn't stop.

"Hazel, it's too dark. You won't do Prudence any good if you're harmed too."

Elijah called after me as I shimmied out the kitchen door, trying to slip out before he could catch me. He was quicker than I anticipated and managed to step out after me as I relinquished my hold on the door.

"Fine then." Thoughts buzzed like a swarm of bees in my mind. "Come with me."

The door slammed shut behind him and he froze. A soft light flew across the kitchen with unearthly speed.

"What was that?" Elijah's eyes shifted across the kitchen window, no doubt searching for an answer.

"Every old house has its ghosts," I replied in a deadened tone. "Now keep up. We need to cover as much ground as we can."

The air bit cold against my exposed skin, but I didn't stop my brisk pace across the yard. I was barely clothed, in only my nightgown, and I drew the shawl tighter around me. I couldn't stop even for modesty. I was running out of time.

"I can't stop thinking that something must have befallen her," I said as Elijah followed, his eyes still wide. "That we missed something."

I stopped short, causing Elijah to bump into me. Too many

thoughts wove through my addled mind to dwell on the feel of his closeness once more.

Ahead, a thick patch of trees marked the end of my husband's property. Beyond that, trees blanketed the canyon as it sloped upward into the mighty Wasatch Mountains. Up and up the canyon the forest would grow and twist, giving way to mines and mills surrounding the winding river that cut through it all.

If I dared to take this path into the darkness, I sensed I'd cross a final boundary and uncover places I'd held myself back from seeing. More secrets to carry and sift through. Every revelation rained like soiled manna, polluting the ground instead of nourishing. What if the worst fears I'd tried to ignore were true—what if Sariah was dead by Jacob's hand? And what if we were all his next victims?

"Perhaps I've been wrong all along," I murmured. "The dreams . . . the blood . . ."

Elijah grabbed my elbow. "Slow down, Hazel. What are you talking about?"

Perhaps there was nothing I could say that would make sense. No way to avoid the role of the fool. But before me stood my oldest, dearest friend—the song of my heart even after these years of separation. I couldn't bear his scorn or reprimand. But nor could I continue to face this alone. I needed him now more than ever.

I tugged my elbow from his grip. "I will explain as we search. Keep up."

Lit by the brightness of the full moon, the way appeared clear enough. In hushed tones, as we entered the foreboding path I first noticed all those months ago and walked into the wilderness, I explained the nightmares to Elijah.

"The house is, well, sometimes I believe it's alive. The way it moans and shakes, the lights, even an apparition that mimics Abby." I swallowed hard, picking up my pace so I wouldn't have to see his reaction. "I've been having these terrible nightmares since I arrived. So much blood. And in them, Abby lies dead in the study from some unnatural cause. I think the house wants me to know something. I thought it was a warning for Abby, but now, I think it may be something worse.

"I learned Jacob had another wife. Sariah was her name, the second wife, and she just disappeared. Only Abby and Jacob know what happened to her, but Abby won't say more, if she can at all. But I'm certain Jacob had something to do with it. Part of me even worries that she might be dead. That maybe death is coming for us too. And now I have to know what happened here. That's what it's trying to tell me, but I can't put it together yet."

Elijah stopped. He looked at me solemnly, and my heart ceased its frantic pounding. The moon cast shadows from the treetops, the shifting leaves like faces staring down at us. An owl hooted in the darkness and a creature rustled in the nearby bushes.

"Say something, Elijah," I begged. "Do you think I've been deceived by the Devil?"

"Do you believe you have?" Elijah said.

He trusted me. I could feel it as much as I could feel the bitter air nip at my ears. If he was also chilled by the night air, he made no display to show it. Instead, his focus was steady and single-minded on me. Only Elijah ever looked at me like this—as if I was all that mattered in the world.

"No one's ever asked me that," I confessed. "Or if they did, it was only to use it to condemn me for being faithless." I allowed my fortitude to solidify. "No, I haven't. I know what I've seen."

Elijah nodded. "Then tell me how I can help you."

And that was it. Someone—a man no less—believed me. I'd been shown a warning, and now I would wield it to save us from destruction.

"If we can just find Prudence and know she's safe. I need to grasp at least one thing into my control. . . ." I trailed off.

Elijah nodded, knowing not to say more on it. "Let's keep going before it grows too late."

I would find her. I would find her. My own hope withered, but I didn't let it snuff out completely.

We walked on. Elijah drew closer until our elbows brushed against each other. Neither of us moved away. Somewhere in the distance, an animal howled, piercing the stillness of the clear night. I pushed down the throbbing fear inside me.

A twig snapped beneath Elijah's boot and I jumped.

"Hazel, are you certain you want to do this?"

"Yes," I said. "I have to. I can't abandon Prudence."

"I know, but I could look without you. You'd be safer at the house."

"No, I'm fine."

He gently touched my arm and I shivered. "Do you truly think Prudence would even have come out this far?"

"No, probably not." I hated confessing it aloud. "But I can't go back, Elijah. I can't stand another mystery in that horrible house!"

"Then don't go back."

His words shook me down to my toes. As if it were that easy. As if I could simply pull myself out of the ground I'd been planted in, like Flora's carrots from the soil.

"I'm sure for you it'd be that simple," I shot back angrily. "After all, you cast me off on your mission on whatever whim you had. Now you've come back claiming to love me still. You men can do whatever fits your fancy! Meanwhile, we women remained trapped to your choices."

Elijah's grip on my arm tightened. "I never discarded you. *Never*. My father lied to you."

"Why would he do that? He speaks for God."

"He speaks for himself and his own ambitions."

The trees rustled around us, whipping with growing wind that stole my breath.

"My father wants me to be just like him, a leader of the church. But I can't do that without living in polygamy. I told him vehemently that I wanted you and you alone as my wife. That's why he sent me away in the first place, to try to distract me from you. He learned of our continued correspondence, though. When he couldn't persuade me to give you up with his usual threats of losing my soul, he decided to solve the issue himself. That's why he called you into his office that day, Hazel. To tell you a falsehood and persuade you to quickly marry another before I came home."

In the silence following his words, the remains of my unsteady foundation crumbled to ruin. Elder Crowther—an apostle I'd been taught my entire life to follow without question—had lied to me. He used his position and my tender faith to manipulate me into doing as he wanted—not God's will, but the will of him and the church that demanded more patriarchal men to uphold its power.

I wanted to scream into the wind. I clenched my fists, pulling away from Elijah. He let me go without struggle.

"But the wife. The second wife. How did you know about Sariah? That I was the fifth wife?"

He exhaled, pushing back displaced strands of his dark hair.

"I pressed for all the details about Jacob Manwaring again and again. I was devastated when I realized what had happened in my absence, and I simply couldn't let it be. The whole situation was nonsensical to me, and I thought that if I could somehow find the crack that made it so, I might change this reality. I became obsessed. My father was the one who finally told me the truth when he realized I wouldn't let up on my search. He told me that Jacob's second wife had run away. When I pressed him, he admitted no one knew what had happened to her. That was right before I came here to board."

The final blow of betrayal hit like a slap.

Every part of my body hurt with ache, but no doubt remained in me. The apostle had lied to me, twice over. "How could I have been taken for such a fool? He's supposed to speak for God."

"He called it *lying for the Lord*." Elijah spat the words out like they were poison.

I dug my fingernails into my palms.

What did it matter to a man if he wrought horrors in order to create the vision he saw? He'd be called righteous for it. The same as Brigham and Joseph. These men could do as they saw fit without consequence, without worrying about those they crushed in their path.

"Do you think he suspects Jacob had something to do with Sariah's disappearance?" I asked.

"He said Jacob thought she had fled Utah to sin, but . . ." His voice trailed off. "But I know he didn't truly believe that. Someone else would've known if she'd run off. She couldn't have done it alone and on a whim. I think my father suspected Jacob's hand, though he was never questioned. He wants to lift up Jacob as a leader."

Though I fully expected the answer, a scorching horror burned up my throat. An apostle of the Lord led me to a marriage with a man he knew full well might be responsible for the disappearance of his wife. Elder Crowther promised me it was the Lord's will for me to accept Jacob and he knew that commandment lead me straight into the arms of a dangerous man. He never cared about me—only that I obeyed him.

"Hazel, are you all right?"

I stumbled and pressed against a tree for support. My mind flashed back rapidly through every moment with Jacob. So much of what I thought was kindness and love was a ploy for dominance. He'd lied, taken affection from me without my consent, abandoned his family at the slightest hint of difficulty, and then threatened me to keep me in line.

"What do I do?" I whispered to myself.

"What do you mean?"

Elijah drew closer, his face close to mine. A lifetime ago we stood beneath a tree just like this. The world then was painted in flashes of color and hope, now it was dark and lonesome.

"I'm trapped," I said. "I'm his for forever, even after death. I could try to obtain a divorce, but there's no possibility he'd simply let me leave him."

"Even Brother Brigham had wives divorce him."

"Yes, but what if it's still wrong?" I bit my thumb. "All my life

I've tried so hard to be the perfect woman that's obedient and faithful. Who never complains or stirs up contention, that doesn't harbor wicked thoughts or give in to temptations. That listens to her leaders without complaint and doesn't speak her mind aloud."

A sob escaped my lips, but it didn't stop the rush of words pouring out of me. "I've tried and tried to squeeze myself into their boxes—into their cages. But I never seem to fit or be content. I just keep shoving down the wish for something more so I'll be what I'm told I need to be."

Though my natural inclination was to draw back or beg forgiveness for my rash speaking, I couldn't bring myself to do it. I truly didn't want to. Invisible roots of hope sprouted at my feet, entwining up my ankles. The wind's whistle through the branches quieted for a moment. If I wanted, I could reach out and trace the lines of Elijah's face with the tips of my fingers. Or throw myself into his embrace and kiss away every piece of heartache carved into him.

"Elijah." I rested my forehead against his. My voice trembled. "What if I did leave? With you?"

His breathing hitched. "You mean, you want to marry me? Even after all that's been done in my name?"

"Yes. Damn Jacob. Damn your father." My words grew into a sharp cry. "Damn Brigham Young and every man who made this place a living hell."

Elijah's fingers caressed my jawline. "We deserve a choice."

The roots at my feet flared with his words, shooting up to wrap up my legs like ivy climbing a tower. All the brick I'd built up around me crumbled.

"Yes," I said. "Is there ever truly a choice to be had when the threat of eternal damnation is the only other possibility? When you've been taught over and over until it is stained in your mind that there is no other conceivable path?"

The words sunk their teeth into me, piercing at places I'd always buried deep down.

"We've never been truly free, have we?" I continued. "Every step of our lives had been outlined and prescribed by others: a bible, a parent, a deity." My palms grew clammy with sweat despite the night cold. "They told me to obey so I could be worthy. But I've never felt the acceptance. Except from you. And you've never demanded anything of me."

A heat started within me unlike anything I'd ever experienced. Potent, brilliant, and encompassing, as if flames had lit inside my chest and burned through my limbs without consuming my flesh. It wasn't a fear or a pain—it was a strength. It was truth in its rawest form, undeniable and earth-shaking. For the first time in what felt a lifetime, peace blossomed within me. Clarity cleared out the clouds. I *was* acceptable, just as me—and I was capable. I could reclaim myself, my own authority. I could save myself, and my sisters.

Unable to stand the magnitude of the power coursing through me, I fell to my knees.

The movement broke my euphoria. At once, I was back in the dark forest lit only by the pale of the moon. The trees quivered around me, their leaves rustling and stirring noises from the creatures living within. The strength within me passed, leaving me devoid of energy. I inhaled short, stagnant breaths.

Elijah dropped to the ground. With careful hands, he reached out and cradled my face, his thumbs stroking my cheek. The heat I felt now was a roar of desire lodging deep in my center. I didn't dare move away.

"Hazel?" Elijah's voice was a breathless whisper.

I leaned my cheek into his palm and he made a soft noise in the back of his throat. Longing sparked quicker than it could be dampened, spreading out of control.

"I'm fine, more than fine. Especially with you here." I let the truth pour from me. "Elijah, you're who I love, who I want."

With a tug of his hands, Elijah drew me closer until our noses brushed together. His eyes drew down to my lips, his breathing shallow and hot on my face. My fingers moved of their own accord, searching for purchase in the sea of his dark curls and caressing the back of his neck. Sliding his fingers down my sides, he carved a fiery trail until his hands gripped my waist.

"Hazel, my love."

The night stilled once more and cocooned around us, protecting us.

At last, he brought his lips to mine. My body awoke. His mouth moved delicately, gently, like he sought to worship me with exact precision. I parted my lips to allow more of his devotion. The kiss grew harder. Every flame of passion we'd held back between us now ignited into a fire. We were a crush of hungry lips, wandering hands, and gasping moans.

When he broke away reluctantly, he pressed his forehead against mine. "What will we do now?"

"Hmm," I whispered, my fingers still twining through his hair, not completely understanding his words or wanting to leave this moment. This kiss.

"Does the brave Hazel have a plan?" he asked with a slight laugh.

The cocoon around us burst open and the night broke through in a cacophony of sounds—branches rustling, animals howling, owls calling. Once again, we were in the threatening wilderness shivering against the cold.

"I don't want to say it, but I don't think we'll find Prudence tonight. We will find her, I won't give up, but right now we should return to the house and we can start our search again in the morning, leaving no stone unturned." I pulled back but kept my hands interlaced with his. The autumn chill had all but disappeared to me. "For tonight, we can begin planning our escape. It won't be easy."

"I'm with you every step."

"He won't grant the divorce, I know it. He's—" The words of his letter ran back through my mind. "He's threatened me before."

A growl escaped Elijah's pressed lips. "I won't let him harm you."

He wrapped my hands in his and tugged them against his chest. My fingers sparked at the heat of his body. They fit so perfectly in his. He held within his palms my every dream, hope, and prayer, as well as every pain, sorrow, and torment.

I stole another kiss from his lips.

"I'm scared, Elijah. But surely we deserve to be happy. I refuse to believe that we've been sacrificing our whole lives just to endure utter misery until the end."

He lifted my hands up to his mouth, kissing between each knuckle. "*You* deserve every happiness, my dear. What if we simply left before he returned?"

"Without the divorce? Without getting married?"

"I know, Hazel, I know." His tone trembled. We were daring to be bold enough to step into unchartered territory. "But he's a dangerous man."

The wind whipped through my unpinned hair, both threatening and soothing at the same time. "You're right. We'll leave and then I'll write back for the divorce."

"Where will we go?"

I glanced up between the trees to the infinite stretch of sky and stars above. "Anywhere, Elijah. Anywhere but here. California, perhaps?"

Even as I kept my eyes heavenward, I could hear the smile in his voice.

"I've always wanted to see the Pacific. Perhaps I could become a fisherman."

I snorted. "You'd smell terribly all the time."

"And here I thought fish were the most romantic of foods."

"That's chocolate." I rolled my eyes to make him laugh.

His fingers gripped my hip, bringing us together again. "Then perhaps I'll become a chocolatier."

"Sounds delicious." I met his lips halfway as we came back together.

Reluctantly, I broke us apart. "But for now, we need to return."

"Yes, we'll find your sister wife."

Hope brimmed like a fire against my skin. "What if I can convince them to come with us? We could all leave this dreadful place behind."

"If that is what my bride wishes, then of course." Elijah scooped me up by the knees and spun me around, my feet brushing against stray brush. "Oh, Hazel. I've waited so long to call you that."

"As have I." I found his lips once more, my center aching with his touch.

As soon as my feet touched the ground again, though, the anxiety returned. But at least there was something now to cling on to—the hope of future joy in a place far away from here, married only to Elijah, Jacob and his secretive house left behind.

With one final kiss, we grasped hands. I turned back to the path that'd led us from the house. It was somehow brighter than before despite its twisted trees and low moonlight. We made our way back to the house, saying little, as few words could truly contain our shared joy. Branches and brush lashed at our legs, and the wind roared louder like a storm approached. But it didn't deter us.

As we approached Manwaring Manor, our pace slowed. Its towering gables glared down at me. The windows were dark and unwelcoming. Then all at once, a bright light flashed in the attic window. I held out my hand to stop Elijah, my pulse rising. The light flashed again and again.

A warning.

"Something's not right," I said.

"How do you know?" he asked.

I pointed to the top window.

"What should we do?"

"We shouldn't be seen returning together." I tugged him behind a tree. "You go around the house and enter from the front in a few minutes. I'll go through the kitchen like I was out collecting laundry."

Elijah didn't break his stare with the upper window.

"That's probably wise. I'll see you soon." He pressed a kiss to my forehead, then stalked away, staying as hidden as possible in the trees.

I approached the house cautiously, retrieving a forgotten laundry basket as I crossed the yard. I swallowed past the burning lump in my throat. A blanket of hush dropped over me as I came to the kitchen door.

Then I clamored to a stop.

Prudence stood in the kitchen doorway, the hopeful smile I hadn't seen in so long lighting her face.

"Sister Hazel! I've been looking everywhere for you."

CHAPTER 34

I rushed forward, throwing my arm around her.

"And I was looking for you. I thought something terrible had happened."

"I'm sorry."

"Where did you go?"

She stepped back, her smile quaking. "To find Jacob."

The basket dropped from my other hand. "What?"

"Last night when I realized you've been carrying so much for us, I knew I needed to do something to help. I've been drowning. We all have been. So, I went to find him."

Her words suddenly sounded as if miles away.

"Our burdens will be eased with our husband back, even if only for a short time. I rode to a man I knew Jacob was close with, Elder Crowther, and he took me to the safe house Jacob had been at."

I swallowed past the panic choking me. "Did you find him?"

The kitchen door swung open. Jacob stood in the doorway, a vast smirk across his face. He appeared the same as ever, if only a bit scruffier and less clean-shaven. His eyes were bright and focused, peering directly at me as if he could read every sin on my skin.

"Yes, I'd say she found me," he said with a chuckle.

The floorboards rumbled beneath our feet. The house spoke its warning in the only way it could. All my plans for us with Elijah dashed to pieces. How could we ever hope to escape now?

Prudence's face still hung heavy, but she mustered another smile. "And we're so grateful you're here, Jacob. There are a few things that need to be set in order."

"So I can see." His gaze never left me, cutting me up heel to head. His tone wasn't angry or menacing. If I closed my eyes, it would be as though I had been transported back in time to one of our walks during our brief courtship.

Across the house, the front door slammed shut, probably caught in a whip of the growing wind. My heart skittered. *Elijah.*

"Who was that?" Jacob asked, finally breaking his examination of me to glance over his shoulder.

"Abby," I said.

Jacob shook his head. "She's asleep, as good as the dead when I tried to wake her."

His choice of words cut into me.

"No," he said, "it must be the boarder that I've heard so much about."

"Yes," said Prudence, unsure. "Sister Hazel's idea to bring in extra funds."

I hardened my face to remain as neutral as possible.

"Indeed. How clever." Jacob's penetrating stare returned.

I fumbled to retrieve the dropped basket for something to keep my hands busy. "I should finish and go to bed."

"Oh no, I would like to meet this boarder," Jacob said.

Prudence nodded. "I could fetch him, if you like."

"Oh no, Prudence, it's late." I tried to hide the pleading in my voice.

Jacob waved her on. "Bring him to the parlor for a proper introduction."

Prudence slipped out of the room before I could raise another protest.

Behind me, the line of clean plates rattled on the shelf.

Jacob stepped closer until he drew up against me, his sour breath hot against my cheeks. "I'm so glad to be home, my dearest."

My throat was clenched too tight to say anything in return. Silent accusations danced in his eyes. Across the room, the woodpile beside the hearth toppled to the ground.

"Later we will need to discuss where Flora is. I was so terribly disappointed to come home and find her and the children gone." Jacob cupped my cheek. "I wonder if my letter didn't reach you."

"It did."

His fingers ran down the column of my throat.

"I see. Well, I suppose things happen. It's hard to keep everything under control."

He pressed a hard kiss against the base of my neck, his tongue against my skin, tasting my wild pulse.

"Don't worry," he said, his mouth hovering at my throat. "All will be forgiven. Eventually. I'm simply so grateful to be home."

Jacob released me and I inhaled sharply.

"Come, introduce me to the boarder."

His hand, firm on the small of my back, directed me through the kitchen door. As we passed the dining table, the hanging light above shook as if with a mighty wind. Two chairs toppled over. But Jacob said nothing.

I'd never prayed more fervently in my life. *Please, don't let Jacob find out it's Elijah.*

Prudence and Elijah stood in the parlor conversing softly when we entered.

"Ah, so this is the famous boarder," Jacob said, stretching out his hand to clasp Elijah's. My pulse thundered in my ears.

"A pleasure to meet you at last, Brother Manwaring," Elijah replied, politely. A mask of civility pressed tight to his face, but I noticed the twitch of his fingers at his side and the blink of anger in his eyes.

Prudence yawned. She appeared as if she might fall asleep standing.

"Jacob," I said, "she's exhausted."

Jacob dismissed her with the wave of his hand.

"Good night, dear. We'll speak more in the morning."

I brushed past Jacob to follow Prudence up the stairs.

"I should go too."

"No, dearest. Please fetch us glasses."

I froze, uncertain what to do. If I stayed and played along, would it assuage any suspicions? Leaving them might be worse than bearing it with Elijah.

I fixed a small smile to my face.

"Of course, I would be happy to. I'm glad to see we can all get along so well."

I shared a quick look with Elijah as I passed him, praying he'd understand what I meant. There was no reason to start a fight in the parlor now. We'd never manage to escape this horrible place if Jacob was on alert.

I retrieved the first two glasses I could find from the kitchen and returned just as Jacob reentered the room with a dark green bottle. He took the glasses from my hand but didn't dismiss me. I hovered, waiting on the balls of my feet.

"I know the Brethren can sometimes be concerned about this, but I've seen them drink it plenty of times," Jacob explained as he poured the dark red liquid.

I watched Elijah out of the corner of my eye to see what he would do. Wine wasn't strictly forbidden but was generally considered a sinful vice.

Jacob seemed to be thinking the same thing and held a glass out to him like a challenge. Slowly, Elijah took the offered drink, but didn't taste it.

"Forgive me, I didn't catch your name," Jacob said.

My heartbeat intensified. This moment could sink us.

"John. John Smith," Elijah said.

"Another damn Smith. You seem to grow on trees in Utah."

I breathed out in relief, drawing Jacob's focus back onto me.

"Are you married, Brother Smith?" he asked.

"No," Elijah said, glancing over at me. "Not yet."

Heat from his small look simmered through my body in a strange mix of anticipation and horror. Thankfully, Jacob didn't seem to notice the flush surely growing in my cheeks.

"Well, I will tell you, it's the greatest blessing of the Lord. Take Hazel here." He signaled for me to come closer. "Couldn't even wait for me to get home, she's already in her bedclothes."

Elijah let out a forced laugh to mingle with Jacob's.

"Have a seat, Brother Smith."

Jacob gestured to the checkered sofa across from him as he sank into a high-backed, threadbare chair.

"Join us, wife."

I kept my head low as I crossed the room to sit beside him when an arm scooped me up by the waist. I bit my tongue to keep from screaming as Jacob settled me into his lap.

"I've been away too long, you see," he said to Elijah, who held his glass so tight his knuckles had turned white.

I thrashed, trying to extract myself. "Jacob, perhaps—"

"Sit." He wrapped his free arm tighter around my waist, locking me against his chest, and took another drink. "You know, Brother Smith, you do you look awfully familiar."

Could Jacob hear my pulse racing?

"Which Smith are you related to?"

"None of the great ones." Elijah's tone was tight. "Simply a common name."

"I see."

A loaded silence crackled among the three of us. Elijah sat on the edge of the couch, his drink untouched, but Jacob quickly finished his off.

"Hazel," he said, dropping his glass without care onto the table beside him. "It's so good to see you again after so long."

And then his mouth was on mine, crushing my lips against my teeth as I gasped. His tongue darted out to taste mine.

I managed to pull away.

"Jacob, dear, we have company."

He only smiled, so disarmingly charming.

"Just giving the boy a look at what his future holds. You should get married right away, Brother Smith. I've got a good connection to an apostle. You might know him—Elder Crowther?"

The air tugged tight, a string between Elijah and me. I tried not to catch his eye but couldn't resist a quick look in his direction. He held his shoulders back, his tone was casual, but not a bit of his body stayed at ease.

"I've heard of him, like all the Saints."

"I can put in a good word for you. Might be able to scrape up two at once for you."

I forced back a taste of bile, even as something plucked at me.

"I'm uncertain plural marriage is prudent at this time," said Elijah. "The new laws and all."

Jacob raised an eyebrow.

"The government doesn't scare an apostle of the Lord. Shouldn't scare you either, I'd say. What the Lord commands, He commands. Isn't that right, Hazel?"

His hand glided up my ribs, pausing briefly at my breast before stroking at my neck. Surely, he felt my erratic pulse beneath his fingers.

"Jacob, please," I begged, as softly as I could.

He kissed me again in response, this time nipping at my bottom lip.

Elijah was at his edge. His eyes shined with what I knew were pent-up tears of anger and frustration. My heart tore.

"Perhaps," Elijah said through gritted teeth, "you should listen to the requests of your wife."

Shifting back, Jacob released his hand on my throat but gripped the flesh on my leg.

"Do you know the sign of a great wife? A true helpmeet as the Lord made her to be? Simple obedience. Hazel wants what I want."

He leaned toward Elijah, taking me with him.

"I could tell her to get on her knees right now and she would."

I was going to vomit.

"Unhand her." Elijah's words cut through the room as a knife.

Jacob studied him, his gaze tracing back and forth between the two of us.

Suddenly, I fell to the floor. He had dropped me as he rose, pushing me off like a troublesome cat.

"I didn't mean to make you *uncomfortable.*"

A loud groan tunneled through the chimney. The line of books atop the mantel toppled; some fell to the hearth below with repeated bangs, stealing Jacob's attention.

Elijah began to rise and I shook my head as subtly as possible. He sat back in his seat, his ears brimming red.

"Brother Smith." Jacob swung back toward him. "Where is it you work again?"

"The Henderson farm, just down the road."

"Ah yes. Brother Henderson is a stalwart man of God."

Jacob kicked a fallen book with his toe, staring at me. Lancing holes into me. I stayed as steady and unreadable as I could. I wasn't ready to pick myself off the floor, uncertain what move I might make that would not set him off.

"Say," Jacob said. "I know Brother Henderson has troubles with coyotes and his chickens. Let me show you something."

Before either of us could reply, he slipped into the dining room, probably headed to his study, but what he wanted to fetch I couldn't guess. Weight pressed against my chest, heavy as a dozen devils. I blinked to hold back tears.

"Hazel," Elijah whispered as he leaned down to pull me up. "Are you all right?"

"Are you? I thought you would break that glass in your fist."

"Or his damn nose."

I hushed him. "We can't—he can't know who you are, Elijah. We'll never escape."

"Believe me, that was the only thought keeping me from ripping his hands off you." He kissed my knuckles.

Part of me warmed with his declaration, even as the panic held me.

"Here it is!" Jacob called from the dining room.

We both jumped back into our seats. Was he warning us of his presence, or simply overly excited tonight?

He held up a slender brown rifle. I gripped the arms of the chair.

"This is the newest Browning rifle I picked up in Ogden. Might be of interest to your employer. You need to catch the rascals before they get to the hens," he added.

I didn't dare breathe. Elijah seemed to agree. I stared at the firearm, waiting for Jacob to take aim. My head rushed with images of blood flowing across the floorboards and Elijah's battered body . . . I was losing air. Losing the fight when I needed to be strongest. My mind went to Sariah, to my nightmares, and the house dripping with fresh blood. Had this scene played out here before?

Elijah found his voice.

"New model, you say? I remember when I left on my mission a few years ago, it was just rumors of something coming from his shop. I'll mention this to my employer. I'm sure he'll be grateful."

We balanced on an invisible tightrope pulled taut across the parlor. One false move would send us plummeting to our demise.

"I would like to go to bed, please, Jacob," I said, hardly above a whisper.

Jacob smiled his most benevolent smile. "Of course, I've kept you up late, my dearest. I know how eager you are for us to retire together."

Elijah's glass tumbled to the floor. Several other objects rattled on their shelves.

"Forgive me, I must be tired as well." Elijah stood. "I'll go and fetch a rag from the kitchen."

"Thank you, Brother Smith. You know, it's such a pleasant surprise to know there's been a priesthood man watching over the house in my absence."

His hands brushed the small of my back. They were cold.

"Yes, a true blessing," I said.

Jacob placed a tender kiss on my brow, and Elijah disappeared into the kitchen. It didn't appear Jacob knew. Perhaps we would make it through the night. First, I would hurry to my room and try to lock Jacob out. I needed to conjure a new plan. Even though it'd be far more difficult with my husband lurking around, I couldn't stay here any longer.

A light flickered above me as I walked into the entry. My gaze caught by the faintly lit figure at the top of the staircase. Her face was stern. The specter looked so unlike Abby in this moment, it was jarring. I slowed to a stop, studying her.

And then I was overcome with knowing. This wasn't Abby, or a simulacrum of her. Her face was painted with a different pattern of freckles and wider eyes. Her beauty was different. Even the movements of her body, the mannerisms of her expressions. I saw it now plain as day. This was *her*. The second wife.

I swallowed.

"Sariah."

Chapter 35

She offered me a pained grimace in confirmation, and then she was gone. I opened my mouth to call after her, but no sound came out. Guilt rushed through me. Was abandoning Jacob abandoning her? Doubt heavy as lead stopped my feet.

I wrung my hands.

"What if the others won't leave with me now that he's home?" I whispered to myself.

Prudence, who still thought of her husband as her savior. Flora, who only waited for his call to obey. And Abby, who'd known all along and never left.

I buried my face in my hands, allowing my held-back tears to flow freely. My quiet sobs echoed off the entry walls. Months ago, I'd stood in this same place, greeting the women who were my new family. We struggled and disagreed, always a thick, invisible chain around our necks binding us together. Our fates entwined for eternity, held fast in Jacob's hands. I could run now and try to sever that chain, but would that only tighten his grip on theirs?

I pressed my palms against my burning eyes. Panic heaved in

my chest, and I struggled for air. I couldn't do this. I couldn't forsake my sister wives to this fate. Opening my eyes, I wiped the tears and the room came back into clear focus. If only my resolve would follow suit.

I took a step toward the stairs.

Suddenly, a blur of darkness and a stream of fractured light descended on me.

I screamed and scrambled desperately backward.

A crash shattered through the clammy air.

Shards of glass and metal volleyed at me, ripping my nightdress as they scattered across the entryway.

I stood paralyzed, my heart in my throat.

The chandelier lay smashed into a thousand pieces at my feet. It had missed me by only inches.

I'd nearly been crushed.

Momentarily, I was cocooned in silence. And then the world exploded.

Doors slammed. Walls whispered in hideous voices. The floorboards refused to stay even beneath my feet.

Prudence came running down the upstairs hallway.

"What happened?" she cried, her eyes widening as she took in the mess.

We looked up. The place the chandelier had hung from was now an ugly cracked hole. New fissures twisted across the ceiling like a spider's web. Like it had rotted and finally gave way.

The house wasn't finished with its dangerous revelations.

"It's all right." I tried to keep my voice calm so as not to alarm her. "The chandelier simply fell."

"Simply fell? Hazel, you could've been killed!"

The faint light returned, just behind Prudence, who was leaning over the railing. The specter—Sariah—hovered out of her sight, holding my gaze. Her expression was serious. It dug into me.

"But I'm fine," I said, speaking to both of them.

Splinters of glass cascaded from my nightdress as I moved

around the wreckage to the stairs. Glass crunched beneath my feet in sickening pops. My mind hummed, trying to piece together the shards of this mystery.

Sariah commanded this house. Sariah kept this house silent. Sariah made the chandelier fall. But I didn't think she wanted to harm me; I doubt she would've missed if so. No, she used the house as her voice where she had none, and she wanted me to know something.

"Hazel! What happened?" Jacob's footsteps crunched through the debris behind me.

"Nothing."

"The ceiling is breaking, Jacob," Prudence said. "Should we be concerned?"

Sariah's face tightened. *Yes*, she seemed to say. She glared down at Jacob for a moment, then, instantly, she faded from view.

Jacob leaned back to inspect the broken ceiling. "There's never anything to be worried about here. Go back to sleep."

A laugh came from the shadows and Abby slinked forward.

"Oh yes, all is well. I'll remember that when the house caves in on us," she said.

"Go back to sleep, Abby," Jacob growled.

"Shouldn't we help to clean this up?" Prudence asked.

"It'll keep till morning. Go on, dear. We've had a long day."

She bit her lip, then reluctantly turned on her heel and strode back down the hallway, lit only by the faint moon from the windows at the end. Abby made no signs of retreating, watching her husband with an intense stare.

Jacob ignored her and snapped to me, standing on the other side of the broken chandelier. My lungs cinched tighter.

"Brother Smith left. Said he had something to do. In the middle of the night."

"Oh?"

"Thought you might want to know."

"Why would I . . . ?" I trailed off.

And suddenly, Sariah's message became perfectly clear—*Jacob knew*.

He didn't break his pleasant, almost too-casual look as he watched me, probably waiting for a reaction. For a confession.

This was what Sariah wanted to tell me. She warned me in her loudest shout that I shouldn't stay here with Jacob. I needed to get us all out of here before something worse than a crashing chandelier harmed us. And I needed to keep Jacob as distant as possible.

I yawned.

"I should go to bed."

"I'll join you."

"Perhaps you should first make sure there's no danger here from the chandelier?" I suggested with a soft, pleading expression.

He hesitated, his eyes narrowing.

"I'll help you. I wouldn't want anything to happen to our children," Abby said, slowly walking to the staircase.

"Of course," he said at last. "Anything to protect my family."

I took the stairs slowly, feeling every step measured by Jacob's careful gaze. As Abby passed me on the stairs, she grasped my hand briefly but didn't look at me. Her hand was cold, but her hold was firm.

Was she trying to help me too?

As soon as I reached my door, I threw myself inside, shutting it tight. I likely had only a few minutes before he came up. Even if Abby was attempting to distract him, it wouldn't last all night.

And what would he do to me once we were alone?

I staggered to the bed.

This couldn't be how my story ended. Trapped in a monstrous house, the fifth wife of a dangerous man, tied forever to him and his other wives in a tangled mess.

And what would happen when Jacob determined I was no longer of use to him, like Sariah? I thought about my nightmares, all the blood. I felt more certain than ever that Jacob had murdered her.

Would my family spend the rest of their lives wondering what became of me, while apostles acted as gods and found more wives for my destroyer? How could it be that our Creator cared more for the satisfaction and increase of men than the broken and torn bodies of women?

"Sariah?" I spoke into the quiet room.

Her light gathered softly beside me. It stung my eyes, but I refused to close them. I trembled, my chest beginning to heave with the weight of a panic. The cacophony of worries and fears didn't dissipate, but I waded through them. They were not a weakness. *I* was not a weakness.

"Tell me what I can do. There must be a way to escape this, to escape him."

For the first time, the ghost's despondent face warmed. She understood.

"Perhaps if you can tell me what truly happened to you, I can piece something together."

She tilted her head, considering me, then nodded slowly. Lifting her hand, she stretched toward me. Scant inches vibrated between us. Though I felt nothing, her fingers brushed over my forehead.

I blinked. Sudden drowsiness overtook me, making it hard to keep my eyes open. I let out a staggered breath as my knees plunged to the floor. Was I dying? I tried to scream, but my mouth didn't obey. My body slumped against the bed. Sariah's brilliant face was the last thing I saw as my eyes drooped closed.

A clang startled me. I poked my head up, trying to recall what had happened. I was on my knees leaning against my bed, but the dark of night had given way to brilliant day. Light poured through the window, the golden glow suggested it was already late in the afternoon.

My heart thumped with distrust as I took in the room. Its usual musty odor had dissipated, instead a sweet lavender and vanilla sharp enough to coat my tongue. Cheery blue curtains, without a stitch of fraying, rippled in the breeze from the open window. A vibrant floral bedspread was neatly tucked into the mattress. I brushed my fingers across it. I'd never seen this linen before. Fresh yellow flowers sat in a vase on the table, and the large armoire was a stunning spring green, no chipping paint or scratches. This wasn't my room, but also, it was.

I seemed to only think of standing and then at once I was up on my feet. From this vantage the room was even more splendid, welcoming even. Every spot shined and sparkled with the obvious care of an attentive owner.

A noise caught my attention. At the table across the room, a woman sat humming to herself as she worked. She hunched over a tray of bright colors and a jar of water and brushes. Her hair was stunning red tucked tight in a bun on the back of her head. A few loose strands hung at her ears to frame her face. Her dress was a fern green, giving her body the illusion of a spring flower sprouting to life.

Abby?

No sound came from my throat.

She didn't appear to notice my presence. I drew closer to the table to watch her work. She didn't stir from her painting. I reached a tentative hand out toward her, but she went on as if she didn't see it. I was invisible.

I'd never known Abby to paint, or to appear so light and joyful.

She dipped her brush in the jar and tapped it before selecting the next color from the palette. I looked over her completed watercolor drying beside her. My pulse jumped. There, in the corner of the paper, was her artist signature. And it didn't say Abby.

Sariah.

At last, here she was in her full splendor—Sariah, the second wife.

The woman who stalked my nightmares couldn't have appeared more different. Her cheeks were no longer hollow, nor her eyes haunted. Her low hum of "Come, Come, Ye Saints" was cheerful and her movements carefree. At this moment I witnessed, Sariah was very much alive. Radiant.

I'd asked her spirit to show me what happened to her, and now I was seeing it. Living in it.

I looked back down at her painting, a white page spread with pink and orange flowers. I recognized those flowers. They were the same ones that lined the frame of the front door. Sariah had been the one to paint some hope and life into the house long ago.

The door hit the wall with a snap, startling both of us. Jacob stepped into the doorway. He was younger, his face lineless and smoothed. His moustache was shaved cleanly off, and his hair was a deep blond without the gray. His gait was lighter as he approached Sariah, who turned in her chair with a smile.

"Do you ever knock, Jacob?" Sariah said. Her dulcet tones were so different from what I'd expected after watching her ghost gesture sadly in the study.

Jacob laughed.

"And miss the beautifully incredulous look on your face? Not a chance, my dearest." He held out his hand to her. "Come. Let's take a walk."

"I have to finish this painting for Abby to hang in the nursery."

"I promise I won't keep you long. You must come."

The scene was too perfect, too jarringly different from everything else I'd witnessed in this house. Though I wished the vision could bring me a measure of joy, instead I sank with dread. The air seemed to agree with my fears, and the smell of the room shifted from heavenly floral to a dark tang.

Sariah accepted his hand and stood. The couple scarcely made it to the doorway when Jacob stopped and wrapped his arms around her, pushing her against the open doorframe.

"I thought you said we were going for a walk," she said as he began to place kisses down her neck.

I averted my eyes as the kisses continued, waiting for the moment to end.

Jacob's hands wandered down her body until they tugged up the edge of her skirt.

"Jacob, we should at least close the door this time," Sariah protested.

"Ah, but that's the fun of it," he replied.

His lips crashed into hers with a fervor. Heat stirred in the room as they continued, hands groping and skirts lifting higher. I glanced down at the floorboards when I heard his belt unclasp and his pants fall to the floor. Moans filled the room and escaped down the hallway. Panic rose inside me even though I knew they couldn't see me and I clamped my eyes shut, praying my feet would suddenly move again and take me from the room so I wouldn't have to witness this scene anymore.

A screech broke through their lovemaking.

My eyes darted back up. Between the doorframe and their tangle of bodies, I could just make out Abby standing against the far hallway wall, her eyes wide as she took in a wife and her husband in their compromising position. The couple stopped mid-motion, their mouths hanging open and panting. Sariah's cheeks turned as red as her hair.

"You think my witnessing this again is funny, Jacob? You're a beast—a monster! And *you*. My own sister." Abby ran, her footsteps echoing off the walls.

My knees nearly gave way.

The resemblance between them. It was too plain now for me to ignore. Sariah was Abby's natural sister.

Why hadn't Abby told me? Two women, sisters by birth, yoked to the same man by virtue of plural marriage. Forced to live every day in each other's shadows within the same house. Perhaps it was simply too painful for her to speak of, sharing your husband in such an intimate way. And then that sister disappeared at the hand of your mutual husband. It was little wonder Abby had broken down into the shifting woman I now knew.

I squeezed my eyes shut again, trying in vain to erase the sordid image etching into my mind. The smell hit me first before I opened my eyes—a putrid leak of spoiled water and rotting flesh. The couple was gone. The light of the day had faded lower, proving that night was fast on its way. I still stood in my room—Sariah's room.

Anticipation surged through me as I looked around. The house's secrets were unwinding before me in all their horror and tragedy. Inevitability settled and cracked in my bones.

Sariah leaned against the open doorframe with her back to me. "Abby, I've said I'm sorry, but you can't hold it against me forever that I love my husband."

I crept forward to catch a better view of the conversation. To my surprise, there was no sign of Jacob, only Abby stood in front of her sister in the hallway. She glared at Sariah. Beneath her blue dress and apron, I could make out the faint signs of a growing bump.

"My husband, Sariah. *My* husband," Abby said. "He was mine before he was ever yours."

"It hardly matters who was first. He is mine the same as yours. I have every right that you do."

The air pulsed with fury so strong it was almost visible.

"He would never have married you if the prophet hadn't told him to. Jacob *chose* me. You were his obligation." Abby's words dripped with disdain.

Sariah pushed off the doorframe. "This isn't worth arguing over. You agreed to the sealing the same as Jacob, and now there is nothing to be done about it. You know it can't be changed."

"You speak as if I had a choice," Abby said, her pitch rising. "Brother Brigham would only agree to seal us if we brought you along too. Jacob loved *me*."

Sariah lifted her chin. "Well, he loves *me* now just the same. Perhaps more, given the attention he's been showering on me lately."

The house seemed to suck in a breath, squeezing all the air from the room.

In a flurry of motion, Abby sprang forward and grabbed her sister by the hair. Sariah yelped and tried to pry her fingers from her head, but Abby held on, dragging her from the doorway into the hallway. I followed a step after, my heartbeat climbing.

"You. Bitch." Abby spat out each word. "You're just as unfeeling as he is."

Sariah pushed back against her sister, but Abby was like an immovable boulder, barely registering her sister's struggle.

"You two deserve each other."

With a heavy thrust, Abby shoved Sariah away from her. Sariah flailed backward, her feet stumbling as she fell back a step, and then another. And seemingly in an instant, Sariah plunged from view. Her scream pierced the air as she crashed down the stairs. Abby joined her sister's chorus, screaming too. A hideous final thump reverberated off the walls.

Then all at once, silence.

Chapter 36

The house groaned, loud and shaking. The floor shifted beneath me.

Abby screamed. "No, wait. I didn't mean . . . no, no!"

The same pleading repeated in my own head. *Please, this couldn't be true.*

I peered down the staircase. I gagged, unable to tear my eyes away from the gruesome scene. At the bottom, Sariah laid in a crumpled mess. Crimson liquid pooled out from her head like a crown. Her neck bent awkwardly, misplaced almost to her shoulder. On an impulse, I shouted for help, but there was no one to answer my cries.

Abby jumped down the staircase several steps at a time until she collapsed at the bottom. At once, I stood a few steps above her watching her through a rain of tears. Abby knelt on the floor beside her sister.

"No, Sariah, no." Abby gripped Sariah by the shoulders. Blood poured faster from a large gash at the back of her head as she lifted her.

"Get up. Get up!" She shook Sariah, but her head only lolled back and forth. Sariah's eyes stared upward, hollow and empty.

Abby whimpered as she cradled Sariah's head into her lap. Blood dripped onto her skirt as she sobbed. My own heart fissured as I watched, unable to aid her. In all of my most horrible imaginations, I could never have dreamt up this reality.

Abby scanned the room.

"It's going to be okay, Sariah," she murmured, like she was trying to convince herself.

She carefully lifted her sister off her lap and stood.

As she bit down on her red-stained thumb, I realized what she contemplated. The next step in the nightmare.

Abby dashed back up the stairs. Within moments, she returned carrying the vibrant floral bedspread I'd seen earlier on Sariah's bed. Her hands shook as she dragged the body onto the blanket. Red soaked through the beautiful quilted squares in seconds, staining them with a permanent reminder of this sin. Bending down, Abby took hold of the edge of the fabric and pulled.

Slowly, the body inched across the entryway. Blood smudged against the grain of the wood as the sickening procession—Abby dragging the body of her dead sister—moved, leaving a soiled trail of scarlet in its wake. Sariah's head flopped to the side and more drops of red splotched onto the floorboards. But Abby didn't stop or even look down at the mess she was creating.

Abby managed to drag Sariah through the doorway and across the parlor. She hesitated as she noticed the crimson soaking into her hands and she wiped them against her apron. She began to pace.

But I already knew where she would go.

Abby's eyes lit up. She flung open the door to Jacob's study with a kick of her foot. She bent down once more and hauled Sariah over the threshold, only stopping when Sariah's feet hung just outside the doorframe. I moved toward Sariah's boots and then, all at once, I found myself in the study tucked up in the corner.

Abby frantically wiped her hands again. She began to rummage around Jacob's desk. Throwing open drawers, she dug, tossing items that rolled away or fell to the ground. Her fingers held up at last what she sought—a small vial of yellowed liquid.

Consecrated oil. Priesthood brothers used this substance to anoint and bless the sick.

Abby glanced up at the shelves. Jumping to her feet, she reached up and pulled a book down from the shelf. My heart slammed into my chest as I saw she was carefully holding Jacob's black book of scripture.

"He said he kept those notes from Brother Brigham's instructions in here," Abby murmured to herself.

The book from my nightmares popped open on the floor beside her. Rubbing her hands repeatedly down her skirt, she reached out and with the barest touch flipped open the pages. They flew with the flick of her thumb until they landed open on the page marked with the folded piece of paper.

Abby unfolded the note and read it aloud under her breath. Her fingers left dark prints on the edge of the paper. Rolling the vial between her finger and her thumb, she unscrewed the lid and lifted her sister's lifeless head, then shook the oil until drops poured over the hideous, gaping wound. I pressed my fingers to my mouth to hold back sickness as the oil congealed with the blood over the exposed bone and tissue. Abby didn't bother to replace the lid, instead tossing the vial to the side.

I inhaled through my mouth, barely able to keep myself standing; the metallic stench invaded the small room. I knew already she was reaching into a well of desperation.

"I will heal you, Sariah. This will be fine. I can heal you," Abby said to her sister's lifeless body. Trembling, she placed her hands onto Sariah's head. She glanced down at the instructions for a blessing scrawled in Jacob's looping words, and cleared her throat.

"I command you, Sariah Manwaring, to return to your body. Be whole."

Sariah didn't stir. The room breathed heavily with me.

Abby pressed her hands again to Sariah's head. I could hear the squish of blood and flesh as she shoved harder. Crimson soaked her front as she leaned over the body. My nostrils stung with the rising bite of the rusty gore.

With a strain in her voice, Abby tried again.

"Be ye whole, Sariah. I command ye."

But nothing changed. Sariah's head drooped back into her chest with a squelching plop.

Abby placed Sariah's head back onto the floor and curled up into herself. Her hands grabbed her own cheeks, streaking them red. Her eyes grew wilder and brighter as she rocked herself.

"No, no, no . . . Sariah." Tears rolled down her cheeks, smearing the mess of red. "I couldn't have—I didn't . . ."

I pressed my eyes shut, praying this nightmare would end, but when I opened my eyes again, I was still in the study. Death hung heavy in the air.

Abby let out a gruff shout and picked up the scriptures beside her like she meant to throw them but stopped midmotion. Dropping the book carefully back down so it wouldn't touch the mess around her, she leaned over and reexamined the note. I remembered the words I'd read in the middle of the night.

What you bind on earth is bound in heaven.

"A binding," Abby said. A smile cracked her miserable face like this sentence was the answer to all her problems.

"This is it, Sariah. If we bind you here, you'll have to be—you won't be . . ." She trailed off and again placed her hands on Sariah's head and cleared her throat.

"Sariah Manwaring, I bind you to this earth. To this house. I bind you to stay here with me."

Her profane words ricocheted through me.

I watched as if in slow motion as her hands pulsed on Sariah's head again.

"You will obey me, Sariah. You will obey me," she shouted. "I. Bind. You. Here. In the name of—in the name of God, the Devil, whoever!"

She gritted her teeth.

"I will keep you here, in this house, forever."

She let go of Sariah and smacked her bloodied hands against the floorboards.

"For once, someone listen to me and what I want! Give me back my sister!"

I knelt to the floor beside her. Blood was all around, but it didn't stain me. I reached out to grab Abby's hands, to comfort her, but my arms went straight through her.

Around us the floor rumbled. Abby's eyes widened. An iridescent light broke through the lines in the floorboards like the foundation of the home turned into a brilliant sun. All around, the walls shook and heaved, sending items falling from shelves and furniture bounding across the floor.

A loud clap like thunder struck the room, at once silencing the shaking house. Light cracked in the air like a door opening slowly. With each second, the light widened in the air. Abby sat back, her hand shielding her eyes. The light wasn't brilliantly white, but it glowed strong against the darkness of the falling night.

I shrank back, unable to believe this truth.

The radiance formed into a shape. A body. It manipulated and pulsed until a final burst revealed the figure floating right before us. Sariah stared down, her eyes blinking as she gazed around in confusion.

Abby let out a cry of excitement and climbed to her feet.

"Sariah! You've come back. It worked, it worked," she said, hope edging into her voice.

But Sariah appeared as only a husk. Her eyes sunk hollow into her face, her visage dim and lacking. As if staring into a distorted mirror, the wrongness of her presence sent a shiver through me.

Extending her hand, Sariah gestured toward the floor. Abby followed her movement and gasped. The body still lay on the floor, lifeless and empty. The apparition glided backward, her cold and accusing stare boring holes into Abby.

"No, Sariah—this cannot be. You're here, you're here."

Abby began to sob, her whole body shaking.

"What have I done to you? What have I done?"

Sariah faded away, piece by piece.

A shadow darkened the doorway.

Hope lit Abby's voice.

"Sariah?"

But as she turned, her eyebrows raised in panic.

"Jacob, I . . ." she trailed off.

Jacob took in the scene, blinking back what might have been a moment of shock and then it was gone. Without saying a word, he squatted, leaning his arms on his knees as he examined Sariah's body. His expression was now stone.

"Well, Abby. I see you've finally done it," he said.

Abby sobbed once more.

"I knew I'd break you eventually. You see now why you need me? If you'd only been more obedient, then it wouldn't have come to this! But not to worry, dear. I won't tell a soul, as long as you obey."

His finger grazed the pool of blood, then reached out to slowly paint it down Abby's cheek.

"Remember you're always mine, Abigail Manwaring."

He crushed her jaw, blood dripping from his finger to floor.

"That Sister I spoke of, Flora, has already agreed to join the family, so nothing is lost. There is still time for your redemption."

His words drifted off as the scene blurred before me.

Someone gripped my shoulder, and I screamed.

Chapter 37

"What are you doing?" Jacob hissed.

He knelt beside me on the floor, his charming veneer at last wiped away for the day. He grabbed me by the arm and forced me up. I swayed, unable to find my footing as the dark and dusty room spun back into place around me.

"I fell asleep. I had a nightmare."

He pushed me toward the bed, but I caught myself before falling onto the mattress.

"Impossible. You've been up here less than five minutes. Though I suppose you've been having trouble with the truth tonight, so it's to be expected."

Sweat trickled down my neck. I now knew the horrible past. Jacob wasn't Sariah's murderer as I'd been convinced. But still my body screamed at me to flee from him, from his house, from this marriage. Within hours of our wedding, he swore there was no piano, even though he knew it sat collecting dust right above us. He withheld my letters, isolating me in this strange home with only him as my savior. But when trouble arose, he ran without a second thought, leaving us behind to fend for ourselves. Worst of all, he knew the truth of his second wife's demise and did nothing but marry again, leveraging her death to entrap his first wife in their joint misery. And now he stood over me, all remains of the façade he'd convinced me of washed away.

How dare he accuse *me* of dishonesty. He couldn't paint me as the villain, not when I'd done nothing but break myself over and over to obey his commands.

I straightened up, praying for every piece of fortitude within me to come forth. His eyes raked me up and down, but I didn't cower.

"Do you think I'm an idiot?" he said, too calm.

"No."

"Then why did you think you could fool me?"

"I haven't—"

He drew closer.

"I know who *Brother Smith* is. Did you really think I wouldn't realize it was Elijah Crowther? That you've been fucking him while I was away?"

My stomach turned, but I steeled myself.

"I've done no such thing." The truth would need to come out. I let the words fall. "But we're leaving. Together. I'll write for a divorce."

It all happened too quickly. One moment, I was staring up at Jacob, and the next he barreled toward me digging his hands into my hair. I screamed as he pulled me up by the scalp.

"As I said to you before, no one is leaving," he growled. "This is my family and my kingdom. You have no say in any of this."

My feet struggled for purchase as he jerked me away, dragging me by the head to the doorway. I thought of Abby and Sariah's struggle that I'd only just witnessed. Would I be the next thrown down the stairs? I screamed again as I fought him.

Jacob heaved me from the room but didn't relinquish his hold at the top of the stairs. Instead, he dragged me down after him. As we moved in a blurred tangle, the walls shook again. Books fell. Dishes smashed to the ground. Even chairs wobbled out of place and onto their sides.

"Shut up!" he yelled into the empty abyss of the house. Even in death, Sariah wasn't free of his commands.

With a hard thrust, Jacob shoved me into his study. As I scrambled to standing, he shut the door with a thud. I wasn't certain if I wanted to be sick or to whimper for mercy. My husband hadn't thrown his second wife from the stairs, but he'd knowingly grated Abby for his own amusement and chained her to his side. I wasn't safe with him. I'd never been. I glanced around for the rifle he'd produced earlier.

"I will fetch Flora and the children soon enough. She'll see the error of her ways." Jacob took a step closer and I backed up, bumping against his desk. "We'll all be together soon, back as my family."

"And what about Sariah? Is she a part of your happy family?"

"In eternity, she will be." He shrugged as if his own wife merited little care.

He bent over to light a lamp.

"You have nothing more to say about the dead wife you've been keeping as a secret?"

"I'm a man of great faith and I've done all things in righteousness. What is bound on earth is bound in heaven. Sariah will be my wife after death, as will you and all the others."

Anger surged through me. I wanted to rage as I'd never had in my life. I wanted to scream and shout and rip and tear. This man held us all in his cage, for this life and the next.

"*You* planted the wedge between Abby and Sariah, and then used her death to bring Abby to heel without a second thought! How can you care so little for the women you're supposed to love and protect? You kept marrying without sharing the truth. What if you'd pushed Abby again to madness and I fell victim? Would my blood stain your conscious at all?"

Jacob looked at me. No remorse, no sadness, nothing showed on his face.

"I buried Sariah's body myself and I kept Abby from hanging.

I protected her and our family from ruin. I'd say that makes me a rather benevolent husband, Hazel."

I laughed, hollow and cold. "Does a benevolent husband also lie?"

"I've never lied to you, Hazel."

"The piano!" I shouted. The bookshelves rattled with my words. "You knew all along it was there. And my letters!"

I reached over and ripped the desk drawer open with shaking hands. "You could have at least told me they wrote. You could have . . ." I trailed off as I rifled through the envelopes I'd left stacked inside the drawer earlier.

There was familiarity to the paper. I pulled one out and gasped.

Staring up at me was my own handwriting, the letter addressed to my mother. This was a letter *I* wrote to my mother months ago.

"Hazel, you're being hysterical and must calm down. I'd hate for one of your devilish panics to overcome you," Jacob said with little patience.

"My letters. These are all of *my* letters!" I shouted.

Jacob opened his mouth, but I shoved the pile of envelopes into his chest.

"You never posted a single one. You could have at least let them know I wrote!"

"You're mine now. Not theirs. Can you blame me for wanting you all to myself?"

I tried to push him away, but he stood firm. He caught my hand before I could pull away, gripping my wrist tight.

"Prudence never complained about it. Didn't Flora teach you to be a better wife than this?" he said.

My chest heaved trying to find my breath. He'd done the same thing to Prudence. She probably never knew that her family had written her and they never heard from her. How long had she written before she gave up on them as I did? It suddenly made sense why she was so attached to Jacob despite her independent thoughts on women.

"You're a monster," I murmured.

His other hand shot out, grasping me by the chin. I didn't dare take my eyes off him even as my body screamed in pain.

"This is the man I was made to be. In the world to come, I will reign as a god, and I intend to start now. Just like Joseph and Brigham. It is my right to do so, and for you to obey."

"And when will it end, Jacob? When will you have enough women to satisfy your eternal lusts?"

"When I say I am fulfilled," he said, his fingers grinding into my jaw. "When God declares the work is finished. I serve only Him and this is what He wants for me. For us. Obey and your place in my kingdom will be great. Try to run and your place shall be one of damnation. I will not be denied you, Hazel. You're mine and I will drag you from hell if I must, but I will keep you."

His words sounded like every sermon I'd heard since childhood. Somewhere in my girlhood, I'd absorbed all these lies into me—that if I didn't obey perfectly, I'd be damned. That if I wasn't flawless enough to be on a man's arm, then I was nothing of merit. That if I didn't stay small enough to make men comfortable, then I was out of my place. But did I truly need a man to be saved? To find happiness and peace? Why could I not be something for myself, as big and broken as I needed to be?

Jacob's touch softened, his hand on my chin suddenly a caress.

"My poor Hazel. You've been deceived by the Devil. I knew when I first saw your strange panics that Satan's hold on you was strong. I'd hoped you would overcome it with my help, but I see it wasn't so."

Doubts crept into my mind. Like so many times before, I saw flashing in my mind a lifetime of being scolded, guilted, and shoved into compliance. The way I constantly berated and beat myself for the slightest imperfections. All the shame I carried from the judgments of others for my panics.

My husband's touch was gentle, but his words were sharp as briars. He was almost convincing. Was I truly so weak, so wrong for simply being myself?

Suddenly, I didn't believe that at all. I didn't believe *him*. I didn't need to hide my panics that weren't a flaw. I didn't need him to take me to heaven. His claims on my life and my soul meant nothing to me. He could search hell over, but he'd never find me.

I flicked my chin from his grip.

"You can't have me, Jacob. I don't choose you."

"Because you choose Elijah?" he said in a mocking tone.

"Because I choose myself. I'm done being a pawn in any of your games. I don't belong to you or to Elder Crowther or any man. I belong to myself."

The air around us pulsed. It seemed to expand the room, placing distance between myself and the menacing husband watching me with an insatiable hunger in his eyes.

"You leave me no choice then."

Slowly, he stalked around the desk, a vulture circling me.

"You will stay in this room until I bring back Flora. By then I expect the lack of food or water will humble you, for you truly need to be humbled, Hazel. You need to remember that *I* am your head."

He ripped open a small case on the shelf and dug within. When he withdrew his hand again it held a gleaming knife. I froze.

"Don't worry." He slammed the case shut. "This isn't for you. Yet. I imagine Crowther won't be out all night in this darkness. I'll be ready on the drive for his return."

"Wait, no—" I reached for his arm and caught only wisps of his shirt as he tugged away. "Jacob, please."

He shook his head. "You're out of second chances and bargains, Hazel. I'll see you in a few days, I suppose."

Faster than I could catch him, he slipped through the door and slammed it shut. I pounded against the wood. "Jacob!" The lock clicked.

I shouted and beat the door with my fists to no avail. Only silence called back. With tears streaking down my face, I slid down the door and buried my head in my knees. I prayed to whatever deity would hear me that Jacob wouldn't find Elijah. I couldn't have his blood on my hands. And I wouldn't be trapped forever in this house with nothing but my guilt over my failures as company.

I let out a sob. I could see it all so plainly—so horribly. If I remained trapped in Manwaring Manor forever, one day I'd have a daughter of my own and I'd condemn her to this same life. I'd watch and wait and know that I couldn't save her. That one day this same cruel fate would be hers as well. And so, the cycle would turn on and on, generations of women pressed too hard beneath the boots of men, who heard none of our cries.

The door shook behind my back.

I peered up as a light flooded the room.

Sariah crouched in front of me, her face long.

"I can't let this happen."

Her light flickered.

"I have to stop him," I said.

Her eyes watched mine with what looked like profound care. My tears stopped. In silence, my strange ghostly companion sat with me, not demanding or pushing, but simply there. Though we couldn't touch, I sensed her arms around me, encompassing me. She did what few others were willing to do in my life—she mourned with me.

Heat radiated up my arms and lodged in my chest. I found myself overwhelmed with warmth. It was like earlier as I'd searched through the canyon with Elijah. The heat once more generated from within me, spurred on by Sariah's acceptance. It stirred my convictions, of the strength hidden within me that I needed only to draw out. I sucked in a long breath, then slowly let it out.

I meant what I said to Jacob. I didn't choose him. I wouldn't stay here.

Hope. Tenacity. Need. It all rose and bubbled out of me. They were things that I could hold and shelter that weren't shame or worry. I gazed up at Sariah once more, her brightness lighting my face.

"Can you help me one more time?" I asked her.

Without hesitation, she slipped through the door. I didn't have to wait long. The doorknob quivered and shook. I heard Abby swear to herself on the other side and I almost laughed at the absurdity of it all.

At last, she picked the lock and the door swung open.

Abby sighed, pocketing a long hatpin. "My God, it took forever for him to leave."

Chapter 38

Abby ushered me out of the study. "Clever of you to finally figure it out, little Hazel. Though I suppose it's unsurprising. Sariah's been louder than ever since you arrived. She tried befriending Flora once, but I'm sure you can guess how that went."

I shrank away from her. Though she wasn't a cold-blooded killer, Abby had still ended Sariah's life, and part of me wanted to keep my distance.

"I know what happened to Sariah," I said.

Abby straightened up. Closer now, I noticed her eyes were rimmed with red as if she'd been crying.

"I see." Her words were only a whisper.

"You pushed her down the stairs and she died. It may have been an accident, but it was still a murder."

Abby's expression diminished until it faded from her ashen face. "I know."

She stepped back into the dining room and I trailed behind her, anxious to see what she would confess.

"Then you cursed her in a profane act," I continued. "You cursed this whole house."

Abby bumped against the edge of the dining table. Placing her hands back on the tabletop, she hung her head. The house and I waited; I was barely breathing.

She gripped the table edge tighter. "Did Jacob tell you all this?"

"He didn't have to," I said. "Sariah showed me herself."

Abby whimpered.

"You don't understand, Hazel. You can't understand. Everything was taken from me. Everything."

"Then for once, tell me the truth, all of it."

"You must believe me, I never intended to harm her." Her shoulders curled in to ball herself up. "She was my sister—my twin sister. Our whole lives we only had each other."

The entire house shivered with me, walls and windows rattling.

"I was so angry at her in the moment, but I—I've done a lot of things, Hazel, but I never would've killed her on purpose."

I believed her but still felt disgust for her actions, so I said nothing.

She went on, her eyes glazed over as if she didn't even see me standing there anymore. "I was so in love with Jacob. We were going to have a beautiful life together. And then on the day of our marriage we came to the Endowment House ready to be sealed, so proud that Brigham Young himself would conduct the ceremony. But do you know what he said?" Her eyes searched mine now, tears streaking down her freckled cheeks. "He refused to marry us. He said he knew that I had a sister and he wouldn't seal us unless we left and came back with her so Jacob could marry us *both*."

I saw it almost as if I were there myself—a devasted Abby being told they could only be united if another came along. Sariah watching them return from the porch, forced to acquiesce to the prophet's sudden demands or to squash forever the happiness of her sister. Abby fighting back tears as the love of her heart swore himself to another over the altar on what should've been her own—only her own—joyous wedding day.

My heart sagged heavy with a misery that wasn't my own.

How many heartaches and sorrows were required for the church to flourish? Perhaps at final judgment day God would weigh our exaltation in tears.

"Of course, I begged Sariah to agree to it. I couldn't lose Jacob," Abby continued, her voice rasping. "I didn't know—I couldn't have imagined what it would feel like—how we would live. I lost everything as I watched him fall in love with her too. But it was already too late to change anything."

"You could have insisted on your own household," I said, trying to fit these final pieces of their story together.

More tears splashed down her face. "No, he said he wanted something special for us by keeping only one house. It didn't take long for Jacob to start believing himself entitled to quite a lot."

Entitled to Flora, to Prudence, to *me*. Did he ever once worry for our safety? That the sins she had committed, that lived on in the house, could do more than simply haunt us—that they could harm us?

"And now, neither of us will ever find peace. Sariah's everywhere in this house, her and that godforsaken hymn. She plays it to remind me, I think, that I'll never find solace after what I did. That she'll never be at rest either. She uses the house to swallow all sounds, to continually berate me for silencing her in death. I've tried everything to ignore her, but I've known for a long time there's something she needs me to do and she won't stop until it's finished."

Abby stood lost in her thoughts for what seemed an eternity.

The grandfather clock ticked louder in my ears. I was running out of time. Jacob could return any moment. Elijah could be hurt or worse. Dread for his possible fate hummed loudly, and I continued my unspoken prayer that he wouldn't try to return tonight. But questions continued to pile in my mind.

"Why did you never harm us?" I asked. "We too took your husband."

Abby wiped her tears on her sleeve, though it did nothing to hide the bright splotches on her cheeks. "Any last remains of love I had for Jacob were destroyed the minute he carried in a shovel to dig a hole for her grave. I just kept wondering why—why hadn't he said anything when Brigham told us to fetch Sariah? Why didn't he protest or even apologize for destroying my dreams? Why did he find it a lark to let me catch them time and again in compromising positions, even as I birthed his children?

"It was like the scales dropped from my eyes and I finally saw him for who he truly was, how he'd really treated me. When he'd blamed his lust on me and demanded I take the brunt of repentance, or when he took Sariah to wife without hesitation or sadness. The little games he would play to make us compete with one another. He'd been torturing us for his own amusement for years. And my God, the guilt of bringing my sister right into his arms was almost as devastating as having killed her.

"And then he simply carted Sariah outside and buried her body without even saying a prayer over her grave. I realized I was nothing to him in the end. *We* were nothing to him."

Was that all we were to our husband? A thing to be used and discarded? Tears slipped down my own cheeks, tasting salted and bitter.

"But you never left him, Abby. And you never warned us of all this," I said, betrayal and devastation battling within my chest.

"How could I? He held my secret crime over me! I have children to protect that I couldn't leave to his sole care if he turned me in. Jacob held all the cards! But I grew to love the thrill of hitting back at him where I could, rebelling only to hurt him. I hoped that somehow one of you would see it and be wary of him. But what else could I do when he married you all without so much as telling me first? Once you were here, it was already too late."

Too late. Too late to dwell on what should've happened or what she could've done.

My hand warmed at my side as if someone had slipped their own into mine. I shifted slowly. No one stood there, but I felt her presence. Sariah strengthening me. Reminding me. I gave the ghostly sensation a squeeze, then turned back to Abby.

"It may be too late to change the past, but is there anything we can do to release Sariah now and try to right at least one wrong?" I asked.

Abby shook her head.

"I've tried everything. Why do you think I've been studying Brigham's words in Jacob's journals?" She let out a choked laugh. "I'm that desperate for answers."

My heart sank. But we were running out of time, and perhaps I could at least save Abby.

I closed the final gap between us, standing inches from Abby's face.

"Listen to me. We can't stay here. We know Jacob's a monster and it'll never end if we do."

She coiled her fingers around her own neck. "But my sister . . ."

"She can't leave this house, but you can. We need to get Prudence and the children far away from here."

"Oh, little Hazel. You think it's so simple? You think Jacob won't find us, wherever we go?" She dug her fingers into her skin. "You think he won't lay claim on us in the next life? This is our eternal burden. We can run and run, but men will always hold the invisible cords around us. Even in death there is no freedom. We'll always be tied to them—their wives, their daughters, their muses, their sacrifices—a woman they can look back on as part of *their* story, but never our own.

"To Jacob, we're the silent queens of his eternal, Mormon kingdom, covenanting to him as our God. Nothing but a means for his own exaltation."

Abby gripped me by the shoulders. Her tear-stroked expression was desperate, despairing. Squeezing against my shoulder bones as if she could wring redemption from my flesh, she wrenched me closer.

"This is a woman's lot," she said. "A poisonous salvation we're fed over and over, never realizing we're consuming our own destruction."

A hatred I'd never before experienced devoured me. It was for all of them. For Jacob and the prison he'd locked us in. For the years of torment that ground Abby down. For the prophets of God and men of this world who fashioned the disease of patriarchy and called it exaltation.

I wanted to crumble beneath it all. Panic rose in my chest, ready to steal my next breaths. But I threw my arms out and fought. On command, the house ceased its trembling.

"Then we run as far as we can so our children won't have to live what we've lived."

Abby stared back in disbelief.

"Sister Hazel, I . . . I can't. I can't leave my sister. Not alone in this house with only *him* for company."

Until the next wife.

My heart cracked open for her, blood spooling into my chest thick with sorrow and frustration that could never be overcome. But in the back of my head, the clock continued to tick. I was almost out of time.

"Very well, Abby," I said, a plan slowly forming. "Then you'll at least help us escape."

Abby nodded but seemed uncertain. "How?"

"We need time to get away without him following behind." I began to pace. "First, we need to draw him away from Elijah before he harms him. I knew him before he came to board here."

She snorted.

"What?"

"Don't think I never noticed your lovelorn face every time the boarder entered the room," she said.

Heat warmed up my neck. "Yes, well, I'm going with him, far away from here."

"Then I suppose we better hurry before your current husband finds your husband-to-be."

I pushed down the mix of awkwardness and excitement, as well as the fear, her words brought me.

"We need to get Prudence to go along with this," I said. "I can't leave her behind."

"No, I suppose not. . . ." Abby trailed off, her eyes searching around the dining room. "Sariah, I know you're here somewhere!" she called.

The large windows that once had terrified me over dinner rattled in response. It was strange how normal all this madness had become to me.

Abby continued speaking to the house. "Go and wake Prudence and bring her down here, quickly."

A faint light shot across the room and disappeared into the hallway.

She turned back to me. "Do you have a plan?"

"I think so." I fidgeted with a button on the nightgown. "We'll tie him up. Imprison him in his office for the night. If we catch the first train tomorrow, we'll be long gone before he can make it back to the city."

A scream cut through the anticipation brewing around us.

Prudence ran through the doorway, her unpinned hair wild around her face.

"Abby! Oh goodness, there you are! I saw—I thought I saw . . ." She trembled.

Carefully, I wrapped my arm around her shoulder. "I know and I'm sorry. Come, there's something I have to show you."

As I led her to the study, out of the corner of my eye I saw Abby speaking softly with a faint light lurking in the hallway.

"I think I finally know what you need me to do," she whispered.

Chapter 39

The front door hit the wall with a bang that echoed through the house's deep silence. Abby and I watched each other in the darkness from either side of the parlor doorway. Every wall, shelf, and window held its breath with us. Abby clutched a heavy candlestick. I twisted the rope we'd hastily taken from the laundry line between my hands, my pulse frantic in my chest.

Prudence's voice drifted in from the entry.

"She wishes to repent for her sins against you." Her tone was stronger than I'd heard in months.

I pictured her face as I handed her the letters hidden in the drawer only half an hour ago. The way she bit her finger to keep from screaming as she looked through the stack of letters from her family all the way back in England, never delivered or mentioned in four years of marriage. That moment broke her, and it shattered me to witness. But she arose from the ashes of it, faster than I'd imagined possible, with determination. After sharing all we knew, Prudence volunteered to venture out to lure Jacob back to the house.

Jacob let out a loud exhale as his shoes clicked off the entry floors. The house amplified every step for us.

"Very well, my dear. Get back to bed and don't come down, no matter what you hear. Do you understand me, Prudence?"

"Yes." Her lie was breathless. Now she'd pack our things and ready the children for our flight, as we planned.

"Hazel," Jacob called as he entered the hallway. "I hear you're stricken with contrition already. You'll be happy to know I didn't find your lover. The slippery bastard must be halfway to the city by now. Though that doesn't bode well for you, I suppose." He chuckled as he neared.

Across the way, Abby nodded. Steeling myself, I watched her jump from her hiding place just as Jacob stepped through the doorway.

He only grunted in surprise as Abby swung the candlestick at his head, landing with a resounding crack. As we hoped, he stumbled forward. I pounced next, throwing the rope around his chest and arms, twisting it as tight as possible. His weight set me off balance, nearly toppling me as he crumbled to the floor, where he lay motionless.

A light flickered on near us, though neither of us lit it, revealing a gash of crimson across his temple. Blood dripped onto the floorboards. My stomach clenched.

"Do you think he's . . . is he?"

Abby leaned in closer to his face. "He's breathing."

Guilt lessened its hold on me. "I'll take his legs and you can take his arms."

As she shifted him, a gleam of silver reflected in the lamplight near his waist. The knife he'd pocketed earlier to hunt Elijah. My grip on his ankles tightened. But Abby made no move to pick up his shoulders. She stared at the knife.

"Abby," I hissed. "We have to hurry!"

Jacob groaned. I froze. Abby's face calcified. The groan turned into a hacking laugh.

"You two. I should've known better."

He heaved himself up to sitting. No, no, no . . . this wasn't the plan. The tangy stench of blood hit my tongue as he attempted to wipe it off his temple. Glancing at the ropes now weakly hanging from his chest, he shoved them down to his elbows.

"I should've known Abby would only corrupt you, Hazel. Everything she touches turns bitter. Or dead," he said, his gaze piercing through her.

But Abby didn't cower. She stalked back across the room to circle her prey.

"I could say the same for you, husband."

"Surely, you don't trust this Jezebel," Jacob said to me. "She killed her sister in jealousy and cursed this house in a profane act mocking God's priesthood."

"And your hands are just as filthy." The words slipped from my tongue, but they fortified me. I unfroze, slowly stalking closer.

Blood from the gash on his forehead dripped into his eyes, turning his stare a sickening red. "What were you planning to do? Tie me up and run off with your lover? You know what God does to adulterous women—He destroys them."

The windows rattled above us, sending a cascading wave through the walls. A snake sprouted beneath the floorboards, slithering toward Jacob. He cried out, attempting to escape it, but it coiled around his ankle, as if his foot had sunk into the floor. He staggered, struggling to stay upright as the house sucked him in.

"I think my God is on my side," I said.

All at once, Abby sprang forward, tackling Jacob back to the floor. Even with Jacob's height, she was quick and decisive. Using her full weight and trusting Sariah's tight grip on his foot, she thrust against him and he lost his position, striking his nose hard against the floor with another sickening crunch.

Jacob rasped. Abby pressed her knee between his shoulder blades, immobilizing him.

"Abby," he pleaded, disoriented from the double blows.

"What do we do now?" I said.

I stepped toward them but stopped. Something more than the raging house and the taste of blood in the air was unexpected.

Shifting back, Abby revealed the sheen of a silver knifepoint. My heart clawed into my throat. She'd taken Jacob's knife.

"Abby. . . ." I trailed off, uncertain what I was saying.

"I must do what my sister needs me to do," she replied.

She fisted his hair and pulled his lolling head back.

"Ab-by," he stuttered again, shaking his shoulders to get her off.

I sprang forward, throwing my weight with Abby's to hold his trembling body down. There were no thoughts, only pulsing power in my arms that needed to hold Jacob in place. To help Abby with what had to be done to take back what was rightfully ours—our own souls.

The tip of the knife dug into his skin just below the left ear.

In one smooth, practiced motion, she slid the knife across his throat to the right ear. A long slash dropped open. Hot crimson rushed out, spilling across the floorboards. They lapped it up hungrily, the blood soaking into the floor at an impossible rate, almost as quickly as it poured out of Jacob's neck.

Here were the true sinews and marrow of a man, bright red and slopping from the skin. No power or priesthood simmered over to save him. Jacob gasped in a way that made my stomach turn, but I didn't relent my hold. His eyes bulged.

Abby lowered the knife to her side and released his head with a flick. Jacob slumped forward. His body continued to twist and wheeze, struggling to keep its slipping hold on this life. But neither of us made any move to save him. The pool of his lifeblood grew faster than the floorboards could consume now, skirting out around him and licking at the furniture.

A final, long rattle told us it was finished.

I rose slowly, watching Abby instead of the gore. She stood, her legs on either side of his now-still body. Crimson soaked up the edge of her skirts. The knife dripped drop after agonizingly slow drop of blood into the waiting pool below.

"Perhaps his black soul is clean now," she said, tossing the weapon into the mire. "I doubt it, though."

"We killed him," was all I could manage.

"Many wrongs needed to be corrected. Now the blood is spilt and Sariah will be avenged and free. We'll all have peace at last."

A white light broke through the floorboards, just as it had in my vision of Sariah's death. They shook hard enough to send us both toppling down. All around us, books, shelves, objects, furniture rained down. Both of us lost our balance and fell to the floor.

Could this be it? Had we saved or condemned us?

A clap of thunder silenced the tumultuous room. And then a light, brighter than description, rested on us. I cracked my eyes open.

"*Sariah*," Abby cried. "Are you free at last?"

Her sister's expression was exuberant, but also menacing, her eyes dark and narrow.

Hair rose on my arms.

"Abby, wait." I tried to call her back as she stumbled closer to Sariah's burning visage.

"Please, tell me that worked and was what you needed."

Sariah sent her a knowing look, one Abby seemed to understand. The tinderbox dropped from the mantel with a metallic clang.

"It's time then," Abby whispered.

I grabbed her arm, tugging her back from Sariah as the walls began to shake once more. Windows boomed strong enough to crack. Items toppled from everywhere, dropping to the floor around us. I crouched down, trying to drag Abby with me even as she twisted away.

"We need to leave. Now," I shouted over the tumult of the house. "Someone will eventually come looking for Jacob. We could hang for this."

"I'm not leaving my sister," she replied, tugging her hand back and cradling it against her chest.

"Abby, please. You can't stay here with your children alone!"

Sariah glowed brighter, hotter somehow. The edges of her white light singed yellow and orange. My head screamed at me to run.

"I know. Take my children, Hazel," she pleaded, her voice cracking with fresh tears. "They deserve better."

"Come with us."

She collapsed into the checkered sofa and swung her legs over the arm, just as I'd seen her do months ago. The image burned into me.

"No, I'm not leaving. And I'm not implicating you all in this either! Just leave me here with my ghosts."

The tinderbox shook and burst into flames. I screeched as the fire rose up, instantly covering the large hearth with a wall of flames. Sariah whipped her arms out to her sides. Fireballs gathered and jumped to the edges of the parlor.

"No, Sariah!" I reached out as if I could stop her. "What are you doing?"

A flame rose on the fraying old curtains. Then almost at once, the flame spread and licked up the window faster than anticipated.

Abby sat up, strangely calm for the fire rising around us.

"Isn't it obvious? She's helping us and saving herself. She's burning the house down because it's the last thing tying her to this earth. And it'll hide all evidence."

Another flame whooshed up from an armchair. The table linen beside it went up quickly along with it. The inferno grew. Heat like I'd never felt oppressed my skin. The entire parlor was ablaze in minutes.

Sariah moved almost too fast to track her, a blur of white and yellow light blending into the fire as she stoked it. She truly controlled this house—its moans and magic, and now its death. It dawned on me that she could've done this before and left the house as ash. But she'd waited all these years, biding her time to extract herself from its ties until we finally did what needed to be done: destroyed the oppressor.

This was the true sacrifice and atonement.

While a part of me filled with righteous justice, I couldn't remain calm, nor still. A house this old, surrounded by mountain brush and deadened trees on a night of howling wind, would be eaten by fire in precious few minutes. And even if Sariah needed to destroy her final household appendages to find rest, we needed to survive, especially the children upstairs preparing with Prudence.

"Abby, come!" I screeched once more. "We have to wake the children and get out!"

"I'm staying." Her stare cut through the smoke and flames across the room.

"But—"

"If Sariah must burn the house to end it all, then I'll make sure the work is finished. I want to be in this blaze." She choked. "You must go quick, little Hazel, and get the children out."

A coughing scream came from the entry.

"Hazel, Abby!" Prudence called into the fire.

Abby motioned me for me to run. "Now! You must go!"

I offered out my hand one last time across the flames.

She shook her head. "No, I'll die in this place, just like my sister. You can blame me for everything. Now take care of my children."

I hesitated another moment. I couldn't let her do this. A flame shot up between us and I jumped back. Sweat trickled down my back now from the growing heat.

Abby's eyes pleaded with me. "Please."

At last, I nodded. "I will, I promise." Then I turned on my heel and ran.

Chapter 40

I grabbed Prudence's hand as we took the stairs three at a time. We thought we'd have more time to prepare, but now we needed to get out before it was too late. Our feet pounded across the floor.

We would leave this horror behind forever. I wasn't the same young woman who had come into this house. Perhaps plural marriage had refined me into something sharp and fierce, unafraid at last to claim my own needs and desires.

Smoke seeped into the hallway. The wooden smell drifting in was sickly inviting like a bonfire, but I could hear the fire crackling with a thickening fury. I knew there was no hope for it losing steam. As soon as the flames breached the walls, the autumn wind would whip it into a frenzy and consume the house in minutes. The dry grass and dead plants around us would be quick kindling for it to feast. The danger would spread and spread.

Prudence coughed as we slowed in the darkness. "What's happening, Sister Hazel?"

"Sariah started a fire."

"The ghost?" She nearly screeched. "But what of Jacob?"

I took in her soft, uncertain expression. Prudence didn't deserve to have blood on her hands, to carry any more weights and poor memories of this house. I couldn't help feeling glad she hadn't been there at the end. She would've helped us and it would've destroyed her. Despite all the pain, her kindness and hope were her true power, and I wanted desperately for her to keep that triumph.

"He's gone. I'll explain later," I said. "We must get out! Where are the children?"

"Still asleep! I was working on preparing our trunks before I roused them," she replied.

With a shared glance, we ran together, throwing open the door to the nursery.

"Children! Wake up!" I shouted.

Esther already sat up in her bed. "What's happening, Aunt Hazel?" Esther's voice quivered as she pulled back the covers.

I ripped open the armoire and began tossing out dresses and coats. "The house is on fire. We must leave *now*. Here, put these on quick." I shoved an armful of clothes into Esther's arms. "We'll get the horses and leave as fast as possible."

Nephi climbed into a pair of pants with shaking hands. Esther threw the dress I handed her over her head and scooped up the coats.

"Where's Mother?" Esther asked, her voice small and uncertain. My heart ripped open for Abby. For her suffering. For her terrible misdeeds. For what she now chose.

"I'll explain later. We must get out now."

Loud crashes careened through the tumult as furniture broke down around the house. The taste of ash settled on my tongue. It was growing stronger.

Prudence tore at the bedsheets in the corner. "Where is Edward?"

Esther's eyes went wide. "He went to sleep in Flora's bed. It was a silly dare."

A screech tore through Prudence's throat. But I was already out the doorway.

"Go, I'll fetch him and bring him out. Leave now!"

Prudence reached for me. "No, I should—"

"I'm already halfway there," I called back from down the hallway. "Now, go," I demanded, a sense of finality settling into my gut.

"Hazel!" she called after me, leaning into the hall hung dark and gray now with heavy smoke. It burned at my nostrils and I did my best to cover my mouth with my sleeve as I tore down the hallway in the opposite direction.

"Go to the horses!" I yelled, choking on the smoke. At least they would be safe, I repeated over and over in my mind as I blinked past the streaks of tears in my eyes from the sooty air.

Flora's room was at the far end of the hall, directly above the parlor below. I braced myself as I shoved the door open with my shoulder. A flame gushed up in front of me. The fire below had begun to penetrate through the floor.

A faint cry sniffled in the far corner. My heart lost all sense of its rhythm. *Edward.*

I jumped around the shooting blaze and into the room. Sweat drenched me in seconds as the temperature rose. The smoke was thicker here than in the hallway, almost blinding. I ducked lower to try to avoid the worst of the smoke. The floor groaned and cried beneath me. I stifled a cry of my own as the walls wept around me, their wallpaper peeling from the sides to feed the flames.

Perched on the corner of the bed, Edward sat in a ball cradling his knees. Tears poured down the sides of his cheeks as he cried.

"Edward, I'm here, I'm here, darling."

He climbed into my outstretched arms without protest. He molded into my chest, his body too warm from the fear he'd been forced to endure alone for too long. I swallowed a sob.

But there wasn't time to mourn yet. I had to get us out now. I turned back to the door, but the fire had spread too quickly. Flames licked the door, trapping us inside. I forced my mouth shut to keep from screaming out and inhaling more of the strangling smoke billowing through the room. I glanced around as fast as I could through the thickening air for a solution.

The window, a strong voice shouted in my head. I didn't hesitate.

"Try to keep your mouth against my nightgown." I spoke directly into Edward's ear, and he obediently pressed his face against me. Cradling him tight, I crossed the floor carefully. Holes began to show in the bottom where the fire had eaten straight through the ceiling below. My gut told me we had only minutes before the entire floor collapsed.

Using one hand to hold the child and the other to shimmy the window, I drove my fingers beneath the windowsill. It resisted at first, but I forced it open. The smoke flooded out around us into the open night sky. With gasping breaths, I took in a few hopeful gulps of the fresh air but couldn't rest. The danger was too strong.

I looked down below, instantly feeling the rush of elation from making it to the window dissipate into the cold wind. We were up on the second story and below was nothing but hard dirt. How could I jump and save this child's life? I tried to think quickly through a plan, but my thoughts muddled with the horrendous smoke choking us. The heat of the flames scorched my back. The floor creaked louder beneath my feet in final warning.

"Hazel!"

Elijah.

My heart beat again with a strike of hope as he came running from the wilderness. He'd come back. He was safe. My chest fizzled. From this far up and with tears pouring down my cheeks from the smoke, I couldn't make out his face, but I could sense he was frantic as he stared up at us helplessly. Prudence, Esther, and Nephi ran up behind him, their cries mingling with the cracking in the air.

Edward's breaths sputtered against my breast. I needed to get him out of here. Now.

"We're trapped!" I shouted down to them. "The floor is going to cave any moment."

"You'll have to jump then." Elijah extended his arms up.

"We'll catch you!" Prudence barreled forward, her arms shaking as she tried to form a landing spot with their entwined arms.

There was no time to deliberate. "I'll send Edward first," I called out.

Working quickly, I pried Edward from my chest. "Stay upright! They will catch you below," I instructed him. His eyes grew wide, but he nodded. I lowered him by his arms as far as I could lean out the window. Holding back a cry of fear, I let go. "Catch him!" I screeched as he went, my heart in my throat.

He was safely caught in the pair's outstretched arms. I cried out in gratitude.

The floor shifted beneath me, then disappeared altogether. Screaming, I grasped the window opening as my feet struggled to find purchase below me. There was no time to waste now. Summoning every piece of courage and strength I had left inside me, I dragged myself up into the windowsill. Elijah drew up his arm again toward me as Prudence stumbled back with Edward tight in her arms.

The air whooshed past my ears as I fell.

I landed half in Elijah's arms and half on my feet. Together, we tumbled forward in a crashing roll, but we were alive. I couldn't help my cry of relief.

"Are you all right?" he asked over the smash of something exploding in the house.

"Yes, but let's get away from here."

He didn't wait for further instructions. Urging the children forward, we dashed away from the structure, now surely in danger of total collapse. Hand in hand, we ran until we came to the front. From somewhere within, a voice screamed. Beams cracked and hurtled to the ground, spreading the fire to the trees around us. Manwaring Manor was almost gone.

"Where's Abby?" Prudence asked, tears pouring down her cheeks as she wheezed.

I grabbed her shoulder, a knot in my throat. But before I could respond, another scream cut through the night. We both turned toward the house as a figure staggered through the collapsing doorway, a bright light illuminated behind them.

My eyes widened in amazement. It was Abby.

"Mother!" Esther screamed as Nephi sprinted forward to catch her as she attempted to jump over the smoldering remains of the porch.

The light shielding her flared, then flickered out as she nearly collapsed onto her son's shoulders. Elijah and I ran over to help.

"What happened? Abby, are you all right?" I cried. I couldn't believe what I was seeing. She'd been so determined to stay and lose her life with her sister, but here she was, wheezing and covered in a layer of black ash. How had she survived that long in the inferno?

Abby coughed. "It seems my sister is determined I should live. Despite everything I've done."

I glanced up as Elijah took Abby's other side and wrapped her weak arm over his shoulder. Against the raging flames, Sariah's white glow flashed in the window. Somehow, she'd saved her sister. Even after bringing her into this house and her accidental murder, Sariah wanted Abby to live, to forgive her. Heat that wasn't from the fire burned through me.

I reached out and carefully stroked Abby's cheek, painted red and black with a mixture of frustrated tears and soot. "It's all right, Abby. You didn't need to sacrifice yourself in order to save her, or any of us. I think all Sariah wanted was for you to finally end the torment."

Her tears leaked onto my fingers.

Abby looked directly at me, as if seeing me for the first time. "I don't deserve it. But at least, I finally understood her."

The heat scorching up my back from the fire reminded me we couldn't stop now and wade through it all. I stepped back so they could carry Abby farther from the house.

"We need to find the fire brigade before this fire spreads out of control," Elijah yelled as he and Nephi carried her to the others.

I nodded. "Yes. And Abby needs a doctor right away."

Prudence led us to the hitching post nearby, where Jacob's horses were tied up along with Elijah's. The poor creatures stomped and whinnied in worry, trying to break free to escape the oncoming inferno.

"Shh, we're here," I murmured, gesturing for Esther to help me. "It's going to be okay, I promise," I told them, tears thickening in my eyes.

Working as fast we could as the flames spread across the drive, we threw the saddles onto the horses and steadied them. Prudence climbed up, clutching Edward to her as she took the reins. I helped Esther on behind her, while Elijah placed Abby onto the other behind Nephi. The horses clomped their feet anxiously.

At last, I pulled myself up on Elijah's horse.

"Ready?" Elijah called as he swung his leg and grabbed me, pulling me tight against his chest.

"Yes, I never want to see this place again," Abby said.

Prudence took off with a nod, Nephi on her heels.

I allowed myself to sink in exhaustion into Elijah's comforting embrace. As we rode away, I turned for one last look at the pile of burning timbers that had been the house. I swore the fire moaned, then sighed in relief. It was finished.

A flash of white light caught my eye.

Sariah stood at the end of the drive, a smile tracing her lips. Unlike I'd seen her before, she was clothed in brilliant white, her presence serene and hopeful. She was free. She wore an undeniable look of relief and joy, as animated as if she were alive once more. She gave us one last look before disappearing into the night air.

And somewhere from the ashy ruins a cold hymn played on:

Come, come, ye Saints . . .

All is well! All is well!

Chapter 41

Four weeks later

Flora's family table was set with a starch-pressed gingham tablecloth and a tall white vase holding carefully arranged wildflowers. Seated across the bench from her, I wasn't surprised in the least bit that every inch of this kitchen was scrubbed, polished, and symmetrically organized. Perhaps if Manwaring Manor had had an ounce of beauty, the kitchen would've looked like this all along. The thought brought a bittersweet smile to my face.

For all her faults, this was Flora in her prime and I couldn't help hoping that her newfound freedom would bring her happiness. Judging by the pained frown on her face, though, she wasn't keen on embracing that reality yet.

"I can't believe it's all gone," she said. "Everything our husband built destroyed."

I spoke softly, unsure if I was trying to comfort or reason with her. "The house was wretched, Flora. We both know that."

"And what matters most was saved," Prudence added. "You and all the children are safe."

Flora's fingers pressed harder into the table. "But our husband perished in a fire! Abby too." Her voice cracked with a rare glimpse of emotion.

Though part of me wanted to confess, I knew I could never tell Flora the full truth. I sensed that she truly did care for all of us, perhaps even more than she did for Jacob. She'd been harsh and demanding, but in her strange way she worried and worked for us. Her true love was for the family she'd helped build, not her husband. I knew that she had her own scars she refused to acknowledge out loud. But when confronted with the jarring truth, she'd cleave to her fears and innate beliefs. No matter how justified, Flora would never accept Jacob's murder as right.

My heart splintered anew remembering the knife poised against Jacob's throat and the sea of blood seeping into the floor. My weight holding down his fading body. At night, I sometimes cried out from the nightmare of it, crawling into Elijah's arms as he slept beside me.

I kept my expression calm so as not to betray the truth behind the lies; ones even Prudence knew only in part.

"We won't have all the answers in this life, but they are both at rest now," Prudence said.

Flora sighed. "Where are her children?"

"They've been placed in loving homes."

Silence sunk around us, heavy and warm. How strange to be having such a conversation, to watch Flora struggle to hold back her obvious sentiments. My chest tightened with more sadness for what could've been if only life were different.

Outside the open window, children's laughter carried across the yard. Elijah had organized the children into a game of tag to give us space to converse freely. Gratitude for his unending kindness swept through me.

"I will find the funds to give them both a proper gravestone," I said, breaking up the quiet. "But I won't bury Abigail beside him. I know that's what she would've wanted." It was only partially a lie.

Even though Abigail still lived, leaving the Territory with her children in secret right after the fire, I would make sure it was done properly to cover her tracks. Most importantly, the stone would read *Abigail*, the true name she called herself.

Flora pushed her glasses up her nose. "I suppose I won't bother telling you that I don't agree."

"No, and you don't have to agree. I know Jacob was the father of your children and that he provided for you for years." Hurt rolled through me and I allowed it to spread and settle in my bones. "But not all of us cherish his memory."

Every possible piece of joy from that short life had turned to ash in the fire and I wanted nothing more than to leave Jacob, Elder Crowther, and all the men who led me to Manwaring Manor in the rubble. From now on, I would control my own life, my own choices, by virtue of my own authority.

Like Prudence sensed my thoughts, she cleared her throat. "What are you going to do now, Hazel?"

At last, I smiled. "Elijah and I will be heading to California tomorrow."

Flora shook her head in the same disapproving movement I'd come to know so well, but it didn't ignite shame within me. "It's disgraceful to marry another only weeks after your husband perishes."

I shrugged as I picked up my long-forgotten glass of lemonade. "Then it's a good thing my marriage to Jacob was never real in the eyes of the law."

"Man's laws," she chided. "Remember, God will judge."

"And I suspect He'll understand me perfectly." I stared at her over the rim of my cup, unmoved. I could see the agitation in her eyes that I didn't squirm beneath her accusations. I knew that Flora only acted and said as she did because of her own deep convictions, but they still were not my own anymore. Part of me mourned for her remaining lot in life, though such a sentiment would truly shock her if I admitted it.

"Well, I think it's marvelous," Prudence said. "How long must we stay in black before we get back to our lives? The world won't wait for us."

"I suppose it won't," she said reluctantly. "Prudence, when does your train leave for the East?"

"Tomorrow," Prudence replied. "I'm so nervous."

I clasped her hand. "You'll do wonderfully. You'll be brilliant in school and become the best midwife in the entire country."

She laughed. "Well, I don't know about that."

"But you will, Sister Prudence," said Flora in a matter-of-fact tone.

Now we shared a surprised look.

I reached across the table and placed my hand on Flora's. She glanced up at me, paralyzed with discomfort, but she didn't remove from my touch. "I know your life will be hard after this, and I will pray for you."

"We both will." Prudence joined her hand to ours.

"I've no doubt your industry and dedication will give you strength," I said. "But you could come with us, you know."

She scoffed. "To San Francisco and abandon Zion?"

"Or the East. Midwives are an important commodity," said Prudence.

"There's a whole other world out there, Sister." My chest thrummed with the possibility.

Flora slid her hand out from ours. "I'm glad for you two, I truly am. I know you'll find a place for yourself." Her eyes met mine. "But I'm not like that. I need Zion and the church. This is my home and all I've ever worked for. I couldn't start again and I couldn't abandon my God."

"I understand." And I meant it. We each had to take our own paths.

"Besides." She sat up and lifted her chin. "California is a den of iniquity."

"Right, Sister Flora."

The kitchen door cracked open and Elijah poked his head

through the opening. He gave us a tentative look that made him look so boyishly handsome I had to fight the urge to stand and kiss him on the spot.

"You about ready to go? Sun's starting to fade and we've got to ride back to make our final preparations."

I nodded. "Yes, I'll meet you outside."

I stood, my legs trembling beneath my skirts. There was a finality in every step, in every breath of air. "Thank you, Flora, for everything. I will write you; I promise."

Prudence replaced her hat as she stood. "I will as well."

"Very well." Her shoulders dropped some. "I would like that."

I stopped toe-to-toe with her and tilted my head back to memorize her face one final time. Before she could protest, I threw my arms around her neck and tugged her tight against me. Slowly, her arms wrapped around my back. My pulse beat faster knowing well what I would lose and what I could gain over the next few weeks, months, years.

Elijah and I slipped back out the kitchen door to our waiting cart. At first, the ride was silent. Unspoken conversations carried back and forth—worries, fears, joys, sadness—an entire universe contained between us. But threading through it all was hope. As we drove down the road to Salt Lake for probably the last time, it didn't feel like a goodbye, but a yawning opening to possibility and future. To find a place prepared for us, far away in the West.

Elijah prodded me with his elbow as he held the reins. "Do you think Sister Flora will ever realize Abigail's grave is fake and that she's alive?"

I laughed. "I doubt it. I don't think she'll ever find herself in Oregon, where she might run into Abigail and her children."

Elijah's hand found mine.

"And we're about to leave ourselves for San Francisco. Are you ready for this, Hazel?"

My lips pressed together as I searched through my own body. My heart ticked quickly, anxiety rolled through my pulse. There was no denying I'd struggle possibly forever with my panics, but

I realized now that fearing them and filling myself with shame would never bring me peace. I needed to embrace them as part of me, as part of my unique soul.

"I'm worried," I confessed, tugging us closer. "But I'm also excited. This will be our first big adventure."

He smiled at me as I glanced up at him. "Indeed, my dear. The first of many."

I shifted back to Elijah, leaning on his arm. He placed a kiss on the top of my head. All, at last, was truly well.

Author's Note

In 1872, my third great-grandfather George Kirkham married Mary Russon in Salt Lake City, Utah Territory. Three years later in 1875, George also married Mary's natural sister, Sara. Both sisters remained married to him polygamously for the rest of their lives.

The formal practice of polygamy in the Church of Jesus Christ of Latter-Day Saints ended in 1890, but its long shadow continues to haunt Mormonism. I grew up on stories of Mormon pioneers sacrificing everything to come to Utah and live their religion. I was taught that polygamy—also known as plural marriage, the Principle, Celestial marriage—was a commandment of God and that my ancestors obeyed even though it was hard. The narrative surrounding it was told only through a faith-promoting lens. It wasn't until I studied the true history of polygamy as an adult, the untold stories of abuse, neglect, and poverty, that I realized the stories of my childhood were whitewashed and often inaccurate.

I was drawn to my ancestors Mary and Sara but disappointed that the record of their lives was mostly silent. Many family stories, images, and biographies exist about George, but only a few memories of Mary and Sara. Their own short autobiographies contain no mention of plural marriage or that they were both married to their sister's husband. Sadly, this is common in Mormon pioneer family histories. The realities and traumas are conveniently not remembered, not written, or sanitized into faith-promoting narratives.

As I wondered what Mary's and Sara's life might have been like, I knew I wanted to write a book about polygamy. I needed to help heal this generational wound within me by giving a voice to the women of the past who were censored or censored themselves. Ironically—or perhaps inspirationally?—I was sitting in an LDS church meeting when the idea struck me: what if that book is a *Gothic*?! From there, the story of Hazel, Abigail, Flora, and Prudence came quickly. I knew I needed to tell this story in this way because the horrors of ghosts and creepy houses mirror a reality of abusive patriarchy and religious manipulation.

The history of plural marriage in Mormonism is complicated and at times controversial. Joseph Smith began the practice sometime during his life, most likely in the 1840s in Nauvoo, Illinois. He secretly spread that practice to his inner circle, who also married multiple women. Joseph's wife Emma knew about only a few of her husband's plural marriages. Joseph took great pains to cover his adultery, including penning a revelation from God that supported his right to marry virgins, and threatened Emma (and any other opposing wives) with destruction if they didn't agree. This revelation is still canonized in LDS scripture as Doctrine & Covenants Section 132.

Life in polygamy was different for every woman in the nineteenth century. Only approximately one-third of Latter-Day Saints practiced it. Some did truly love it, many secretly struggled, and a few openly rebelled. Primary sources demonstrate a system full of problems and abuses. Polygamy reduced women to objects and entrenched the power of patriarchy in the church.

Priesthood authority was viewed as supreme in both religious and secular matters. Men were often required to have multiple wives in order to move up the priesthood hierarchy. Women were frequently traded, gifted, coerced, or manipulated into plural marriages. As numbers of available women diminished, teenage girls were married off as well. Joseph Smith, Brigham Young, and other prominent leaders had several underage brides who were decades their junior. Marrying sisters, or even mother-daughters, was also common. Divorces were easier to obtain in Utah Territory, but legal protections afterward were difficult since the original marriage wasn't legally recognized. Religious and personal shame could also accompany leaving plural marriages.

The LDS church formally abandoned polygamy in 1890, but it

wasn't until 2014 that the church publicly acknowledged that Joseph Smith had up to forty wives. The church continues to struggle with accurate representation of polygamy in church materials. Some members also spread conspiracy theories to deny Joseph's polygamy despite historical evidence. The church as a whole does not appear ready—and may never be ready—to honestly look at their past and see polygamy for what it was outside of a selective narrative. To me, this is a tragedy that will continue to cause harm, especially to women, and spread generational trauma.

In *The Fourth Wife*, I strived to make the story and characters as historically accurate as possible. At times I deviated from history for the sake of the story and modern readers' understanding. I moved up the threat of federal intervention from the Edmunds Anti-Polygamy Act of 1882 in the official timeline. I placed Elder Crowther's office in the Council House to mimic the present-day Church Administration Building, but I couldn't find any direct evidence that such apostle offices existed in the 1880s. Manwaring Manor and its location are fictional, though homes were built throughout the valley and canyons in the nineteenth century.

All the characters are fictional, but I used the experiences of Mormon women to create their personalities and experiences. Flora and Prudence, for instance, represent two different perspectives on living polygamy: feminist women who fought for suffrage to defend their polygamous lifestyle and religiously dedicated women who martyred themselves for their faith. Hazel's struggle with anxiety and panic attacks are my own struggle. Many of Hazel's thoughts are my attempt to capture what it's like to be in my own head and body, especially when I was at my most religiously devout. Hazel also shares my ancestor's maiden name as a tribute to their remarkable lives.

I created a fictional apostle, Elder Crowther, to avoid unneeded controversy, but Brigham Young is portrayed as I see him in history. The quotes read from Jacob's journal are documented teachings of Brigham Young. Blood atonement was a real, though short-lived and infrequent, teaching and practice. Young did preach that some sins required death for redemption. Documentation and stories of Saints killed under blood atonement do exist. Young and other leaders also taught that only those who practiced polygamy would be saved in the highest degree of heaven, and that righteous men would become gods in the next life and create their own kingdoms and worlds.

I also pulled many specific stories from primary sources to infuse throughout the book. Emmeline B. Wells was a suffragist and early feminist writer who publicly supported polygamy and then went home and wrote of her misery in her private journal. Many women in plural marriages lived in poverty as their husband's resources were spread thin over multiple women. Some were left in remote towns to fend for themselves, only for their husbands to show up every year or so to get them pregnant and then leave again.

I based the plot of Abbey being forced to bring Sariah as a sister-wife on her wedding day from the lives of Madeleine and Emily Malan in 1858. According to their family history, Brigham Young refused to marry Madeleine to her fiancé, Isaac Farley, unless they returned to Ogden to bring her twin sister, Emily, to also be sealed to Isaac. Most accounts of this story frame it as a faith-promoting narrative, but this ignores the real trauma this family would've lived with every day, inflicted on them by a spiritual leader. It also highlights the lack of true choice many women had in joining polygamous relationships.

The Edmunds Anti-Polygamy Act of 1882 made polygamy a felony in federal territories and prohibited polygamists from voting, holding public office, or serving on juries. Under this act and the following Edmunds-Tucker Act of 1887, many polygamists were prosecuted, sent to jail, or forced to pay high fines. Polygamists frequently went "underground" to hide from federal officials, including the church prophet and highest leaders at times. Mormons saw this as religious persecution.

Although the LDS church now officially disavows the nickname, I chose to use the term "Mormon" throughout the book. For nearly two hundred years the church openly embraced this name as their culture and identity. Members like Hazel in the late-nineteenth century would have identified as Mormon, and so I used the term that would be historically accurate to them. I also grew up identifying as a Mormon, and Mormonism is part of who I am, regardless of my level of personal religious orthodoxy.

It's impossible to cover all that should be said about Mormon polygamy in one book or author's note. I've striven to create a story that honestly reflects lived experiences while also connecting with modern women who've experienced life in a high-control, high-demand religion or group. Although this story is Mormon, at its heart it's a feminist manifesto for *all* women who've ever been in an abusive relationship, who've struggled with a religious doctrine that harmed them, or who've felt that they had to be someone they weren't in order to be safe in a patriarchy.

To learn more about Mormonism and Mormon polygamy, I recommend the following books and podcasts:

American Zion: A New History of Mormonism by Benjamin E. Park
A House Full of Females: Plural Marriage and Women's Rights in Early Mormonism, 1835–1870 by Laurel Thatcher Ulrich
In Sacred Loneliness: The Plural Wives of Joseph Smith by Todd M. Compton
The Polygamous Wives Writing Club: From the Diaries of Mormon Pioneer Women by Paula Kelly Harline
Mormon Enigma: Emma Hale Smith by Linda King Newell and Valeen Tippetts Avery
The Ghost of Eternal Polygamy: Haunting the Hearts and Heaven of Mormon Women and Men by Carol Lynn Pearson
Year of Polygamy Podcast
Sunstone Mormon History Podcast

If you need a Mormon feminist community to express yourself and share your stories across the faith spectrum, I recommend *Exponent II*'s magazine, blog, and retreat.

Acknowledgments

As a little girl, my dad used to read us bedtime stories about my ancestors, the Mormon pioneers. Falling asleep on my bunk bed while Dad read about people being found frozen to death under handcarts might be where my Mormon history interest began. I'm grateful my parents fostered and encouraged my love of history and writing. This book wouldn't exist without my dad's lessons on Joseph Smith's plural wives and my mom's example of how to be a strong and independent woman.

An enormous thank-you to my agent, Rach Crawford, who saw the potential in my niche, creepy Gothic and for her continued support of my unique projects. To Elizabeth Trout, my fabulous editor, thank you for all your insights and efforts to make this book a reality. Thank you to everyone at Kensington for giving *The Fourth Wife* the perfect home.

A special thank-you to Rose de Guzman, who didn't run away screaming from my first book, who coached me through the writing process, and was the first person I pitched *The Fourth Wife*.

To all of my early readers, thank you for wading through the mess and giving me so much support and helpful critique. A special thanks to Laurel, Rachel, Gena, Lizz, Marielle, Giselda, Genalea, and Bethany. Thank you to the Pitch'n'Bitch chat for being there to both pitch and bitch about querying and writing.

Thank you to my siblings, who understand that quoting Monty Python means "I love you," and to my in-laws, who all put their support behind my writing schemes.

To Taylor Swift, thank you for the soundtrack to my writing daydreams.

To Paris Paloma, thank you for the anthem of this book and women everywhere, "Labour."

A shout-out to the historians and scholars whose research

helped me not only write this book but also discover more of my own Mormon history: Laurel Thatcher Ulrich, Lindsay Hansen Park, Bryan Buchanan, Benjamin E. Park, Todd M. Compton, and Paula Kelly Harline, among many others.

Thank you to the readers on social media who've seen my videos and jumped right in to support this project! To all the creators who instantly wanted to support, asked me on podcasts, and just shouted out my Mormon Gothic, I will be eternally grateful.

Most of all, to my silly, wild, adorable kids: thank you for tolerating your mother's constant history lessons and rants during school drop-offs. And to my amazing, handsome husband, Peter: I cannot express in words how much you mean to me. You've shown me support and grace like I've never known, and you help me pursue all my crazy dreams without hesitation. I love you.

And a final thank-you to my Heavenly Mother. I feel your divine feminine inspiring my writings and my work every day.

A READING GROUP GUIDE

THE FOURTH WIFE

Linda Hamilton

ABOUT THIS GUIDE

The suggested questions are included to enhance your group's reading of Linda Hamilton's *The Fourth Wife.*

Discussion Questions

1. *The Fourth Wife* is a Gothic novel with many classic tropes, such as creepy mansions and the supernatural. How do these Gothic elements reflect the real horrors Hazel experiences in her world?

2. The title *The Fourth Wife* is in part a nod to Ann Eliza Young's famous exposé, *Wife No. 19*, where she shares about her life as a plural wife of Brigham Young. Hazel is, in her own way, exposing the reality of polygamy to her readers as well. What did you learn about polygamy that you did not know before? What surprised you?

3. Each of the sister wives represents a different viewpoint on polygamy shared by real Mormon women in the nineteenth century. How did Flora, Prudence, and Abby feel about polygamy?

4. Hazel chooses to marry Jacob without truly knowing him because a religious leader tells her to. Why do you think she makes this risky decision?

5. Hazel's character struggles with what we would now diagnose as anxiety and panic attacks. How does her religious upbringing play into her understanding of her mental health struggles over the course of the book?

6. Hazel chooses to stay with Jacob, even as she learns the truth of his lies and abuse. Why do you think she stays?

7. Flora mentions that she once thought she saw something in the house and later Abby says Sariah tried and failed to

befriend her. Why do you think Flora never truly noticed Sariah's presence?

8. Who is the true villain of the story?

9. In the final scenes, Abby believes she needs to stay in the burning house with her sister's ghost, but Sariah forces her to leave. Why do you think Abby wanted to stay and die? Why would Sariah want her to live?

10. 1880s Utah is distinctly Mormon, but many of the sister wives' experiences are universal to women in other high-demand religions, insular groups, or patriarchal structures. How is your lived experience similar or different from these women's experiences?

11. Considering the themes in this book, how has our world changed or not changed since the nineteenth century for women?

12. How does abuse manifest in this book? What makes it difficult to immediately identify?

13. Who was your favorite character and why?

14. If you cosuld fancast your own film version of *The Fourth Wife*, who would you cast as the main characters?

www.ingramcontent.com/pod-product-compliance
Lightning Source LLC
LaVergne TN
LVHW031924090826
845145LV00018B/2826

* 9 7 8 1 4 9 6 7 5 6 8 9 3 *